Shards

By Jo Bannister

JO BANNISTER

Shards

A CRIME CLUB BOOK
DOUBLEDAY
New York London Toronto Sydney Auckland

A CRIME CLUB BOOK
PUBLISHED BY DOUBLEDAY
a division of Bantam Doubleday Dell Publishing Group, Inc.
666 Fifth Avenue, New York, New York 10103

DOUBLEDAY and the portrayal of a man with a gun are trademarks of Doubleday, a
division of Bantam Doubleday Dell Publishing Group, Inc.

Library of Congress Cataloging-in-Publication Data

Bannister, Jo.
    Shards / Jo Bannister. — 1st ed.
        p. cm.
    "A Crime Club book."
    I. Title.
PR6052.A497S5   1990   89-49364
823'.914—dc20
CIP

ISBN 0-385-41443-9
Copyright © 1990 by Jo Bannister
All Rights Reserved
Printed in the United States of America
August 1990
First Edition

Shards

I

Sojourners

The land shall not be sold for ever: for the land is mine; for ye are strangers and sojourners with me.

Leviticus 25

THE BOMB lay like a beast in darkness, breathing softly. The men that hunted it knew it was there—close, very close, they could sense it and smell it, feel the tension generated by its presence run like threads of electricity in their fingertips. Its proximity turned the palms of their hands damp.

They knew, too, that this was as close as they could approach it in safety. In comparative safety, rather; safety was always comparative on these streets, if the beast reached the end of its patience it could kill any one of them without further provocation, where they were. Or it could spare them and take instead some woman hurrying with her shopping past the end of the street, and cut her in half with a hurtling scythe of steel shrapnel.

But if they were to cage the beast, so that the woman doing her shopping, and her husband and children, and their friends and neighbours and also the people they could not abide like the man with the "Present from Cyprus" T-shirt and all the cats, could get on with their lives in some semblance of normality, someone had to go closer. Someone had to get close enough to that bomb to hear its heart beat, close enough to see the shreds of other men's flesh on its back teeth.

Then, if he was both good and lucky, he could tame it. If he was not good or lucky enough, all the padding and protection he wore—the helmet, the visor, the armoured apron, the big gloves he could only do so much in—would do him no service, would only complicate and make messier the job of reassembling the bits required for a funeral.

In the normal way of things—because, like the people living here, the men working on the bombs had created their own normality—it would have been their climbing into the suit of armour with the integral radio. But only yesterday Meir had been involved in a professional contretemps with a colleague, a demarcation dispute of a kind, and now his hand was heavily bandaged and his backside tender with tetanus antitoxin. His dignity had also suffered, and he strongly suspected his chances of promotion had too. An army which cared deeply about credibility would find it difficult to forgive him for being put out of action by a sniffer dog named Shoshana.

So Meir stood by while another knight donned his armour and waddled gracelessly toward the lists, and he had to be told three times to take cover behind the blast screen erected round the command vehicle. Even after the other ATO had disappeared into the building, Meir looked after him wistfully, for all the world as if there were a party there to which his invitation had unaccountably gone astray.

Gichon followed the wire that was the robot's umbilical. They called it Geronimo: he could not remember why. It had found the device while he was suiting up. Rather, the men in the command vehicle operating its tracks and sensors and watching with its closed-circuit eyes had. He had done their job often enough to know that the spindly robot was no more than a sophisticated tool like the other sophisticated tools at his disposal. Still he thought of it as a colleague named Geronimo.

Geronimo pared the amount of time he had to spend with the bomb, which automatically improved an ATO's chances. Its television camera allowed him to make his initial assessment from behind the blast screen. Sometimes it was possible to have Geronimo finish the job by means of a controlled explosion. But not this time. This bomb was the work of the man they called Sinbad, and though no one in the Israel Defence Forces knew who he was, they all knew that he did not leave devices that could be disabled by a well-judged blast from a shotgun. He left devices that flattened streets if somebody coughed too close. They called him Sinbad because his first consignment of Sentex was smuggled in from Lebanon by sea.

The building where Gichon went was a small one-man workshop off an alley off a side street. The name in peeling paintwork over the door was that of a motor mechanic who had used it for a couple of years. Before that someone had made kitchen units in it, and before that someone else had serviced solar panels. It was a backstreet workshop like a hundred others in the dusty byways of this city, and a million others on the shadow side of cities all over the world.

The fact that this city was Jerusalem, sacred to three of the world's great religions, that these streets had been tramped by some of the most famous feet in history, did not make the needs of its modern citizens any more romantic than those of the residents of Birmingham, or Detroit, or Munich. Motor mechanics and plumbers have inherited the earth; even in Jerusalem, there is not much trade in ceremonial palm fronds. Perhaps the dust is older; that is all.

But the mechanic whose name was over the door in flowing Arabic script was not in fact the last tenant of these premises. In its recent history this workshop had broken abruptly from the tradition of small one-man workshops in backstreets the world over. This workshop had been used for the assembling of bombs, and when he had pulled out, Sinbad had left a present for the security forces whose proximity had dictated his departure.

The device was in a fifty-gallon oil drum against the front wall of the building, to the right as Gichon followed Geronimo's wire through the door. There was as yet no knowing how much of that fifty-gallon capacity was occupied by explosives, how much by packing, how much by the shrapnel material designed to maximise the human devastation of which the thing was capable.

But some of that space, Gichon was sure, would be given over to antihandling devices of one kind or another, and if this was one of Sinbad's children they would be clever and devious and deadly. Another man might settle for a mercury tilt switch, or a pin suspended in a metal tube; but Sinbad had a new trick for them every time they met. His circuits and detonators came from no bomb-maker's manual but straight from his own fertile imagination via his agile fingers. The man must have had hands like a surgeon's just to set up his surprises. A man had to have hands like a machine's to begin dismantling them.

Once he was within sure-kill range Gichon began divesting himself of some of the armour he had pulled on so carefully minutes before. It had already done its job: if the bomb had gone off early it would probably have saved his life. Now that he was ready to bend over it and infiltrate his fingers into its innards, the plate and the padding could do him no service and some of it would be in his way. Since he would only turn his back on this thing and walk away from it after the detonator was in pieces on the concrete floor, he needed to be comfortable, relaxed and deft more than he needed to be protected. If the thing went up now it would push his front plate out through his backbone anyway.

Back in the command vehicle Meir was acutely aware of everything Gichon was doing, everything he was thinking. He knew because he could see, courtesy of Geronimo's camera, and because he could hear, through the comlink in Gichon's helmet by means of which he reported every move he intended to make. But more than that, he knew what was happening in Gichon's belly and mind because he had been there so often himself. Ammunition technical officers—known outside the trade as bomb disposal experts; they did not call themselves that for fear of tempting fate—die, but they never die alone. When they go, a bit of every other ATO in the world goes with them.

Yet there was no sense of urgency or moment at either end of the radio link. The voices were quiet and calm, and though mostly the information that passed between them related to the bomb, at intervals snatches of conversation intruded, startling in their almost banal domesticity. Gichon asked if it was still raining outside, and if anyone had tickets to spare for Kol Yisrael, but no one in the command vehicle shared his enthusiasm for orchestral music. Once the men in the vehicle heard Gichon humming a little tune, as it were a lullaby, to his bomb.

After forty minutes the man at the bomb had reached a kind of impasse. Sitting back on his heels, still talking in that quiet academic voice like a man in the safety of his study wrestling with a theory, Gichon explained it to Meir. Meir of all people needed no explanation, knew the threads that were braiding in Gichon's mind, many and complex and as yet more holes than lace. Still he listened carefully because two heads were better than one and, even apart from that, just telling it would help Gichon focus his thinking.

"If this was anyone but Sinbad," Gichon's voice mused over the comlink, "I would go in there with some idea of what he wanted me to do, and some idea therefore of how to avoid doing it, and anyway the awareness that probably I'm better at my job than he is at his and ought to be able to outthink him and outperform him. Almost any bomb that can be put together can be taken apart—note the careful avoidance of absolutes here, Simon—and I have the hands and the experience to be as good in there without a blueprint as anyone but Sinbad is with one.

"But it is him, Simon. I can smell him—his vibrations are packed into this oil drum along with the explosives and the shrapnel and the mechanism. He's right here with me, watching, waiting for me to make a move. And I can't guess what he's thinking, what he's done. Whether he's left me a box full of lies in the hope of catching me with one if I sidestep another. Or maybe he expected me to think that, and this time the Yellow Brick Road is straight ahead and the traps are waiting for me to turn aside to check the culverts. I can't second-guess him—do you know what I mean?"

Meir said quietly, "David, do you want me in there? I can't do much, but we can look it over together."

Another man—a man in another job—might have been offended, might have seen the offer as a slur on his abilities. Gichon only gave a soft, wry little chuckle. He was a young man, but he had grown old and wise in this job. "No, Simon, thank you. I can see all there is to see. From here it's by guess and by God. I'll keep you informed."

When the bomb went up, there was a perceptible moment in which the wall of the building bulged outwards into the street before the bricks flew apart and hurtled into the alley and into the sky with the velocity of bullets. Waves of sound and shock washed over the surrounding houses, breaking glass. A single gout of flame jetted out where the wall had been and licked the paint on the doors opposite into blisters. Black smoke and white dust billowed through the gap between the frontages and into the aching air above ancient, injured Jerusalem.

In the fraction of a second that he knew he was going to die, Gichon remembered why the robot at his elbow was called Geronimo. Its name was on his lips when the blast took him.

Mickey Flynn had been drinking a good part of the afternoon and was consequently both more garrulous and more argumentative than usual. He had discovered a new recruit to the ranks of the Jerusalem press corps, fresh from the moral high ground of quality reporting for a discerning home readership, had pinned her in a corner and was proceeding to demolish every idea she had ever cherished about her profession.

His long body, loose-limbed going on disjointed, barred her escape. Fever-bright brown eyes, candlelight and madness dancing in their depths, transfixed her. His wide mouth twisted in a lazy and ironic curve, and poured words like a slow torrent, muffled slightly by his glass and the New York accent.

"Yeah, sure," he drawled, "you're only doing your job, I'm only doing mine. I bet you're really good at it too. Point is, who benefits? We do, sure, it's a nice living—I take photographs, did I tell you that?"

He had, several times. "Newspapers make big money out of it too, which is great for the people who own them, and as long as you think of it in purely commercial terms there's no problem. But if you think you're doing mankind a service, your elevator is not hitting the top floor. If you became a hooker tomorrow, and I joined a travelling circus, and everybody else here found something useful to do with their lives, nobody—in Jerusalem, in the Middle East or anywhere else in the world—would be any the worse for it, and quite a lot would be quite a lot better."

"I don't see how," said the girl, at once amused by his manner and outraged by his argument. All the same, as soon as she had said it she knew it was a mistake. There were only two ways she would get free of him before bedtime: one was agreeing with him, the other was kneeing him in the groin.

Flynn's mad eyes kindled in triumph. He closed in for the kill, his long body leaning over her and only kept approximately upright by his spare hand, the one without the glass, propped against the wall by her shoulder. "Because," he said, with the air of a man proving a clever point with devastating skill, "if we weren't here, most everybody else would go home too. Half of everything done here is done for the publicity. People get killed not because of who they are or what they've done but for the publicity. People stage outrages the way Broadway stages musicals, to grab the headlines.

"OK, maybe the Palestinian movement is a grass-roots thing, with or without us there would still be young Arabs lobbing stones at passing tanks and Israeli soldiers beating the crap out of any they get their hands on. But how much of the rest of it is inevitable? The bombings, the raids, the machine-gun attacks, all the big set pieces—they aren't done because the removal of a few schoolkids and middle-aged mothers will make it easier to overturn the state of Israel. They're done because the people who do them know they can count on our cooperation in reminding the world of their grievances and aspirations.

"Want to put your case to millions? Forget the UN—blow up a few children, preferably somewhere that'll look good in the pictures, and the great god Media will noise your deeds unto nations, yea even unto the corners of the earth. You don't have to be a majority, you don't have to be democratic, you don't even need much of a cause—all you have to be is nasty enough to think up some atrocity nobody's reported this month and we'll take it from there. Any excuse will do: a united Ireland, a divided Palestine, independence for the Basques, dominion for the Cypriots. We're not particular: however few you are, however little support you command, however vicious your campaign and impractical your objectives, we'll do your PR. If any other kind of victory is beyond you, we'll help you win the propaganda war. All you need do is hurt enough people in enough imaginative ways. Care more about what happened to your grandfather than what will become of your children? Roll up, roll up, you're our kind of people."

The girl was becoming more and more incensed. "So what are you suggesting we should do—ignore it? Write about dog shows and bonny baby contests while innocent people are being murdered in the streets where they live?"

"Why not?" asked Flynn, disconcertingly, his eyes agleam. "Nobody would be any the worse off except the terrorists. Without the publicity we give them, most of these firecracker stunts wouldn't be worth pulling at all—their practical effect on the balance of power is marginal or nil. So there would be less terrorism, fewer victims, and less army activity for people to resent. Insurgents would have to find other ways of advancing their causes—you never know, they might even try democracy. And if they did, and if they turned out to have the sort of popular support they always claim to have, a whole bunch of politicians would find themselves having to work for a living too. The day of the free lunch would be over."

"What about the man in the street, the guy who buys newspapers?" demanded the girl. "Doesn't he have some right to know what's happening around him—particularly when it's done in his name?"

"Screw his rights," said Flynn, succinctly. "He's been kept fully informed, in glorious Technicolor, for longer than I've been alive, but what's he done about it? Has he made any effort to understand the situation here—or in Ireland, or any of the other places you've sweated your guts out writing deathless prose about? Has a word of it altered his perception of how democratic institutions work, or what scale of threat can be posed by armed insurrectionists in urban society? Does it mean anything at all to him besides a quick thrill and something to wrap his fish and chips in? If he doesn't care about the consequences, what claim does he have on the facts?"

Almost every other conversation in the hotel bar had petered out as one by one the press gang had realised what was going on and drifted over to spectate. Most of them had reeled under the shock of one of Flynn's attacks at some time or another, and mingled with their natural sympathy for his new victim was a shamefaced pleasure at seeing it happen to someone else. They knew how it felt, the terrible impotence of being assaulted from an unexpected quarter with unreasonable accusations derived from apparently rational arguments, and now they wanted to see what it looked like.

Finally someone came to the girl's aid. A broad hand clapped on Flynn's stooped shoulder and the American looked round with a lazy grin. "Hi, Gil."

The older man did not smile back, except possibly in his eyes which were dark grey and recessed into a deep mass of wrinkles. He was nearly as tall as Flynn, and much broader, and most people thought he looked like a policeman. It was an impression he did not hesitate to exploit. Even the voice was the right combination of sepulchral authority and brisk disfavour.

"Michael Diarmid Flynn, you are charged with possession of an offensive argument, assault occasioning actual mental harm, and conspiracy to empty a bar before closing time. How do you plead?"

Flynn drew himself up to his full six-foot-two. It took a little time but it was worth waiting for, except that the effect was somewhat marred by a filter falling out of one of the more marsupial pockets of his combat jacket. "Fifth Amendment."

Gilbert Todd clucked impatiently. "You can't, they don't have one here."

Outrage flashed in Flynn's eyes. "I am an American citizen, sir. I have a constitutional entitlement to life, liberty and the Fifth Amendment. I'd have thought that was self-evident."

Todd grinned. Flynn grinned. The girl looked puzzled but relieved. Someone ordered another round of drinks.

A flat thump, like somebody dropping books in the next room, fell into the quiet space between the voices. A half-open window rattled, and glasses clustered together on the bar made music like wind chimes. The sound of the explosion, perhaps a mile away across the Old City, was not so great but everyone in the bar, except the new girl who had not heard it before, knew what it was.

And she guessed. She stared at Todd, wide-eyed and somehow stricken although this was what she was here for. "Was that—?"

"Yes." Todd was ferreting through his pockets, came up with a bunch of keys. He took Flynn's glass off him and put the keys in his hand instead. "Come on, hotshot, let's go to work."

The girl stared at him in horror. "You're not driving there?"

"Certainly not," said Todd with dignity, "I've been drinking. Mickey'll drive."

She hardly knew what to say to that. Finally she managed, "And what do you suppose he's been doing all afternoon? Apart from boring me, that is."

Flynn was already on his way, taking the stairs at a speed which would have been reckless for a man who had not spent four hours in a hotel bar. Todd paused a moment longer, and smiled, and put Flynn's glass into the girl's hand. "L'chaim." Then he followed Flynn downstairs at a rate which, if less than breakneck, still made scant concession to his bulk and his age, which was the trying side of fifty.

Perhaps half the press gang moved towards the door in their wake. Before she followed the girl sniffed the glass. Then, frowning, she tasted the clear liquid in the bottom. Then she understood both more and less than before. It was lemonade.

As they drove down David Hamelekh—fast, Flynn threading the hired car through the traffic with a precision compounded of skill and abandon—Todd said, "That line you were feeding her. You know, the one that says she's directly responsible for hundreds of deaths every year. Do you actually believe that?"

Flynn shrugged, threw a hand-brake turn to take them down a side street. "I dunno." Then he grinned, indolence spiced with wickedness. "Is there an *R* in the month?"

[2]

While Flynn drove, Todd talked to his police contact. Not the press office, which tended to be more amiable than helpful when faced with a request for immediate information, but someone in the headquarters building he could rely on to tell him anything that would not actually make problems for the security forces.

The mobile phone had been a major investment, but it had paid for itself four times over. Not so much in terms of Todd's dispatches, which were often better and more cogently written when the passage of a little time had enabled all the details and implications of an incident to emerge, but because of the difference a swifter response made to the quality of Flynn's photographs.

He had always been a good photographer, often an outstanding one, with the reputation—among colleagues and editors and the more discerning readers—for going that little bit further than his competitors, for sticking his neck out the extra inches that turned good photographs into great ones. The car phone cut maybe four minutes off the time it took them to react to an incident in progress.

Those four extra minutes had won Flynn shots of burning buses when everyone else got burnt-out ones, shots of bomb warnings turning into explosions, shots of terrorists and terror victims writhing into death in the bright unforgiving streets. Some of the photographs were close to the knuckle for Western readers, but that did not trouble Flynn. He took the pictures, Todd wrote the words and they sold the package for the best offer—in London, New York, Paris, Berlin, Hong Kong.

Todd got the address from his contact, checked the street map, called Flynn a couple of turns up sneaky back ways, then they rounded a corner and found the street ahead choked with dust, debris, soldiers and emergency vehicles. They left the car before anyone could tell them to move it, Flynn with a camera slung round his neck and his pockets stuffed with lenses and film.

Todd looked round for a familiar face, spotted Simon Meir and started up the street at a purposeful march. There were soldiers posted to keep sightseers away but they saw Todd, thought he looked familiar, thought he was a policeman and let him pass. Flynn did not look even slightly like a policeman: when he was challenged he jerked his head at Todd, grunted, "I'm with him," and kept walking.

Todd came up on Meir's blind side, a little like a square-rigger hoving to in his unbelted raincoat, and said quietly, "If that hand is all you got out of this you can count it a success."

Meir grimaced. He was a man of about forty with a narrow, aristocratic face and the same gentleness in him that Gichon had had. He looked at the bandage, then at Todd. "A dog bit me. She saved my life. When I leave here I'm going to find her the biggest bone in Jerusalem."

Todd looked at the new vacancy in the street frontage, gaping like the bloody socket of a drawn tooth. Six minutes after the explosion it was still belching smoke and thick dust, not vigorously now but wearily, apologetically. The building was gone. Even the foundations were gone.

Todd said, "Was it anyone I know—knew?"

"David Gichon." Meir's voice was quiet, emotionless, but he did sound tired. This was not the first time he had lost friends and colleagues to this iron maiden, their profession. It was not even the first time he had been present, seen and heard it happen, seen the human consequences before they could be consigned to the decent anonymity of a black plastic bag; but still the shocking, devastating thing was not how much it affected him but how little.

The secret that his quiet manner hid from the world was not his own fear or even his own courage, which were anyway terms that had no relevance in the way he thought. It was that, every time this happened, before he had full command of the emotions ripping through his mind, the first was a brilliant crescendo of joy, a celebration that he had got away with it again, that somebody else's number had jogged his out of its place in the queue.

He had no idea if other ATOs felt the same, or if the obscene joy was uniquely his own. Over a period of years he had come to terms with it, exchanged the initial horrified disgust for mere resigned distaste, but not enough to speak of it to anyone. He thought it conceivable that everyone in the business experienced a similar pang of ecstasy when someone else's bomb went up, and that those evenings they spent together afterwards were quiet not with mourning but with the intense effort every man was making to keep the lid on his own delight. But Meir would never know because he would not ask, and even if he was right he could not imagine anyone else asking either.

Todd said, "Shit," feelingly. He had known Captain Gichon—only a little, but his regret was untinged by any paradox. "What happened?"

Meir sighed. "Sinbad. You know, our friend with the nimble fingers and the Lebanese Sentex. Almost the last thing David said was that he was lost in there, that Sinbad had him so he didn't know which way to jump. He must have guessed wrong." He looked round then, mildly surprised. "Isn't Flynn with you?"

Todd looked round too, with resignation. "He was. He must have gone walkabout. He's probably hanging out of somebody's upstairs window right now."

The ambulance with its red Star of David moved away—without speed, without the siren. The security barriers cordoning off the street were parted to let it pass. The men found it easier to breathe after it had gone.

They turned and walked back towards the command vehicle. Meir said, "There's no truth in the rumour, then."

"What rumour?"

"That you and Flynn are getting a divorce as soon as you can agree custody of the car phone."

Todd laughed aloud, a broad full-bellied laugh that turned heads and drew curious and disapproving stares. Remembering then where he was and what had happened here he winced, but Meir was unembarrassed and added a light tenor chuckle of his own. He said, "Where did you find him?"

"Mickey? I didn't find him, I built him. From a construction kit—the Laid-Back New York Press Photographer model in the Little Frankenstein range. That's why he always has that camera slung round his neck. To hide the bolts."

Meir grinned. They continued their perambulation of the devastated street. "Do you always work together?"

Todd nodded, a shade ruefully. "Pretty much. Four years ago when we started, my stories sold his photographs. Now it's the other way round."

It was an oversimplification and therefore not wholly accurate, but essentially it was the truth. Gilbert Todd was and remained one of the big names in international front-line journalism, one of the comparatively small brotherhood who had declined the role of household god open to those who switched to television news. In the industry, and also among those who read newspapers for information and informed comment rather than screamer headlines and shock-horror stories composed of monosyllables with the juicy bits picked out in black type, Todd's byline carried a special authority which still had its price.

After thirty-five years in the business he was recognised, by those capable of making a judgement, as a critical and perceptive reporter, a determined and ingenious researcher, a wordsmith with a precise and evocative command of his language and, through that, of his readers' hearts and minds. His lack of bias, of political fear or favour, was admired though his ability to see more sides to an issue than the popular one was more often a handicap than an asset. Even so his track record demanded respect: whenever the media circus was marching to one beat and Todd to another, precedent advised that Todd probably had it right. If there was a tree of internationally recognised professional journalism, Todd was somewhere near the top of it.

The irony was that, by the time he was getting into the upper branches and beginning to glimpse the overview, the tree itself was already quietly withering. It was no longer words, however, perceptive, evocative and true, which stirred individual conscience and national fervour. The great days of the correspondent were already gone. Readers—or rather, people who bought newspapers—wanted their fare instantaneous, prepackaged, predigested. Pictures had become the name of the game.

In an effort to compete with the visual media, instead of outflanking it in areas where the printed word would always have an inbuilt superiority, editors devoted more and more of their space to photographs. They forgot—perhaps the younger ones never knew—that every word in an hour-long news broadcast would not fill one page of a broadsheet newspaper, and that their natural strength was therefore in serious, analytical reporting at a depth no TV team could match. Instead they offered still monochrome photographs, inviting a direct and rarely flattering comparison with colour television news. By the time their pages were crammed with such photographs, which—however good they were in their own terms—were almost bound to be inferior to the opposition's, there was no longer the space, or the will, to fight back with quality reportage.

Todd had seen it happening, had known it was a mistake and had gone out of step on that one too. But though time had confirmed his fears, it was already too late to reverse the disastrous consequences of the error for the industry he loved. He did not think it would ever get back the status it had enjoyed when he was learning his trade, when the names of great newspapers were synonymous with the virtues of honesty and courage.

So for once in his life, when he had seen which way the wind was blowing, he had decided to bend with it. If henceforth reporting needed to be accompanied by pictures to help a semiliterate circulation understand what the words meant, he would provide his own damn pictures too.

So he picked up a lanky, drink-sodden kid in a New York bar, thrust a cheap camera and a gross of 35-millimetre films at him, and set about teaching him what sort of photographs were suitable illustration for serious journalism. He could have hired an experienced press photographer, but he thought he would have fewer arguments teaching someone from scratch. And to start with the only drawback was that neither of them knew how to develop a film.

"I don't know what Mickey would have ended up doing if I hadn't dragged him out of The Longshoreman, stuck his head under a tap and put a camera in his hands. He might have robbed banks, or become a spy. He might even have made bombs. That cheap camera tapped into a vein of wicked creativity in him, and before I knew where I was he was trying to tell me how to write stories so as to fit with the pictures he was taking. Finally we worked it out that if we went to the same places, my words and his pictures ought to have something in common without either dictating the other, so that's what we do. I detail the general, he spotlights the particular. I still reckon I'm giving a young lad a chance in life. I think he thinks he's supporting the aged."

And if, alongside the satisfaction of having guessed right once again and having survived another revolution, there dwelt a small bitterness that the name and work of his protégé were known and sought after by people who had once known and sought his, Gilbert Todd was old enough and wise enough to recognise the working of human nature in himself as well as in others. He was not envious of Flynn's success, did not begrudge him the exhibitions of his work in New York, the invitations—rarely accepted, unless he was in the mood to scandalise someone—to fashionable gatherings in London and Monaco.

If he was a little disappointed, it was not that Flynn's reputation had grown faster than might have been expected, nor even that his own was already past its prime, but because of the future that painted for a profession he had grown up in and would have liked to grow old in. There were times now, mostly early mornings with the dawn cracking grey over one torn city or another, when he did not expect the job to last long enough to see him out.

They reached the command vehicle. The screens were being dismantled. Sullivan put his head through the back door and exchanged a few words of Hebrew with someone inside. Then he said to Todd, "Do you want to see what's left of the workshop?"

Todd grimaced. He would not see anything he had not seen before, but he would not get any pleasure from it either. "Not much, but I suppose I'd better. Mickey'll want photographs. Where the hell is he, anyway?" They both looked round, without success.

Automatically, although most of the front wall was gone and all that remained of the door were the pillars, one barely to shoulder height, on which it had hung, they entered by the doorway. Neither of them was aware how grotesque that looked, what a parody it made of the devastation. They entered by the nonexistent door and turned up along the missing wall, and stopped at the edge of the crater the device had excavated four feet into the foundations.

The two men looked thoughtfully into the hole. Both were conscious of the third man, who had been kneeling on ground that had since disappeared when the bomb went off.

Todd cleared his throat. "Any estimate of the size?"

"Big enough?" suggested Meir.

The roof was gone. Bits of it were in backyards a street away, other bits were piled as rubble in the surviving corners of the building. Gables on either side framed the sky, blue paling to pearl with the imminent dusk. Both had been damaged, one more obviously than the other. It would require a structural engineer to adjudicate on the safety of the adjoining buildings.

So a man crawling across the roofs in advance of any such survey was taking a certain risk. When a boot at the end of a long leg descended into the limestone quarry that the workshop had become, Todd thought wearily that he should have guessed where Flynn would be. "If you disturb anything up there, the police'll have kittens."

Flynn's wolf-wicked grin fell on them from a height, like the Cheshire cat's but less innocent. "It's a roof. What's to disturb up here?"

"The Defence Minister's peace of mind?" suggested Meir. "Seriously, I've no idea what you'll find up there."

"Angles," said Flynn. He had the viewfinder to his face as he spoke, the Cyclops eye of the camera roaming restlessly over the scene. "That's what it's all about—angles. That's what makes the difference between a photograph and a snapshot. Not the camera. Not the guy behind the camera. Not the fancy lenses or the clever filters, or any of the rest of that junk they make foam-lined compartments for in expensive camera bags. None of that's worth a dime. Angles is what counts. Being there, and then angles."

Todd reflected that the sum of the difference between him and Flynn, and between his generation and Flynn's, was encapsulated in that statement. Looking back, it seemed to Todd that he had been middle-aged before anyone asked him to get an angle on anything. Before that it had been sufficient to offer a story that was detailed, accurate and complete. Angles—the idea that a story could be made more interesting, more catchy, by zeroing in on some aspect of it no one else had thought of, probably because it was largely irrelevant—were the invention of those without the skill to obtain a complete account or the readership to appreciate one. They were the triumph of appearance over content, of facade over substance. He sighed, as a man might who had, quite cleverly, created a monster.

He shook himself then, almost physically, irritated at his morbid mood which he recognized had more to do with the man who had died here than the one photographing the scene. Mickey Flynn was no monster, any more than Todd was Frankenstein. Mickey Flynn was young, overconfident and American; little or none of that was his fault; age would hopefully wither him somewhat, and in polite company he could pass for English—well, a Yorkshireman or a Geordie or some such—as long as he kept his mouth shut. On the other hand, he was capable of hard work, good work and loyalty, of good humour albeit served up with bad language, and of occasional surprising acts of great kindness. Todd would not have married him, but as a partner he was aware he could have done worse.

The camera descended on its strap. "Take this, I'm coming down." Todd took it. He had to reach up for it. Flynn grinned at him. Then he launched himself into space. The damaged gable was fifteen feet above the rubble-strewn floor, and Flynn was in mid-air long enough for Meir to murmur, "Ahuvya," thoughtfully.

Flynn landed in a crouch like a paratrooper and kept his feet, the thick dust puffing up round his boots. Todd held out the camera, but Flynn made no move to take it, seemed hardly to see it. He never straightened up, remained bent over his bent knees with his fierce eyes caught up in the corner by Todd's feet.

"Holy God," he said, and though he was notoriously foul-mouthed even among the not particularly fastidious press gang, there was reverence in how he said it. His eyes were the eyes of Macbeth on Banquo's chair. Finally he said, quite calmly, not to Todd, "Is that what it looks like?"

Todd's every instinct told him to turn round so he too could see what it was behind him that they were staring at. His shoulders began to twist but Meir stopped him, a sudden strident authority running through his mild demeanour like a steel thread.

"Don't move, Gil. I mean it—not a muscle. Flynn, you get out of here."

Todd's blood ran like meltwater. He still could not see what they were staring at—Flynn half on his knees like a pointer, his eyes hollow with shock, and the ATO from whom stillness was expanding outward like a kind of force field—but he knew what it meant when a bomb disposal expert took charge.

Doing nothing—not turning round, not running—took all the strength and all the courage he had. He felt the meltwater drain from his face, leaving his brain light and racing; felt the warm weight behind his knees that would soon be an invisible tremor and soon after that a patently obvious shake. He said, faintly rather than with urgency, "What is it?"

Meir was on his belly, worming through the rubble by Todd's left foot. The ends of his long fingers were brushing mortar dust away with strokes that would not have wakened a sleeper. But his voice was devastatingly normal, the same essentially conversational tone in which he had been talking before Flynn's inspired discovery. Later, when he had the time, he would marvel that Flynn had spotted the lethal significance of something so almost totally covered. But for now his mind had enough to deal with.

He said, "A little afterthought for whoever came in here to tidy up. Or in case David beat him, he could maybe take the legs off him when he stood back to admire his work." When he realised what he had said he looked up at Todd and smiled. "Sorry."

Flynn said, "Is it a pressure plate?" His voice was hard, as if he were working at keeping the emotion out of it.

Meir glanced sidelong at him. "You still here? There's nothing you can do, you know, except maybe get in my way."

The sweat was breaking under Todd's collar and in the palms of his hands. His voice was unsteady. "Mickey, get out. There's no point—"

Flynn ignored him. Hard and fast he said to Meir, "You've only got one good hand. I've got two. I'm a photographer, they don't shake."

Part of Meir's training had been in the avoidance of unnecessary movement, so he did not shrug. But his eyebrows made a minimalist gesture not unlike a shrug. "All right, let's get it done."

In fairness to the man who made the device, he never intended it to be his apprentice piece, an item on which the quality of his workmanship should be judged. That was the big one, the one which Gichon had wrestled with and lost. This little booby trap was just an extra surprise for the unwary, sneaky rather than clever, put together in a few minutes and rendered safe in not much longer. It was never going to present a major problem, not once Flynn had spotted it and Todd had been restrained from disturbing it by the shift of his not inconsiderable weight.

Meir made the thing stable with nothing fancier than the contents of his top pocket and the deftness of his fingers—at least, the deftness of his and the steadiness of Flynn's, keeping the box of tricks still to be worked on. There was a pressure plate: Meir immobilised it. There was also a timing mechanism, run by a cheap child's watch with Superman on the analogue face. Meir grinned at that: so Sinbad had a sense of humour. He stopped the movement with fully four minutes still on the clock. Then he sent Flynn racing back to the command vehicle for some equipment and finished the job. Only then did he allow Todd to move.

Todd took three steps away from the harmless remains, and then the warm tension behind his knees exploded softly, dissolving the muscles and ligaments so that one moment he was walking and the next his legs had folded under him and he had no idea where his feet were.

Flynn, chuckling evilly, caught him as he went down, strong hands rock-steady under his armpits. "Hey, old man, can't you take the pressure no more?"

Flynn drove them back to their hotel. On the way he started chuckling again. "There was four minutes to go when Simon Meir stopped the clock."

Todd was working up to being blasé about it now that his knees had stopped shaking. "As much as that?"

"If we'd got there four minutes later, that thing would have killed you."

Todd did not see what he was driving at. He frowned. "So?"

Flynn grinned his wicked grin, scattered two old ladies crossing to the Damascus Gate. "So you owe your life to the car phone."

[3]

Another man—younger, hungrier—might have spent half the night pounding away, unpopularly, on his typewriter and the rest of it expensively on the telephone. Gilbert Todd ran a bath. He made it deep and he made it hot. He put a stool within easy reach, and laid it out with a bottle of malt whisky and two glasses, one filled with ice cubes from the little fridge in the corner of his room; a cigar in an aluminum tube, a lighter and an ashtray; and a detective story of no literary merit whatever. Thus equipped he settled down—by inches, a Plimsoll line of lobster red ascending his pink bulk—to work the kinks out of his soul.

Mickey Flynn was not working either—indeed, had no work to do. There was nothing in his camera but establishing shots of roofs and rubble. All the time he could have been recording, moment by moment, the successful defusing of a terrorist device at one man's feet and another's face and hands—hand—Todd had been holding the camera and he had been holding the bomb. So he went out on the town.

Flynn could have a cheaper night on the tiles than almost anyone in the civilised world. He no longer drank alcohol and had never smoked. But he liked the atmosphere that developed when people came together over drinks, whether in a Belfast pub or a Turkish coffeehouse, and the arguments it was so easy to get into. For the price of lemonade and peanuts he could cut a swathe through Jerusalem from Mount Scopus to the Hebrew University, leaving a wake of bitterly disputatious Moslems, Armenians and Jews in their various quarters banging their fists on tables among half-drained glasses of their various beverages. Better yet, if someone produced a pack of cards or a chess set in any of the watering holes along his route, he could end the evening with more cash in his pockets than he began it.

By night the Old City was an extraordinary confection of darkness and lights, like a stage set for a pantomime. Floodlights played on the high golden walls, ruggedly individual in their many angles and the massive bulwarks of their mediaeval gates, and on the most prominent buildings within. On two sides deep ravines disappeared in inky blackness from the foot of the walls so that the city seemed to sail on the night like a golden galleon.

Lights around the Temple Mount gleamed off the great gilded dome of the Mosque of Omar, the twinkling blue mosaic supporting it, and the silver dome of the El Aqsa mosque. The ancients who chose Mount Moriah for their showcase—Abraham preparing to sacrifice his son, Solomon raising Israel's first temple, Mohammed ascending to heaven —showed a fine appreciation of the dramatic possibilities offered by this highest rampart of the old Canaanite stronghold. They might not have foreseen such things as floodlighting, and American photographers gazing across the Kedron ravine from the Mount of Olives, but they knew that as long as Jerusalem stood, whatever stood on the high fastness of Mount Moriah would impress the hell out of somebody.

Flynn hitched a lift to the top road then ambled, loose-limbed, hands in pockets, down the narrow high-walled pathway that led under the golden onion-domes of the Russian church towards the ravine. At the bottom he turned north, strolling parallel to the city wall until he reached the Lion Gate and went in. This put him in the Moslem quarter and posed him the challenge of picking a worthwhile quarrel in a coffeeshop.

Having succeeded in this—the comparative merits of Anwar Sadat, assassinated president of Egypt, and President Assad of Syria as leaders of the Arab world provoked a gratifying amount of controversy—he moved on. Up the Via Dolorosa he annoyed some Christians by asking about the Turin Shroud, then he doglegged back out of the walled city at the Jaffa Gate, under the frowning Herodian eminence of the Citadel and the tall finger of David's Tower.

Outside the walls raised by Suleiman the Magnificent, the streets were wider, and better lit, and less hazardous with donkey dung, but only by looking back at the golden galleon sailing the Judaean night could Flynn persuade himself that this was still the City of God (or at least a city of God-botherers) not Madrid, or Le Havre, or Milton Keynes.

In the New Town, where business houses nodded politely at government agencies and religious institutions, Flynn grew to a slow awareness that he felt less at ease in these dull, worthy, well-cared-for boulevards than in the teaming dark alleys of the Old City. He knew that in the huddle of tiny homes and tiny businesses, their faces turned blind to the narrow passageways hiding lives of unexpected richness and complexity like secret gardens, unspeakable deeds were plotted and occasionally carried out. Israeli friends warned him to be on his guard in there, especially after dark.

Yet he could only speak as he found, and in the dense, tense streets of the divided city he had found no hostility, no enmity, only a desperate weariness ground into the very bones of the tough, gnarled, kindly little men and their doe-eyed, covertly watchful women. He supposed that the terrorists lived somewhere; perhaps he had even met them, on their day off when they were as kindly and hospitable as everyone else; all he knew was that he had felt safer in those dark and troubled alleys than he did now, walking wide streets flanked by worthy unimaginative modern buildings.

Of course, that unexpected feeling of vulnerability might have been due in some measure to the fact that he was being followed.

On a street corner he found a cafe. Someone leaving let out a belch of light, the chink of glasses, the smell of spirits and coffee and cigarettes, a ragged chorus of folk music. Flynn turned in as if drawn, before the door had even closed. Pausing only to establish the ethos of the place, and thereby which songs from his extensive repertoire would get him free drinks and which would get him shot, he helped himself to a resting guitar and joined in the entertainment.

The woman followed him inside. She was not so much too old as too independent in her manner to be described as a girl. She might have been a little older than him, perhaps the other side of thirty. She nodded to the waiter as if she knew him, then seated herself in a corner. The fact that Flynn was perched on the bar, long legs dangling, working his way through a protest song of the Vietnam years in a voice both deeper and more musical than people would have guessed from hearing him speak, gave her all the excuse she needed to watch him.

The fact that she was a woman under the age of sixty sitting alone in a cafe gave Flynn all the excuse he needed to watch her.

It was impossible to describe her without resort to the word "average." She was of average height and build. Her face was strongly structured, the skin scrubbed, the overall effect squarely within that universal mean between pretty and plain. She had thick dark hair that dropped straight to her shoulders where it had been lopped off level, possibly with kitchen scissors. She had brown eyes, smoky with depth. She wore no makeup. She wore a denim skirt and a blouson jacket in a kind of white nylon that was supposed to look like satin.

What she saw was a tall young man in his late twenties, all arms and legs, and shrewd brown eyes and slightly long brown hair that was not so much making a statement as trying to remember to visit a barber. She noticed that his face was broad across the eyes and pointed in the chin; that his mouth was wide and slightly ragged, and that the unexpected mobility of it had established well-defined creases on both sides; and that there was something faintly disturbing about his expression, even at rest, which was that of an amiable Mephistopheles. But she made no effort to analyse Flynn in the way that he was analysing her, because she knew who he was and what he was, and also what she wanted with him.

When its owner reclaimed his guitar, Flynn got down from the bar and ambled over to the table in the corner. "My name's Mickey Flynn, what's yours?"

Insolent in their lack of haste, the smoky eyes travelled up the length of him. When they reached his face, suddenly she smiled. "Thank you, I'll have a glass of tea."

Flynn laughed out loud—to the consternation of the singer, who was bewailing an ancient catastrophe of more than average proportions —and got her the drink. He did not buy anything for himself, he was surrounded by enough lemonade to top up the Dead Sea.

Her name was Leila. She drank the tea without either haste or import, just as if it was tea and it was good. When her glass was empty she got up to leave. Before Flynn had to decide whether or not to leave with her, someone rapped on the window. The room was immediately silent—so still Flynn could hear the swift footsteps departing down the pavement—and remained so for perhaps five seconds. Then the waiter sighed heavily and said, "Sorry, folks, it's closing time," in three languages.

Outside Flynn and his friend turned along the pavement. "Where now?" said Flynn.

"Where's your car?" asked the woman. Her voice was interesting, slightly soft and slightly harsh, like the Jordan running over rocks.

He raised an eyebrow. "What makes you think I have a car?"

Leila smiled at him again as she had when she asked for her drink. "Mickey Flynn, I not only know what kind of car you have, and the registration number, I know the number of your car phone."

He felt the insides of him go very still—rather as Todd had frozen with his foot against the booby trap, and for much the same reason. Flynn was a private person in only a very few senses, but he still felt exposed, threatened, by the calculated depth of her knowledge. "You were following me, then."

"You noticed that? Good." She seemed genuinely pleased. "Why didn't you challenge me?"

It was his turn to smile, and he did it slowly. "I did."

She thought back, remembering. "So you did."

They walked together, slowly, without touching. A spring rain was falling on the wilderness city. Neither of them had a hat. Quickly the woman's hair turned to a dark veil that clung to her face. If she noticed she paid it no heed, not even to the extent of speeding her step. Slowly, by wide pavements, they made their way northeast, back towards the city walls.

The woman Leila said, "You're a press photographer."

Flynn smiled gravely at the toes of his wet boots. "Good, but not as impressive as the car phone number."

She smiled up at him briefly. "I saw the spread you did on Ireland in *The New York Times* last year."

That did impress him. He did not meet too many people outside America who took *The New York Times*. He broke his stride, peering down at her curiously. Wet he looked more disreputable than dry. "Is that what this is about? You have something for me?"

She broke away and walked on. Back over her shoulder, casually, she said, "I might have."

"When will you know?"

She glanced at him, a world of knowing in her eye. "I know now. The question is, when will I decide?"

"About me? You can trust me."

Leila laughed outright. "If I had a shekel-piece for every man who'd told me that—!"

Flynn laughed with her, a shade ruefully. "Trust me"—he had used the words himself, in another context, and they had meant nothing. He felt a twinge of shame. If she knew that, it meant all women did, and he did not like what that said about men. Being a black sheep was one thing, but he did not relish being just another sheep in a black flock.

She said, watching him sideways, "What we're talking about. It isn't a flower show."

"If you've seen what I do, you know I'm not into flower shows." The spread in NYT had been on the arrest of a gun-running ship in the Irish Sea. One of Todd's contacts had not only alerted them to the action but got them on board the naval vessel which made the interception.

"I know. All the same, you mightn't want to go this far. It could get rough. It shouldn't, because I'd have it all set up for you, but things can always go wrong. Maybe you reckon no pictures are worth risking life and liberty for, not even these."

Flynn felt as if the woman and he were at opposite ends of a taut fishing line. What he could not work out was which of them had the rod and which the hook. He said carefully, to prolong the play until he could establish whether he was fisher or fish, "There are things I risk them for. If you know that much about me, you probably know what they are. But I'm not committing myself to anything until I know what we're talking about."

She thought, then nodded. "That's fair."

"And who you represent."

She looked at him fast for that. "You won't take my good faith on trust but you expect me to take yours?"

They were back to that word "trust" again. Flynn shrugged. "You already know who I am, what I do and pretty much how I do it. You know that I owe a duty of discretion to people who give me information. That's not me being noble, it's the way we work—all of us—the only way we can get the job done. The job of the news industry is to gather information, not to pass judgement. You're a lot less likely to have trouble with me than I am to have trouble with you."

Her eyes narrowed on the arrogance in her look. "I thought that was what you got paid for."

He laughed, without much humour. "Oh it is, baby, it is. But it's down to me to make sure it's worth it. I'm not about to leave my head on a stake in pursuit of a Pulitzer Prize."

Leila watched him a moment longer, then turned away. "All right. If you don't want it, I'll offer it to someone else."

He felt the ground firming under his feet. "I doubt that. If you'd wanted any old pictures you'd have bought yourself a camera. You want me to take these because you want them to reach the markets I have access to. You think there's publicity in it for you, and that means funds. Ahmed's Snapshot Emporium might take the same pictures for you but he wouldn't sell them the same places. You wouldn't have gone to the trouble of following me—of checking out my car phone—if it wasn't my name you needed."

There was both amusement and exasperation in her look. "You have a fine opinion of yourself, Mr. Flynn!" She tossed the wet hair out of her eyes like a spurred horse.

Flynn grinned. He knew now where he stood. "So what are we talking about?"

For just a moment longer she hesitated. Then he saw her decide, like a door closing in her eye. "All right. I won't tell you who I am—who we are—though you may guess. It doesn't matter, one way or the other. What we're talking about are the first photographs of a new training camp where people will acquire the skills and techniques necessary for the pursuit of politics by other means."

By the time Flynn had worked out what she meant she had moved on, talking in a swift low monotone now that she had decided to go ahead with this. "I can get you taken there, shown round, brought back. Blindfolded, of course. I can get someone there to talk to you about what you'll see, and answer any questions you have. Well, all the questions you'd expect him to answer. Within the limits of natural prudence, you'll be able to photograph anything you see—drill, weapons practice, bomb-making, communications. It's a liberal academy. Are you interested?"

Of course he was interested. He could see the spread already. "What do you get out of it?"

"The same as you: thousands of people looking at those photographs. Some of them will be horrified, but some will be inspired. And some of them will send us money, and things we need more than money."

"You want me to do your propaganda!"

The woman shrugged. "Call it what you like. Our propaganda is your exclusive is your publisher's profit margin. If I don't care that you and your publisher will make money out of it, I don't see why you should care if we do too."

Back home, when Flynn was younger and still acknowledged somewhere as home, there was a vogue for T-shirts that declared: "If you're not part of the solution, you're part of the problem." It was simplistic, but—in this context at least—it was true. He could not reconcile what he told Leila about nonjudgemental information gathering with what he had told the girl in the hotel bar about the media's role in the propagation of terrorism. Usually the dichotomy amused rather than disturbed him; but he resented the very deliberate way these people proposed to exploit his name. Of course, he had made his name, and for four years his living, by exploiting the troubled and troublesome of the world.

He nodded slowly. "OK. Listen, I'll need to talk to my partner about this. Where can we find you—?"

Her eyes flashed at him and her jaw came up. "This is nothing to do with your partner. It's strictly between you and me. I'm prepared to arrange for you to be taken in there, but I'm not organising coach trips."

"We work together," said Flynn mildly. "Always."

"Not this time," the woman said, "or the deal's off. Talk to him if you must. Tell him what the situation is. It's the pictures we want: we have to take a risk with you to get them, but we don't have to take risks with anybody else. If you want to go ahead, Mr. Todd sits this dance out."

"Hell, I don't know . . ."

"Well you'd better know," she said decisively, "or you'd better find out. There's no room for negotiation on this. I'm already out on a limb, I'm not handing out saws as well. Suit yourself, come or don't come; but if you come, come alone."

"Where shall I find you?"

"You won't. I'll find you."

She left him there. They had walked past the great edifice of the Damascus Gate, rising like a castle against the night sky. A fire-tender, two-tone wailing, scurried up the road and Flynn's eyes followed automatically. When he looked back Leila was gone. He saw her compact figure, in its white blouson, stride purposefully away down the concourse to the gate and turn in. He could have followed, but he doubted if she would let herself be caught. Besides, it was not Leila he needed to talk to now. It was Todd.

[4]

He expected Todd to be doubtful, to need persuading. He did not expect the man to jump down his throat in size-eleven boots.

Largely the fault was Flynn's own. If he had exercised a little patience and waited until breakfast, they could have discussed it with a degree of detachment and good humour, and while the outcome would probably have been the same it is an acknowledged fact that hell hath no fury like a journalist before his first cup of coffee.

Also, of course, Todd had had a particularly trying day. A man he knew had been blown up. A man he did not know had tried to blow him up. And now, no more than moments, so it felt, into a deep untroubled sleep, with the hotel finally silent and the clock by his bed ticking its way softly round to 2 A.M., here was Mickey Flynn hammering urgently on his door, hissing his name through the keyhole, likely to get them both thrown out if he did not put a stop to the disturbance soon.

So he climbed out of his warm bed into the cool room, padded barefoot across the floor, opened the door with a flourish of uncharacteristic violence, and said ominously, "This had better be good."

Flynn was straight off the street and still wet. His khaki jacket was black and heavy with it, and his hair hung sodden in his eyes. He made Todd feel damp just by brushing past him. "It is, it is." Without seeking leave he dived into Todd's bathroom and emerged with his head buried in a towel. He dropped the jacket on the floor. He was hardly any drier underneath.

The account of his meeting with Leila came out a shade disjointed, the component parts taken out of sequence, fact and comment interlinked. This was more of an irritation than a problem to Todd, who saw it as further evidence of the photographer's inability to see beyond individual images to the cohesive flow of events in the real world. But he listened, in a silence that became increasingly difficult and strained as the inarticulate narrative proceeded, until Flynn finished—or rather ended, not so much reaching a conclusion as running out of things to add.

Then Todd, who had been surrounded by actual and potential explosions half the day, gave vent to one of his own. Fortunately, in view of the hour and the proximity of other guests, none of them other journalists, he had long ago learned the art of shouting quietly.

He began: "I can't believe you're serious. I've never heard such an irresponsible suggestion from a so-called professional newsman in all my life!" After that he moved up a gear and got rather personal and really rather unpleasant.

The interesting thing, certainly from the viewpoint of any independent observer, though Todd himself was not immune to its curiosity, was that Flynn sat there and took it: sat with his long limbs folded, with his knees drawn up to his pointed chin, with his eyes full of resentment and rebellion and his hair tousled like a schoolboy's, and heard himself denigrated and abused almost without answering back.

It was as if Todd was the one whose work was in demand, this time as always. It was as if Todd could do as he liked, regardless of his partner's inclinations; could get up and leave this room and do as his own will and conscience dictated, and need acknowledge no man's primacy. It was as if Flynn was still a boy, a novice, still somehow overshadowed by the old man with printing ink under his fingernails, not a professional in his own right with a track record of successes to prove it.

It was as if Flynn still owed a debt to Todd, and neither of them was about to forget it. So Flynn sat hunched round his bent knees, bitter coals sparking in his eyes, and did not walk out with a parting obscenity and go his own way as the independent observer might have thought he was entitled to.

And in due course, when the fear and frustration of the day had spent themselves in quiet shouting, Todd grew aware that, while right, he was not behaving altogether reasonably. He broke off in mid-polemic with a little sigh, like the sigh of a third man who had been in the room with them waiting for Todd's temper to abate. There was a kettle on the chest of drawers, with sachets of coffee. He filled the kettle in the bathroom and plugged it in. Then he sat on the rumpled bed and kicked his slippers off.

"I'm sorry, Mickey. It's been a rough day, but it's not your fault. Except getting me up at this time: that's your fault."

Flynn smiled: not his quick, wicked grin but a rare, secret smile out of nowhere, a brief glimpse into the heart of the man where there was gentleness and generosity and other things not suspected even by people who thought they knew him well. Todd had known him for nine months before he saw that smile, and when it came it transformed his perception of the young man he had hauled out of the gutter, dried out and hammered into a useful tool. That smile was the first indication that there was more to Mickey Flynn than met the eye.

Flynn rose from the chair, unfolding his long limbs easily. "Forget the coffee, Gil. Go back to bed. I'm sorry I woke you. If you don't want me to do the job, I'll tell her we're not interested. It's no sweat."

Todd flinched, as he frequently did at Flynn's language, which was offensive even more often than it was blasphemous. At least it offended him. "No, sit down. I don't want you to do the job, but there are better reasons than my sensibilities. For your own safety you should understand them."

When the coffee was made he tried to explain logically what he knew instinctively. "You could do the job, Mickey. You could probably make good money out of it. But you'd have to, because you wouldn't be able to work here again afterwards. The reasons they want you to do it, Leila and her friends—let's not be coy here, I'd guess we're talking about the Popular Front for the Liberation of Palestine—are the best reasons you could have for not touching it with a barge pole.

"Your name means something in the news world. Whatever you choose to photograph will be seen by a wide international readership. You make news these days, Mickey. The rest of us can still claim to be only observers of events, with no share in the credit or blame for them. But people like you stand outside the shelter of that umbrella. Your interest causes events in the first place, and makes little events into big ones. That puts an onus on you that the rest of us don't have to worry about.

"You can't take a disinterested view any longer—probably not anywhere but certainly not here. Anything you photograph you'll be seen as supporting unless the pictures categorically say otherwise. You're going to have to start making moral judgements, whether you like it or not, because your fence-sitting days are over."

"If you're not part of the solution, you're part of the problem," murmured Flynn.

Todd looked at him oddly. "Something like that. At any rate, you're going to have to start picking sides. If you do this publicity stunt for the PFLP, that'll put you on their side however strenuously you deny it. They'll know it, and they'll pump it for all it's worth. The Israeli authorities will know it, and they'll be gunning for you—metaphorically if not literally. You'll never do a balanced story here again, because half of those involved won't deal with you. Once the security forces have the idea that your sympathies are with the PFLP, you won't be able to hear yourself think for the sound of slamming doors. Oh, they'll do their duty by you—but no one will talk to you, everything will come via the press office and that means you'll always be the last on any scene."

"Car phone or no car phone," said Flynn.

Todd frowned. More than usual, he did not know what to make of Flynn's attitude. He was not sure if his prophesies of professional doom were disturbing or amusing him. But the point was important and he felt the need to pursue it.

"Mickey," he said forcibly, "this isn't a joke. It's our livelihoods I'm talking about, our profession—mine because I chose it, and worked bloody hard to get on in it, and spent twenty years getting to the point where people believed what I wrote just because I wrote it; and yours because of a chance encounter in a New York bar at the precise moment that I needed a photographer almost as much as you needed a job.

"Well no, actually," he went on, warming to the theme, "it wasn't a job you needed so much as a wet-nurse. You were about the sorriest looking streak of humanity I'd ever seen. It took me two days to get you clean, and a week to get you dried out. Do you even remember that week?—you didn't seem altogether aware of what was happening at the time."

Flynn said nothing. He remembered it all right: the hurting and the fear. He had been working his way steadily from obscurity to oblivion and had been nicely anaesthetised for the final plunge when an Englishman in a baggy raincoat whom he did not know from Adam had grabbed him by the collar and hauled him back. He had never known why.

Apparently Todd did not either. "God knows why I thought I could make a photographer of you. After eighteen hours without a drink you couldn't have held a chest of drawers steady, let alone a camera. You couldn't eat, you couldn't sleep—all I could get down you was orange juice, and if you weren't quite at the little green men stage you were bloody close. If someone hadn't sorted you out right then, you'd have been dead within the month."

Flynn said quietly, "What do you want me to say, Gil? That I'm grateful—again? Sure, I'm grateful. I owe you my life, and my living. You think I need reminding?"

Todd dismissed that with an impatient flick of his hand. "I don't want your gratitude," he said, though probably it was not true. "I just want you to remember that, however good you are at this—and you are good, you started being good as soon as you worked out what those *f*-numbers were for—you've still a lot of ground to make up in the experience department. Four years isn't long enough to acquire all the instincts you need to survive in this business. Little as you may like it, you're going to have to depend on me for that for some time yet."

"All right."

Todd felt his impatience mounting rather than subsiding, and he was not sure whether it was a twinge of guilt because he was being unreasonable or genuine irritation because Flynn was. "All right's all very well," he snapped. "But left to your own devices you'd have done this thing, wouldn't you? And then neither of us would have been able to work here again. And a newsman who debars himself from working certain places soon starts running out of world."

In their early days together Flynn had taken tongue lashings much worse than this one. But it had been some time now since Todd last laid into him and he had rather got out of the way of it. He started to snap back, "If that's how you feel maybe we should . . ."

"What?" Todd's bejowled jaw jutted pugnaciously.

The answer was obvious: split up, go each their own way, pay for their own mistakes and not each other's. But even angry Flynn could not say it. What he owed Todd was more than lip service, and it bound him to the older man even when the partnership grew uncomfortable. Todd could have ended it with a word, or at least set the genie free of the bottle to leave or stay as he chose. Todd knew that too, and said nothing, which said rather more about him than it did about Flynn.

Flynn backed down. "Nothing."

Todd knew that he had won and grinned expansively. "Do you know the secret of continued success in this business?"

"What?"

"Knowing when to walk away. Walk away from this one, Mickey. Better still, run."

Flynn climbed once more to his feet. Now the passion was gone out of him—first the enthusiasm, then the anger—he finally looked tired. He picked his wet coat off the floor. "Sorry I woke you, Gil."

"Think nothing of it," said Todd, magnanimous in victory. "I'd sooner be woken up by you than about you. I don't want to be summoned to a morgue in the middle of some night to identify your body."

The grin was a weary ghost of its former self. "Sure, Gil. OK." He padded away, closing the door softly behind him. He always looked as if he slept in his clothes: Todd thought tonight—what was left of tonight—he might actually do it.

After he was gone Todd thought back over the day's events. But for Flynn he would very likely be dead, or at best waking up in a hospital bed with a cage under the blankets where his legs used to be. He owed Flynn for that—not only for seeing the danger he was in but for staying until he was safe. Maybe in the strictest sense of the word that had not been wise either, but he was grateful. He should really have told Flynn so, have thanked him.

He made as if to trot after Flynn, to do it now. But he stopped before he reached his own door. It was late, they were both tired. Tomorrow was another day—well, later in the same day actually, but they would be fresher then. He would thank Flynn at breakfast. Or if not then, sometime.

After she left Flynn at the Damascus Gate, the woman cut through the Old City and went by roundabout ways to report to her superior. She was not confident that her plan would be crowned with success.

"If it was just him, he'd do it," she said, with some regret. "He's perfect, from our point of view: the name, the reputation—everybody knows who he is. He could be in and out in just a few hours, no risk to speak of—and even if something went wrong, what could he tell anyone they don't already know? For that we'd have his photographs— Freedom Fighters in Training, Somewhere in Palestine. They'd be worth three battalions to us."

"If they're the right photographs."

"How can they be the wrong ones? It's a new camp, a new development—anything we can learn about it has to be helpful. What the facilities are. What weapons they're training with. They're after the publicity, remember, they'll be showing the best things they have. If they have something capable of shooting down helicopters, this is the one way we can find out that doesn't involve wreckage and bodies scattered over the West Bank. One photograph containing that information would pay for the whole operation.

"The other interesting question is, who's going to be there? They'll hardly let Flynn take full-face portraits, but with an image enhancer and an expert in comparative analysis we should end up with a fair idea who most of the shadowy figures in the background are. And if you're taking bets, I'll put money on one of them being Sinbad. We chased him out of Nablus, now we've chased him out of Jerusalem. He'll be looking for somewhere nice and quiet to work now, country air and the company of friends. Wouldn't you like to get your hands on Sinbad?"

"You think we could find this place from Flynn's photographs?"

The woman Flynn knew as Leila shrugged. "Maybe. From the photographs, plus what Flynn can tell us about it."

"He may not want to talk to us at all."

She raised an eyebrow. "He won't get the choice. When I grill someone I don't turn the heat down until he's nicely done all over."

"Is that wise?" frowned Major Ben Simeon. "Don't forget, Flynn's not only press, he's an American citizen. I don't want this developing into an international incident."

The smile on the face of Captain Deborah Lev became a grin almost as evil as Flynn's. "Oh, I'll pretend to be someone else—Black September perhaps. They've been rather quiet recently and there's nothing like a bit of infighting to stir the pot. After all, the more they kill one another, the fewer are left to kill anyone else."

"What if somebody kills Flynn?"

"They'll still want to use his pictures. They'll appear somewhere, sooner or later. We may just do the best we can with what's published. It won't be the same as having the full reels, but beggars can't be choosers."

The major, who was sandyish and fortyish, regarded her with disfavour. "If you were a man, Lev, you'd be described as a ruthless bastard."

Deborah Lev smiled again, with no humour whatever. "If I was a man, Major, I'd be described as a colonel."

He let that pass. Actually he did not doubt it. "What will you do if Flynn backs out—look for someone else?"

Lev grimaced. "I may have to. It won't work as well with anyone else. It may not work at all—the first priority is that the PFLP accepts him, which means the potential benefit to them has to be greater than the risk. They took some persuading about Flynn; offhand I can't think of anyone else they'll even consider."

"Perhaps you should take up photography yourself."

"Don't think I haven't thought of it. But it wouldn't help. I can't offer them the kind of coverage that justifies the risk—that has to be someone famous, someone whose work they can check out. My cover wouldn't stand up to that kind of scrutiny. I've been lucky getting this close to them. I've only got away with it because I've never posed enough danger that they wanted chapter and verse on me. If I try to get much closer we'll end up with nothing; except me, and I'll end up dead."

Major Ben Simeon stretched out his legs, leaned back in his chair. He was not altogether sorry that the ambitious Captain Lev had come unstuck. "Never mind, it was a good idea while it lasted."

"I'll keep the channels open a little longer. You never know, something may happen to change Flynn's mind."

"Like what?"

"Like Gil Todd having an accident, for instance. Todd's the thinker of that partnership. If I could have got Flynn to say yes while I had him, he'd have done it. But where Flynn would see the byline, Todd'll see the problems. He's the obstacle. If something were to happen to him, so Flynn had to make his own decisions for a while, I could hook him."

Major Ben Simeon peered at her from under sandy eyebrows. "You would not, however, contemplate provoking such a fortuitous accident."

"Of course not, sir."

"Of course not."

[5]

In any event, Todd and Flynn breakfasted not in their hotel but on the Amsterdam plane.

A little after eight Todd's phone rang. He spoke briefly to the caller, and a light like wine began to glow in his eyes. Then he rang Flynn's room.

Flynn took time to answer, and longer to understand. His voice was thick, his mind not yet in gear. He sounded as if he had been summoned back from the deepest part of his delayed night's sleep.

Todd gave up trying to explain. "Pack a bag and meet me in the lobby in fifteen minutes. We're going to Holland."

"What—? Why?"

"Because I say so," Todd said briskly.

It was thirty miles to the airport at Lod. Flynn drove and Todd explained. "There's going to be fun and games in Dam Square this afternoon. Everybody from the South Moluccans to the National Front is going to be there, and if you think they're going to settle for applauding the speeches, or even abusing the speakers, you have another think coming."

"Who actually called the meeting?" Americans do not say "actually": it was a measure of Flynn's association with the Englishman that, between obscenities, he could sound just like him.

"Ah. Well, ostensibly it was an undergraduate group campaigning for more university places for overseas students. Since the group largely consists of overseas students, the Dutch nationalists reckon it's a Communist plot. The feminists want more university places for women, together with the child-care facilities that would enable them to take them up. Gay Rights activists want positive discrimination for homosexual students. The Moral Majority, which probably sounds even better in Dutch, wants hanging, drawing and quartering for homosexual students. The Church of Latter-Day Disapprovers wants hanging, drawing and quartering for everybody, excepting its radical offshoot the Flesh Mortifiers, who might enjoy it too much."

"And they're all going to be in Dam Square this afternoon?"

"Some of them are bringing some extremist friends."

"You ever feel Jerusalem is the sanest spot left in a crazy world?"

"Constantly."

Hours before the demonstration was due to start, Amsterdam was full of police. The marchers had been banned from the great square in front of the palace, and the security forces were out in strength, armed with crash barriers and other things, in an effort to enforce the ban. From the mood of the policemen, long before they had anyone but sightseers to deal with, it was clear that they did not expect to be successful.

So it proved. At first the speakers were denied access to the square and, with their backs to the barriers, began delivering their speeches where they stood. At ground level, with no public address system and with the trams still thundering by, they were virtually inaudible so those who had gone to hear what they had to say crowded forward. The police, thinking their line was under assault, pushed back. As the overseas students fell back into the ranks of the Little Hollanders behind them, tempers frayed; first punches were thrown, then bottles. Then the feminists and the homosexuals got involved in a slanging match with the Moral Majority, and the Church of Latter-Day Disapprovers took exception to the burning of three bras and, inexplicably, a truss; and within half an hour the event had degenerated from a three-ring circus into a full-blooded riot.

Tossed on its surface, Todd and Flynn swirled together and apart like sticks on a torrent. In one close encounter Flynn shouted over the throng, "How did you know?"

Almost as mysterious as the truss, Todd laid a stubby ink-grained finger beside his nose. "Contacts is what this business is about, my boy. Not lenses and light meters, not even angles. Contacts."

After that the thing got nasty. The flying bottles were followed by half-bricks and hefty cobblestones, then by more bottles filled with petrol and streaming flaming rags. A policeman hurrying to the aid of a hurt colleague, downed and burning, was surrounded by the crowd and had his own clothes deliberately doused in petrol and set alight. A water cannon swept both the flames and the crowd from him.

Iron bars were hurled like javelins. Knives winked between the pressing bodies. The crowd became a mob, united by violence as it could never have been in its ideas and aspirations. Like a great gestalt organism it surged across the open expanse of Dam Square, trampling its last defences underfoot, and its voice was the baying of an animal, thick with blood. There were no longer units within the mob, no clusters of students or nationalists or women. There were only those who were trying to fight and those who were trying to flee. Sworn enemies had difficulty recognising one another in the terrifying chaos of a crowd thousands strong from which all the trappings and vestiges of civilisation had gone.

Then the shooting started. For a moment it almost seemed to help, for it cut through the roar and commanded attention and respect as perhaps nothing else could have done. For a moment the instinct for self-preservation almost made individuals out of the mass. That was when they thought the guns were in the hands of the police, who would naturally be firing over the crowd's heads. When people began to drop in the midst of the press, screaming and spouting blood, the madness turned to mayhem. Panic was as boundless as the mob, as concrete as the flying cobbles, as real as the spurt of blood, spreading across the seething square at the speed of flying lead.

Spat out of a little knot of disparate people who suddenly, raggedly, began to run, not from or towards anything in particular but only because a new wave of the panic had reached them, Todd found himself by the corner of a building and sank down gratefully in its shelter. Not for the first time this week, he was painfully aware of the passage of time and that somehow his sharp, agile, adventurous reporter's mind had got trapped in the bulky body of a middle-aged man who ought to have swapped his weatherproof notebook and write-at-improbable-angles Biro for a nice desk with a matching pen set and letter rack long enough since.

He tried to remember what Ernest Hemingway had done when he got here. He was rather afraid the answer was to turn to alcohol and make snide remarks about younger talents. He knew Papa encouraged Scott Fitzgerald to drink because he was afraid his work would not stand comparison with that of Fitzgerald sober.

Is that what I do? he thought then, in a flash of horrid revelation— to Mickey, do I use him like that? To bolster my ego, shore up my confidence? Is it genuinely a partnership we have, or do I ride on his talent because mine is no longer enough—out of fashion, yes, but also worn-out, faded, a mere habit I can't quite kick? Does he *know*? Is that why he stays with me, puts up with me—because I gave him his chance and now he's giving me my day? Is he humouring me, looking after the old man—taking care of Papa? Dear God, he can't really think I'd starve in a gutter if he walked out on me?

Still crouching in the lee of the building, Todd looked out over the surging sea of people with eyes from which a veil had been torn, cringing and clear. Flynn was in there now, making his name, making his fortune, making sure there was a market for the old man's scribblings. Todd could not see him, but he knew what he was doing as surely as if he had been beside him: running with the running crowd, his long limbs driving, his young man's lungs pumping oxygen like sparkling wine to his eager, ambitious, fearless young man's brain. He would be enjoying all this. He would not even have noticed there were places a man could shelter, and rest.

And after his films were developed and he knew what he had, he would lie on his back on his bed—some bed, somewhere—with his hands behind his head and his eyes half hooded and a little half-smile hovering on his lips, and he would go over it all again, enjoying it afresh. And then would he wonder, and did he wonder every night, if today would be the one that tipped the balance, that finally made Papa realise he was an old man in a young man's trade; and would he get out at last, and stop hanging round Flynn's neck like an albatross?

Suddenly Flynn was there, by his side, unseen until the moment he dropped out of the running mass, laughing like a madman. But the laughter died on his lips when he saw Todd's face—saw in it the shock and despair he had not had warning enough to disguise. "Gil, what's wrong? What's happened?" He had to shout to make himself heard. His eyes were concerned.

Todd pulled himself together with an effort, masked whatever it was Flynn had seen in his face. "Happened? Nothing. This, for God's sake! It's a madhouse—there'll be bodies everywhere when they get the square cleared. Did you hear the gunfire?"

Flynn nodded, grinning. He held up his camera by the strap. "Hear it? I saw it—got it in here, some of it." Already he was backing away, back into the mayhem of the square, intoxicated by the shouting and the tumult, unwilling to leave. "Listen—"

Todd saw the bullet hit him. Not in its hot and hurtling flight, of course, it would have taken better eyes than Todd's to see that even if Flynn's long, gesticulating form had not been in the way. What he saw was the moment of impact, when the little thing, travelling at the speed of a jet fighter, velocity multiplying its effective weight by many times, crashed into Flynn's back on a rising trajectory and tore him off the ground.

Nothing Todd had seen in films or read in books prepared him for the sheer horror of that happening, for real, just a few yards from him, to someone he knew and cared about. In one way it happened so quickly it was over, and Flynn lost in the backswell of the running herd, before Todd could take it in. But some other part of his brain had made a fast-film record of it, and time slowed down while he watched, frame by frame, as Flynn pitched twisting into the air.

For a split second his face showed surprise. Then as the velocity of the shot spun him the back of his jacket flowered crimson. Then gravity took him and he disappeared from Todd's view as the running pack surged between them.

The shock had brought Todd to his feet. For a moment longer he stood as if undecided, as if he could not believe what he had just seen and could not therefore bring himself to act on it. Then he pushed himself off from the comparative safety of the wall and plunged into the melee, running heavily, with more determination than grace, opening a path for himself with his hands like a swimmer.

He knew where Flynn had gone down and bulldozed his way there, thrusting aside students and feminists and Moral Majority with vigorous impartiality. When he got there he elbowed a space clear and knelt down in it.

They had gone on running when Flynn fell under their feet. They had not stopped to help him, or even gone round or jumped over him: they had trampled him. There were dusty footprints on his back and legs, even the stamp of a boot in the bloodstain spreading wetly from his right shoulder blade to his spine. While Todd knelt over him, trying to assess the damage, a young girl in Madras cotton and sandals went to scramble over him. Todd knocked her aside with a powerful sweep of one arm, roaring at her. He could barely hear his own voice over the roar of the crowd.

Flynn was facedown and still; Todd could not tell in that moment whether he was alive or dead. His long legs trailed, his boot soles turned up, the toes turned in. His right arm was folded under his body, his left flung out as if his last conscious effort was to regain his balance. In the middle of the dark stain, just to the right of his spine and a couple of fingers below his collarbone, a darker hole in his clothes and his flesh was slowly pumping blood.

Todd waited no longer. If his blood was still coursing his heart was still beating and there was some urgency in the situation. If Flynn stayed where he was much longer he would have the life crushed out of him. Todd hooked his hands under the young man's arms, rose with difficulty to a crouch and hauled him into the shelter of the building.

Flynn was heavy and Todd unused to physical labour; it took longer than he had expected, and while he was sweating at it more running people stumbled over Flynn's trailing legs and one man knocked Todd flying so that he had to start again.

Flynn was coming round, or at least the pain was beginning to reach him where he was. He whined as Todd reached under his right armpit. "Sorry, son," murmured Todd, too quietly to be heard by even a conscious man, "needs doing." After they reached the corner of the building the madness swirled past rather than over them.

Todd eased his partner up against the wall, half sitting, half lying. He was afraid that if he left him prone he would get trampled again when Todd went for help. "OK, son, let's see what we can do with this." He tipped Flynn gently forward and pushed a clean handkerchief up under his shirt and, gritting his teeth, wadded it into the wound. If it did not stop the bleeding it would slow it. Then he took off his coat, which was more substantial than Flynn's, and tucked it round him, covering his arms and chest and pulling it up under his chin.

When he laid Flynn back against the wall, turned slightly to rest on his left side, his eyes were open. "Mickey?" For a moment there was no response and Todd thought his eyes must have fallen open with the movement of his head. But as he straightened up Flynn whispered his name and he looked back, startled, and saw pain filling the vacancy in Flynn's eyes.

Todd stooped again, swiftly. He could not keep from smiling. "Hey, kid, welcome back."

The ghost-white face twisted in reply but could not make a smile. "Gil." The voice was weak with shock, a breath of a voice that barely made it past his teeth. That hurtling fragment of lead had knocked, together with a cupful of blood, all the strength out of him, all the courage, all the brilliant and eccentric animation.

In the split second of its impact it had ended forever that glorious air of invulnerability that is the property of young men. It had ended a phase of Flynn's life with indiscriminate, almost casual brutality. He might do his job again, but never with the supreme confidence which had enabled him to stride joyfully into situations like this knowing—not believing but knowing—that no harm could touch him. The days of his virginity had ended in blood.

As his senses stumbled back, so the pain mounted, like knives shredding up his nerves. He rested his head against the wall and squeezed his eyes shut. Tears squeezed out between the lids.

Compassion twisted Todd's gut into a hard knot inside him. He had seen suffering enough in his time, but thank God it had not lost the power to move him. He wiped the tears off Flynn's cheeks with a thumb, as if he were a child. "Listen," he said quietly, the slightest catch betraying the calm in his voice, "you're going to be all right. You've been shot, but it's not too bad. It's your shoulder, that's all, and I've just about got the bleeding stopped. If you can hang on five minutes I'll round up some help and get you out of here, OK? Mickey?"

The sound of his name called Flynn back from the secret depths of himself where he was seeking to escape the pain and his eyes flickered open. Agony crouched in each of them like a scorpion. He breathed through his teeth, in little shallow pants; still the pain of breathing ripped him up. He could not accommodate the enormity of what had happened to him. All he could do was whisper, "It hurts . . ."

"I know." Flynn knew he could not or he would not say it like that, so easily. "Not for long, though. We'll soon have you patched up."

There was desolation in Flynn's gaze, as though he thought Todd would abandon him. His left hand found its way from under the coat and fisted weakly in Todd's sleeve as he bent over him. "Don't go."

Todd freed himself, straightened. "I'll be right back." He walked away briskly. After four or five paces he began to run.

By virtue of his press card and an English-speaking policeman, it was not much longer than the promised five minutes before Todd was heading back along the margin of Dam Square towards where he had left Flynn. In those few minutes the situation had changed radically. All the panic had died out of the air. There was no more gunfire. The mindless stampeding had come to an end as those anxious to leave the combat zone found their exits and streamed out into the city. The police had substantially regained control, and police vehicles were ferrying away arrested persons in relays.

There was space now to see the injured. Flynn was not the only casualty. Damaged bodies, of men and women, littered the square. Many were ringed by knots of worried friends and some were already receiving medical attention. A few looked to be past the need for medical attention. Todd counted a couple of broken legs, several concussions and some knife wounds on his way back to Flynn. While some were clearly serious injuries, most were making too much noise to be at death's door. Their moans and sobbing, and occasional sharp cries as they were moved, had replaced the screams and gunfire and thunder of feet as the characteristic sound of the episode. The contrast, over so short a time, was uncanny.

Flynn was no longer alone. A man was standing over him, apparently holding his left hand. Todd's warm coat had slipped down to his knees. Todd's first thought was that the medical help he had summoned had arrived and that the man was taking Flynn's pulse. Only as he drew closer did he see that the man had Flynn's camera in his hand and Flynn, with an obstinacy typical of his age and sex, was channeling resources he could ill afford into hanging onto it.

Todd quickened his pace, dropping a heavy hand on the man's arm. "What's going on here?" Only then did he see that the man's other hand held a gun.

The man looked round at him, without alarm. He was about thirty-five years old, heavily built, with black hair and a short clipped black beard. Todd had never seen him before but, partly by deduction, partly by intuition, he knew who he was. "You shot him? Why?"

The man looked surprised to hear him speaking English, but replied in the same language, without hesitation and with a Belgian accent. "The camera. I must have the camera."

Todd understood then. "He got you on film. Probably without even realising it. He got you on film, and you'll do time for what he got you doing."

"I must have the camera," repeated the Belgian. "Or I will shoot you both and take it."

"You'll bring the police."

"I will take that chance." So it was more than the odd cobblestone that Flynn had caught him heaving. That, and his weapon, and his demeanour, told Todd who he was: a mechanic, paid to create a riot where none might otherwise have developed, by some organisation with a vested interest in the disorder. Since discretion was part of the package, the Belgian could not afford to become famous. If—for example—the Little Hollanders wanted a nice riot they could blame on immigrants, in order to benefit politically from the wave of racism thus engendered, a photograph of a Belgian agent provocateur appearing in the world's press would be a lethal embarrassment.

Todd looked at the stubby black gun and swallowed. He had not often seen one that close. "There's no need for that." He bent over Flynn and gently pried his fingers apart. "Give it to me, Mickey, I'll sort it out." He straightened up, holding the camera by the strap. "Here."

The Belgian gave a small half-smile and reached for it. "Thank you."

But he had made a serious mistake—one that had been made by others before him, but seldom by the same people twice. He had looked at Gilbert Todd and seen a man almost twenty years his senior, overweight, underexercised and wearing a suit. He had no idea how tough, both mentally and physically, Todd actually was. But he had been a strong man in his prime, and though the passage of time and the trappings of success had overlaid the muscles with flab and subverted his inclination to pit himself against others, it had done little to sap either the strength or the speed he could call upon at need.

The need had not been this acute for years. He swung the heavy camera through a short and vicious arc, accelerating it with the power of his arm and shoulder, and it crashed into the Belgian's face with enough force to break his jaw. He reeled to the ground, the gun skittering from his hand across the cobbles, and Todd followed him down and hit him twice more. He pocketed the gun, and then, carefully, he removed the film from the abused camera.

Then the police and an ambulance arrived to deal with the consequences.

[6]

Todd went with Flynn in the ambulance. The hospital they took him to
was no great distance, but the journey seemed endless. The way was
blocked at intervals by the swarms of people still circulating in the city.

Flynn was still conscious and still in pain. Every time the little ambulance jolted over a hole in the road where a cobble had been ripped up
for a missile his body convulsed with it and a thin cry sounded in his
throat. Todd held him against his chest, oblivious of the seeping blood,
to cushion Flynn as best he could against the pitching of the vehicle.
But still at every jolt Flynn went into spasm and animal cries ripped
from him. Todd found himself praying that his partner would pass out,
though whether out of concern for Flynn's agony or his own distress he
could not have said.

But Flynn remained conscious until they reached the hospital, although Todd could feel him weakening. Shock was disordering his
mind. Once he whispered hoarsely, "Don't move, Gil, don't move,"
and Todd thought he was back in the workshop in Jerusalem. Then he
said, "Where's my camera?"

"I've got it, Mickey," said Todd. "Don't worry, it's all right."

"Angles," panted Flynn, a white line showing under his drooping
lids where his eyes had rolled up. "It all comes down to angles. And
being there. Oh Christ, Gil, why does it hurt so much?"

Todd had no answer. He held the young man tightly, as if he could
absorb some of his pain that way, and wished the beautiful city past.
"Nearly there, Mickey." He had no idea if they were or not.

There was a lot of rubbish lying in the streets, debris of the battlefield even this far from the square. The driver could not avoid all of it
and the ambulance bucked. Flynn's body arched against Todd's, his
thin cry beating at Todd's brain. Over his shoulder, in English, Todd
snarled, "Won't this thing go any faster?"

Like the man who shot Flynn, the ambulance driver spoke perfectly
good English. "Soon we will be there. He will be all right." He
sounded as if he could soothe in four different languages, as if he had
taken night classes in it.

"He doesn't feel all right," growled Todd, trying to cover the desperation in his voice with anger. "He feels like we could lose him if this bloody journey takes much longer."

The driver observed quietly, "He is your friend, yes?"

Todd could not sustain the anger. He breathed heavily, his breath stirring Flynn's hair. "Yes."

Flynn's mind, disjointed with trauma, was back in Dam Square. He was talking again, mostly to himself, in a thin monotonous whine which made the New York accent sound more prominent than usual. "I know him. Seen his picture. French firm—mercenaries, fascists, something. Did he get away?"

"Not hardly," Todd said grimly. "Quiet, Mickey, save your strength."

"You never listen." It was a woman's plaint—more than that, a wife's —and it betrayed the depth of his weakness as even the pallor of his face and the cold sweat standing out on his brow did not.

"We're here," said the driver, and the ambulance swung in at the casualty entrance. Before it was quite stopped, the back door was thrown open and strong, practised hands took the injured man, still complaining in a voice increasingly bitter and increasingly frail, out of Todd's arms.

When he was gone a sudden chill struck Todd's chest where Flynn's blood had wet his shirt, and for a moment he could not move his limbs that had been cramped with Flynn's weight and the effort of protecting him from the road. Then returning circulation restored a little life to his muscles and stiffly he climbed out of the ambulance and followed.

The hospital was waiting for casualties from the riot and they took Flynn straight down to the theatre. Todd got a brief glimpse more of him, on his side on a speeding trolley, with a blanket humped up over him and an airway down his throat that had finally stopped him talking. His eyes were closed and he appeared to be unconscious. Lift doors closed behind the trolley, and a young nurse showed Todd to where he could drink coffee and wait.

He bought the coffee—at least he presumed there was coffee somewhere inside the plastic ramparts of the filter device—but mostly he dealt with the accumulated tension of the last hour as he dealt with emotional overload the world over: by writing. He settled a thick, grubby notebook on his knee, found viable nylon pen—it did not matter to him that the ink was green—and he wrote:

"Dateline: Amsterdam.

"Not more than a minute after these photographs were taken, the photographer was shot by one of the men in them. The camera does not lie, but the man responsible knew that its truth was more likely to lock him up than set him free." Todd tore the page off and crumpled it up; but then he dropped the ball into his pocket, not the adjacent litter bin. He began again.

"If Mickey Flynn dies of the bullet that smashed into his back as he took these pictures, he will have laid down his life for his readers. Don't feel too badly about that, he was where he wanted to be, doing what he wanted to do; and the man who shot him was a professional thug with a stake in violent disorder who was unhappy at being photographed pursuing it. You bear no responsibility for that.

"My purpose in writing this—in a hospital waiting area while Flynn is in surgery—is not to touch your consciences, or your hearts; not to invite plaudits or to court admiration. There are brave journalists and photographers, just as there are brave grocers: like grocers, most of us are just doing our jobs the best way we know.

The significance of what happened to Mickey Flynn is not what it says about him, or even the man who shot him, but what it says about the job he was doing. News is a serious business. People get hurt for it; occasionally people die for it. It isn't just the grey stuff that keeps the adverts from bumping together, and stops the mammary development of some pubescent female from casting a shadow over the bingo card. Nor is it just an industry, providing profits for a few and salaries for rather more. It is an industry, and a big one; but news is more than the sum of these parts.

"Information is the death of slavery. It is the enemy of corruption. Information is the ally of fairness and decency, both a shield and a weapon to all the decent little people who deserve better than to have their lives emptied into the deep pockets of unscrupulous men.

"There is no freedom without information. There is no choice without information. Information is the difference between superstition and science, between magic and technology. Information is the lamp by which the world's dark places, among them the human psyche, may be illuminated.

"Where information is rationed, the soul of civilisation goes hungry. Where information is polluted, civilisation is poisoned. Where information is denied, civilisation starves and the barbarian returns.

"That is why Mickey Flynn went into the middle of a riot today, and stayed there with his camera long enough for a gunman to draw a bead on his back. Because you have a right to know what happened here, and why, and who was responsible; and because it was his job to give you the information you need to form your judgements. Those who do not remember the past are condemned to repeat it. Those who do not comprehend the present have no future.

"Freedom of information is more than a journalist's mantra. It is the fundamental element of which all our freedoms, all our strengths, are constructed. It is a very real treasure. Today a man was willing to kill for it; Mickey Flynn may still die for it. If for no better reason, acknowledge its worth for that.

"Because the very concept of news today faces the greatest threat in its history, and it will need all the allies it can muster if it is to survive. The threat comes not from the barbarian, the man with the gun in the anonymity of the running crowd, but from the philistine. The mammary development of pubescent females casts a shadow over us all.

"Unless the important business of news gathering and news publishing can be liberated from the trivialising influence of the comic strip, the tombola and the soft-porn pinup, freedom of information will die. No one will be dealing in it anymore: no one selling, no one buying. There will be no more Mickey Flynns. No one is ever going to risk a bullet in the back for a new design of bingo card or the latest thing in silicon-assisted uplift."

Todd tore that off the pad too, but instead of screwing it up he folded it carefully into his pocket. He smiled, a little wanly. It needed a bit of work—paring down some, particularly the more pretentious passages—but there was something there. He would read through it again later. When he knew if it was to be Flynn's obituary.

Some time afterwards someone came to Todd in the waiting area with the message that Flynn had come through surgery well, that the bullet was out, the bleeding stopped and his broken collarbone set. His doctor was of the opinion that nothing should interrupt a speedy recovery.

Todd drank the last of the coffee without noticing that it was cold. Then he went outside and hailed a taxi, to fulfill his promise to make a statement to the police. Halfway there, alone in the back of the cab, he realised that for the first time in twenty years he was crying.

That early expression of medical opinion had to be revised several times over the next few days. Flynn was not making the swift, uncomplicated recovery anticipated. He emerged from the anaesthetic in pain out of all proportion to the surgery he had undergone, and found no relief until his doctor, puzzled by this turn of events, put him under again pending a second opinion.

Fresh X rays revealed nothing. A thorough examination of the inert patient revealed nothing, even with two of them looking. They looked at one another then and shrugged: one of those things, a rogue effect, or something more sinister? After four hours they brought him round again. Again Flynn woke sweating and whimpering with pain.

For three days the surgical team deliberated, exploring every possibility they could think of, while Flynn either sweated or slept. There was nothing in between: if he was awake he was hurting. Todd saw him on the second day and was shocked at the state of him. He looked worse than he had just after he was shot.

Drugged just this side of stupor he was still suffering. It was there in the ashy pallor of his face, in the tight frown, in the sweat that bathed his long body. It sent little spastic tremors through his heavy limbs, turned his head from side to side on the pillow. He could not talk. If there was any meaning in the sounds coming from his throat, Todd could not fathom it. He did not think Flynn understood what he said in reply. He was not sure that Flynn knew he was there.

The visit ended abruptly when Flynn went into convulsions. From lying almost comatose in the bed, only the tiny febrile movements of his hands and head evidence of his scant awareness, suddenly his back arched like a man under torture and a cry ripped from him that cut across Todd's nerves like a blade.

Todd had no time to react. Before he had recovered from that shrill assault on his wits nurses had bustled into the little sideward and bustled Todd out, and a doctor was sliding into Flynn's veins the magic cocktail that let him sleep the agony away.

Todd was still shaken ten minutes later when the nurse came to tell him that Flynn was quiet again but there was no point in waiting, Todd would not be able to see him again today. Todd did a quick translation —from hospital jargon, not Dutch, into English: they had doped Flynn up to the eyeballs once more so that he was safe from whatever hags rode him, but he was as far out of reach as an astronaut on the dark side of the moon. Tomorrow they might risk letting him land again, but they could not predict what the consequences might be.

On the fourth day they established a drug regime that let Flynn be awake without paying the price in agony. It was not, to be sure, the level of alert consciousness required of airline pilots and racing drivers, or even of professional photographers; nor was he entirely free from pain. But it was a compromise he could cope with, a degree of discomfort he could tolerate in return for an acceptable level of awareness.

Now that he was awake he was scared. He asked Todd, "What the hell's wrong with me? I've been here a week. I've got a broken collarbone and a bullet hole in my shoulder. I keep being told how well they're healing. So why does it still hurt so much? They won't tell me. They won't even talk about it. Have they said anything to you? Do they know more than they're saying?"

"No," Todd said, quickly. It was bad enough feeling how Flynn was obviously feeling and thinking it must soon start getting better. It would be intolerable to feel like that and think it was going to get worse. "I don't think they're keeping anything from you. I don't think they know what's causing it. They've repaired all the damage that was done. It ought to be getting easier."

"Well it ain't," snapped Flynn. His voice was stronger now, honed by fear to an edge. In his eyes lay deep despair. He was still in bed. They had tried moving him into the chair under the window but the pain was too great. It was as if a scalpel had been accidentally sewn into the wound in his back and lanced his flesh, nerve and sinew, whenever he moved. He bit through his lip before they could get him flat again.

Flat he remained, the long shape of him under the sheet slightly tense with the need to avoid movement. He spoke without moving his head, barely moved his hands. To Todd, who had counted his endless animal energy among the things he least liked about Flynn, it was tragedy on a more than human scale to see him like this, trapped in the prison his strong young body had become, snared in a cage of pain. For all that he could or dared do, he might have been paralysed by the assassin's bullet.

Todd said quietly, "Is it still that bad?"

Bad? Flynn had been amazed and terrified by how bad the pain could get without becoming its own solution. He had thought there was some natural limit to how much hurting a body could do before closing down nonessential functions and taking a vacation. At first he tried to swallow the pain, in the belief that it would either diminish or knock him out; but soon, when the pain was mounting and mounting and instead of shutting down his nervous system was screaming for relief and it took all his strength, all his young man's pride, to keep from screaming too, he begged for the respite only the hypodermic could give him.

Now it was easier, but only because of the drugs. Plainly they—he thought of the hospital staff as "they," more as a soldier regards the enemy than a man might look on people caring for him—could not understand why he needed such powerful pain relief, but thank God they accepted that he did. Only the drugs stood between Flynn and madness.

"The son of a bitch is killing me," he said. Todd knew by the catch in his voice, by the grief in his eyes, that he meant it. "It's eating me by inches." He was not that far from tears.

When he left Flynn Todd marched round to the doctor's office, but there was no one there. He dropped into a chair in the corridor to wait, with more determination than patience, while a nurse went to track down Dr. Van Rijn.

When he saw the tall Asian woman coming down the corridor towards him, with a long smooth stride that rippled through the painted sari that she wore like wind through a flower garden, his first thought was that she was the anxious relative of some other patient come to beard the doctor in his den. When she introduced herself, in faultless English with a curiously musical inflection, as Dr. Parvati Van Rijn he was momentarily nonplussed—not by her race or sex, or even the combination, so much as by that sari. He wondered that she did not wear a white one, and a green one for operations.

They went into her office and Dr. Van Rijn ordered tea for them. Then she approached directly to the subject which Todd had been trying to broach tactfully. "You are concerned about your friend, and worried that, a week after the bullet was removed, he is still suffering severe unexplained pain. You want to know what is causing it and how we propose to deal with it. You want to know if there are any implications that have not been explained. You want to know how we intend to proceed, and how soon Mr. Flynn may leave here and return home, and to his work."

Todd was an interviewer of skill, perception and tenacity; as an interviewee he was rubbish. He mumbled, "Er, yes," totally thrown by the fact that it had not taken the expected half hour to get this far.

Dr. Van Rijn smiled, and in the olive-shaded serenity of her face came together the brisk professionalism of Europe and the timeless knowingness of India, the compassion of her sex and the distance of her calling. She was a woman in her forties, Todd supposed. He particularly noticed the hands she folded together on her desk, firm brown hands with long tapering fingers, strong and dextrous and undecorated by so much as a wedding ring.

She said, "These are the questions to which I too am seeking answers, Mr. Todd."

They talked at length, Todd appreciating the amount of other business she must have put on hold for him. Then together they went to talk to Flynn.

Dr. Van Rijn began. "I owe you an apology, Mr. Flynn. I should not have left you alone and in ignorance to worry about what is happening to you. I thought to delay this discussion until I had something positive to tell you. I see now that was arrogant and rather cruel. I hope you will forgive me."

Flynn said nothing. He was watching her intently. Todd, back in the chair beside the bed, thought he looked like a young man trying hard not to look frightened, and hoped the doctor would not prolong this unduly.

She did not. With a disarming multicultural smile she came right to the point. "The good news is, there's no bad news we haven't got round to breaking yet. By the same token, there's not a lot I can say to set your mind at rest. But I will tell you what we have been able to establish, what the possibilities are and what we might try in order to get you well again."

Nothing revealed by the X rays or any other test they had run offered an explanation for the pain he was suffering. The broken collarbone was stable and had not shifted; the bullet wound was clean and healing nicely. There appeared to be no other damage.

"You're saying I'm going to be stuck with this?" There was no animation in his body or his face, but Todd could see the horror pulsing in Flynn's eyes. It was worse than a death sentence: if it was true, it was a life sentence of unbearable harshness. Without speaking Todd laid his hand on Flynn's forearm and felt the skin twitch and the muscles underneath tense and relax with the microscopic clenching of his fist.

"No, no," said Van Rijn swiftly, "that is not what I am saying."

But nor could she promise that it would not come to that in the end. Until she knew what caused his pain, all she could do was treat it empirically, in terms of symptom control. The best she could do in the short term was keep it from tearing him apart and hope that the root problem would either reveal itself or begin to resolve itself. Either would be a positive development, and there was every reason to hope for one or the other.

"In the meantime?"

"In the meantime we keep you comfortable, and observe you carefully, and hold ourselves in readiness to act at the first indication that we can do you some good."

"Act to do what?"

Van Rijn hesitated. Clearly there was something more she could say; equally clearly, she was not sure she should say it. But after a moment training and tradition lost out to common humanity and she gave a little sigh. "You understand, this is only a theory. It's only one possible explanation of what is happening to you, it may be quite wrong. But I'm wondering if, when the bullet broke your clavicle—your collarbone —it sent a sliver of bone shooting through the tissues of your back. If it came to rest in the spinal region it could be interfering with the nerves feeding into your spinal cord."

She explained then the difficulties of locating such a fragment by X ray, and the other techniques that might be applied. She talked about peripheral nerves and foramina, the brachial plexus and the cervical enlargement, articular processes and the neural canal. Even trying to make this simple enough for laymen, she was using words Todd had never heard before.

Flynn was following her closely. For the first time there was a burr of hope in his voice. "You mean, all you've got to do is find the bastard and cut it out?"

Van Rijn smiled again. "I understand your impatience, Mr. Flynn, but it's not something we can rush into. I need more information before I do anything. This isn't the California Gold Rush, I can't keep digging holes in you in the hope of striking it rich."

"So what do you want to do?"

"Wait. Observe. Try to establish first whether there is a shard, then where it is and what it's likely to do next."

"Do? What can it do?"

She talked some more about the geography of Flynn's back. She made it sound a desperately busy place: Hyde Park Corner at four-thirty on a Friday afternoon. She made the shard sound like a cowboy mini-cab trying to buck the one-way system. If it stayed in one place long enough to get its wheels clamped it might cause little more disruption. If it kept moving, it could cause an accident.

Flynn was still watching her but the hope in his eyes had given way once more to cold fear. The stillness of his body was beyond that he had adopted to protect himself from pain. His voice was low. "What are you telling me—that this thing can still kill me? Or—no, not kill me. Paralysis. That's what we're talking about here, isn't it? If it moves, it's going to cut me in half." Todd felt a tremor run through the muscles of Flynn's forearm and tightened his grip there.

"That is not what I'm telling you," said Dr. Van Rijn, with some asperity. "Any such assumption would be grossly pessimistic and grossly premature."

"Can you tell me it can't happen?"

Van Rijn brought her patience back to heel and sighed. "Mr. Flynn, I can't make you any promises. I can tell you what's possible, I can tell you what's likely. I can tell you what the current position is—that there is no loss of function to indicate damage to either the sensory or motor nerve systems. I can tell you what we'll be looking out for, and what we'll do if and when we see it.

"I can't guarantee that we'll succeed in doing what all our skill and efforts will be harnessed to, which is ending your pain and restoring you to health. But I can assure you—no, I can actually promise—that we'll do our very best. And these days our best is something to behold." She ran a little impish smile by him.

Flynn was not yet up to responding in kind. The implications—some things she had said, some things she had not said, possibly some things which she had not said but which he had heard—had transfixed him, washing the vestiges of colour from his face, stretching his eyes with shock. But his voice was under control. "OK, Doc. Now I know where I stand." He let his eyes fall closed as if he needed the privacy.

Van Rijn said, "You might want to think about being transferred to a hospital in England. You live in London, I see. It would be sensible to wait a little longer, but once we're sure you're stable we can arrange a transfer, if that's what you'd like. You could be in hospital some time."

None of them said it, but all three were aware that if things went badly he could be in one kind of hospital or another for the rest of his life.

Flynn opened his eyes then and grinned faintly at her. "Are you trying to get rid of me, Doc?"

She smiled back. "Of course not. I would sooner keep you here, where I can see you getting better. Also, such a transfer would mean a lot of paperwork. But no doubt a London hospital could do as much for you as we can, and if you would prefer to be closer to family and friends—"

"I got no family," said Flynn, "and I'm not sure I've got any friends, and if you think I'm swapping maybe the only doctor in the Western world who's willing to talk to me for someone who swore the Official

Secrets Act along with the Hippocratic Oath, you have another think coming."

That was one reason. The other, the one he said nothing about, the one he had not yet had time or the nerve to consider but was already drawing some comfort from, was the difference in attitude between Dutch and English law to the subject of euthanasia.

[7]

Todd went back to Jerusalem, to wind up their affairs there—collect their belongings, return the car. News of what had happened preceded him: Simon Meir called him up the first night he was back, and he lost count of the other soldiers, policemen, waitresses, dancers and folk musicians who also asked after Flynn.

He was touched by their kindness but declined to go into much detail. He said Flynn was not too well yet, that it was hoped he would get a great deal better but it could be some time before he was back in Israel. He was surprised at just how much regret that seemed to occasion. He thought Flynn might be surprised to know how many friends he had made in this warring city.

One of the people who came asking after Flynn was Deborah Lev. She did not introduce herself, by any name, and as Todd had never met her he had no reason to guess who she was. He remembered her for the real sorrow in her eyes when he told her what the situation was. He supposed she was sorry for Flynn.

From Jerusalem he returned to London. The accumulated clutter from their hotel rooms he dumped, unsorted, in the spare bedroom of his flat. Then he packed himself a fresh suitcase, and took another round to Flynn's garret to do the same for him.

Flynn lived, when he was not living out of a rucksack, in the upper levels of the only London River warehouse which had not become trendy in recent years. Trains shunted late into the night under his back wall. A nomadic community of drunks and glue sniffers colonised the lower reaches of the building between raids by the police, social workers and the more militant charities.

Flynn photographed them and provided them with drink—with a curious morality he drew the line at glue—on the basis that the other agencies would provide food and large urns of tea. He saw nothing wrong in being an inebriate tramp for a living, taking the unpopular view that most of the time—at least the ones he knew—had at some time chosen to live that way, and would choose to return to it however many fresh starts were wished on them by do-gooders. So he saw no reason not to treat them to the only largesse they appreciated. In return they kept undesirables out of the place.

All the same, someone had got in. Todd knew as soon as he reached the last flight of steps, the ones between the steel door with its New York-style multiple locks and the front door proper, that the dust had not been falling here undisturbed for the last three months, which was the time they had been away. And when he put the key in the lock of the second door, he could not open it for the brass chain spanning the gap.

With mounting fury at what seemed yet another assault in a concerted attack on Flynn's place in the world, Todd shoved his broad face into the hand-span gap and bellowed, "If you don't come and open this door now, I'll have the police round here with fire axes before you can say squatter's rights."

It was an empty threat—Todd's mostly were—but he heard a quick footstep on the wood-block floor within and then a small pointed face like a blonde pixie's thrust up against his own and demanded in a Glasgow accent, "Who the hell are you?"

Her name was Angus. It was actually her surname, but she stopped using her first name when she took up serious swearing. She was a painter.

"Houses or canvas?"

She fixed him with a green eye. "Both. Depending on who's buying, what they're offering and what they want." She was about five feet high, built like a pampas grass, with straw-coloured hair and the personality of a wolf—the kind of reclusive wolf who minds his own business until someone comes bothering him, and then rips throats out.

"Does Mickey know you're here?"

"Of course he knows. I'm minding the flat for him, aren't I?"

"Where do you usually live?"

"Wherever there's a flat needs minding. Who are you? Where's Mickey?"

He told her. He watched her face for how she would react. For a moment her expression hardly flickered. Then she said, "Tough shit." Todd began to see what she and Flynn might have in common.

"Does Mickey owe you anything?"

The blonde wolf looked scornful. "Naw. Somewhere to live—that's all I need. If I don't have to find rent I can manage well enough."

"Will you stay on—at least for a while, until we know what's happening?"

She thought for a moment. "Aye."

Todd had hoped to be able to return to Amsterdam in a couple of days. But he had matters—business, domestic and personal—that would not be put on hold indefinitely, and as word got round that he was back in London he found himself with more and more demands on his time and attention.

He had contacted all his regular editors and many of the more casual ones during those first days in Amsterdam, when he did not want to be away from the hospital for long but had nothing to do there but write letters. Now the replies were coming in, expressing shock and support, acknowledging that Todd's commitments might have to wait for a while and Flynn's might never be met. Many of them asked if they needed financial assistance. They did not—Todd had never considered the pricy health insurance they carried an optional extra—but the offers were a kindness he had not expected. He wrote back with thanks and updates.

Finally returning to Amsterdam after ten days away, Todd found the situation at the hospital significantly better. Flynn was up and dressed —well, approximately dressed in jogging pants, T-shirt, surgical collar and nothing on his feet. He was in the chair by the window, with his back to the door and an open book on his knee, but he did not appear to be reading so much as looking out over the city. He did not hear the door open.

"Hello, Mickey. How are you feeling?"

"Gil?" He did not turn his head to look, but there was a flattering note of hope in his voice.

Todd moved quickly into his range of vision, planting his backside on the bed. He could not take his eyes off Flynn's face. "You're looking human again. How are you?"

"Oh, better." Some of the old strength was back in Flynn's voice. If there was a certain flatness there too, that was understandable. "At least I'm out of that goddamned bed."

"When did this happen?"

"This is the fourth day. I can even move around a bit, if I'm careful. You should see me walking—like a geriatric turtle!"

"How's the pain?" Todd found it slightly embarrassing to ask, as if a person's pain, like the workings of his alimentary or reproductive systems, was something private.

Flynn grinned, a shade wearily, as if he knew his partner's sensibilities were under strain. "Easing up some. She's cutting back on the painkillers. She wants me to be able to feel it in case it starts moving. But it's not bad."

"Going the right way." Todd could not think what else to say. It had been easier when they were both in shock and he had held the arched tormented body against his with all the strength at his command. There had been no time for talk then, except for Flynn's disjointed ramblings. In time it would be easier again, when Flynn was well enough for them to look back on this as something past and they could talk about it or not as the mood took them.

But this was hard: sitting together in a hospital room with nothing else to talk about except Flynn's pain, past, present and to come, that was as real and nearly as tangible as another person in the room with them. Even ignoring it too deliberately gave it a role, almost a personality, that let it cast its shadow over them. With a sick and guilty feeling Todd realised he could not wait to be walking down the stairs, out of the hospital and away.

Flynn may have guessed something of this. His eyes were gentle. "Gil, I know you have work to do. I don't expect you to hang around Amsterdam until I'm fit to join you. It could be a while. Hell, let's be realistic here: it might never happen."

It was all the opening they needed to talk properly about what had happened, to lay this ghost of silence or—worse than silence—false cheer, false optimism. If Todd had had half the guts that Flynn had, he thought, he would have grabbed it and hung onto it until they had said everything that needed saying.

Instead he shook his head, and smiled too brightly, and said, "Don't let it get to you, kid. You'll be back in business before you know it. Listen, I brought some things from your flat. Do you know someone called Angus who talks like Billy Connolly and looks like Tweety Pie?"

When he was leaving, a nurse asked him to call in with Dr. Van Rijn.

He really did not want this interview, not just now, but he put a brave face on it. "You've worked wonders with the kid since I saw him last."

"Yes indeed." She gestured him to a chair. "I'm well pleased with his progress. Whatever was responsible for the pain seems to be settling down now. As long as he's prepared to be sensible, it shouldn't be a major problem to him. He may need some ongoing pain relief, but it should be well within the limits of what he can administer himself, at home."

Todd nodded cautiously. It was excellent news—lots of people needed to take tablets for something; if that was all, Flynn could congratulate himself on a lucky escape. But there was something in Van Rijn's manner which suggested that was not all. "So why are you still worried?"

She inclined her head to acknowledge his perception. She chose her words carefully. Todd thought this was not due to any lack of English so much as the abstract nature of what she wanted to say. All she said first was, "Mr. Flynn is an impatient young man."

Todd laughed out loud. He realised he was being rude, and that she had other things to say of a less banal content, but taken in isolation the statement lacked profundity. He choked the laugh back to a chuckle. "Oh yes; and then some."

Fortunately she understood and offered a solemn smile of her own. "Not the scientific discovery of the year, no? But relevant. Impatient young men do not make good patients. They look not for treatment but for cures, not for improvements but for miracles. Nobody likes being ill or injured, being left with weaknesses which they did not have before. But young, impatient men tend—uniquely—to treat such misfortune as a personal affront. It is an attitude that can interfere, sometimes quite seriously, with the process of recovery."

She had Todd's full attention now. All the mirth was gone from him. "Mickey?"

"The extent of his physical restoration will be dictated mainly by physical factors: the nature and extent of the damage, the success of medical intervention, his body's powers of healing. His attitude will play a small part in the healing process, but a massive part in the extent of his recovery.

"Any doctor can show you paired sets of X rays of patients with nearly identical injuries that healed in the same time and degree, but one patient is a cripple while the other is a man with a limp. The difference was that one man wanted to be made perfect again, and grieved for every ounce of lost muscle and impaired strength, while the other wanted to get on with his life and directed all his energies into what he could do rather than what he could not.

"The human body has all sorts of spare parts that can be done without. But a life worth having is dependent on the survival of the human spirit. Long after we have done all we can to repair damaged bodies, we are still nursing ailing spirits and coaxing them to take up the fight for life again."

Todd was confused. "You think Mickey doesn't have the will to get better?" He did not believe it. Flynn was young and he was strong, and he was tough too. Of course he was shocked by what had happened to him. Naturally he was depressed. But given a little time to get his feet back under him, he would show her what fighting was all about

Van Rijn pursed her lips. She was still being very precise in what she said, very careful, not to keep the truth from him but to avoid misunderstandings. "That is not quite what I am saying. What concerns me is that he may refuse to accept the limitations this event has placed on him. He's making good progress, but for some time to come any activity will carry an element of risk for him. Even after that, strenuous activity would be most unwise. A good recovery will depend on his learning patience."

Then Todd understood. The way they had lived, had made their living, was out for Flynn now. His body could not take it anymore. The next time someone in a crowd thumped him, or a police horse swung him aside with its rump, or he had to run like hell to keep himself and his film out of hostile hands, the fuse on the time bomb in his back could burn down. An hour in a hot bath would do him no good then: he could spend the rest of his life on sticks, in a wheelchair, or flat in a bed.

It was over. Mickey Flynn's career as a photojournalist, which had begun in a night of drunkenness in The Longshoreman in New York and taken him into the top periodicals, and the offices, studies and drawing rooms of the mighty in five continents, had ended in Dam Square with an incautious photograph and a bullet in the back. He was going to have to live at a different pace from now on. If Todd wanted to continue working, he was going to have to find a new partner.

Rather thickly he said, "What do you want me to do?"

As if she understood something of what was going through Todd's mind, Van Rijn said gently, "Talk to him. He respects you. Convince him that life doesn't need to be lived in the fast lane. I don't want him to risk what I believe he can have—a long life with a reasonable standard of health—in pursuit of something he cannot have, the undamaged body and unimpaired strength of a man who was never shot.

"Help him to understand that what was done to him was monstrous, but it's in the past and irreversible: no effort of will, on his part or mine, can turn the clock back. Somehow he has to come to terms with that. We can help, but the healing has to come out of himself and it won't start until he can accept what happened and that his life has changed irrevocably because of it."

Todd had to drag his eyes up to hers from the level of his knees. "You're sure about this?"

Her eyes were almond-shaped, the dark irises very calm and reassuring and understanding. They were eyes a man could rest in, laying down the grief and anger that burdened him. Then, looking closer, he realised that although her sympathy was genuine it was for him only insofar as he was an instrument for treating Flynn. She might feel for him but she was quite prepared to use him—use his offices where hers had failed.

"Sure?" she echoed. "No, I can't be sure. I can't promise that he will keep well if he follows my advice, or that he will suffer the consequences if he refuses to. But it is the best advice I can offer. If you'd like a second opinion, I shall be happy to arrange it, but I think it's the only advice possible in these circumstances: slow down, take care, and remain under observation. If he was my friend, I'd do all I could to persuade him to cooperate."

Todd said, "I'll talk to him." He did not sleep that night for thinking what he would say.

As it happened, Flynn opened the conversation. He had been watching out for Todd; when he saw him he beckoned to him with his good left hand. His face was grim. "Come and see my new toy."

It was a wheelchair. Dr. Van Rijn had brought it in after breakfast, along with comprehensive instructions.

"Now I can go for jolly little excursions along the corridors," Flynn said savagely. "Drop in for a chat at the cancer ward, compare notes on basketwork with the geriatrics. As long as I can get someone to push me, of course. All I can do on my own is go round in little circles. Even when my shoulder heals I'll have to leave self-propulsion to the fitter cripples. Might put too much strain on my back, see?"

"She thought you'd like a change of scene," Todd said reasonably. "You'll be walking before you could wheel the thing, anyway."

"Is that what she said?" The eyes were predatory.

"Not exactly. She never mentioned it at all. She would have done, if she was expecting you to spend much time in it."

"Discussing me at length, were you then?" Flynn's grin was vicious, feral.

"Of course," Todd said simply. "You're the only interest we have in common—what else would we discuss?"

"I think she's softening me up," Flynn said darkly. "Getting me used to the idea. Help the poor chap adapt, don't you know? Awful pity, of course, used to be quite well-known; quite clever in his way. But what's done is done, there's no point crying over spilt milk. He can't do a lot now, of course; but he's perfectly happy—"

Todd said quite sharply, "Shut up, Mickey. If you've nothing more constructive to say, keep quiet and listen instead. Yes, you've been unlucky. It was a bastard thing that happened to you, and I hope the bastard who did it does life. But you're going to do a life sentence too unless you start getting your act together. You went into a risk business. You got away with it for four years, then your number came up. I'm sorry. But nobody feels the same when a hooker gets raped as they do when it's a schoolgirl."

The brutality of that shocked both of them. But they had never gone in for small talk, and now—when Flynn needed a boot up the backside to kick-start his stalled courage—was no time to start. After a moment Flynn gave a low chuckle, and Todd went on in a quieter tone.

"Hell, Mickey, I'm sorry I got you into this. Van Rijn's sorry she can't wave a magic scalpel and pull you out of it. But you can't afford to feel sorry for yourself. You've too much to do, too much distance to go."

Flynn indicated the wheelchair with a fierce glance. "In that?"

"Damn right in that, if you need it," snapped Todd; "or on your own two feet if you can make it; or crawling on your belly if you have to. You're twenty-eight years old, Mickey. That's too soon to give up on life. You're going to have to work like you've never worked before; nothing is going to come easily to you from now on. The glitter days are over, golden boy. You're going to have to learn to be a bit more ordinary."

"That's your definition of ordinary, is it?" snarled Flynn, the flashing of his eyes compensating for his restricted movement. "Living for fifty years in one room with no sensation below the neck?" It was not impatience flashing in his eyes, or anger or grief. It was fear. He was profoundly afraid of that spectre of absolute dependence.

Todd's heart ached for him. "Mickey, Mickey," he sighed, "that's not going to happen. Van Rijn knows what she's doing—she's not going to let that happen. Give her a chance, don't work against her."

"Is that what she said?"

"Yes. She sees no reason why shouldn't get over this, if you'll go about it sensibly. Take time. Take advice. Stop living as if someone has a stopwatch on you. Be patient: learn what you can do and what you can't. Stop pushing."

"And if I take her advice and settle for living like an arthritic nun, can she promise it won't happen anyway—that the shard won't move and leave me trapped in a body I can no longer control?"

Todd shook his head testily. "Of course she can't. There's no room for guarantees, Mickey, not in our business and not in hers. An honest opinion is all you have the right to expect, and hers is that you'll be all right if you'll just come to terms with what's happened. Learn to live with the body you have now, not the one you had a month ago."

In a low voice Flynn said, "And if I don't want to?"

Todd did not understand. "You don't have much choice."

Flynn's eyes flared up and hit him like a slap. "Oh yes I do. For now I have all the choice in the world. I don't know how a basket case goes about committing suicide, but for now all I have to do is walk out of here and into a canal. Don't forget that, the two of you, when you're discussing my future."

Todd did not think that, deep down, he meant it. He thought Flynn was too stubborn to make that ultimate abdication. But it was a token of his despair that he should threaten it, even think of it.

He said firmly, "This conversation is degenerating towards the maudlin. Listen, Mickey, this is what it comes down to. Nobody can make you live if you don't want to. If you decide to opt out, that's your prerogative: it's a waste, it's a crime, it's a crying shame, but it's your choice if you want to make it. And if you decide to fight for a life worth having, the fact that Van Rijn and I and a lot of people you hardly remember meeting, much less think of as friends, will be back here cheering you on won't make it any less of a struggle. If it goes wrong, you'll have to take the consequences—we can sympathise but we can't share them with you.

"But if you get it right—if five years from now you've made a new career without the riots, if you've sent the wheelchair back and the walking stick is gathering dust at the back of a cupboard, and all you have to show for this is a bottle of pills in the bathroom cabinet that maybe you're glad of now and then when a bit of damp rises off the river and gets into your back—you'll look back and you won't be able to believe the conversation we've just had. And you'll still be sending Van Rijn flowers on her birthday."

As usual, when the call came he had no time. He dropped in at the hospital on his way to Schiphol, left his bag in the cab and left the cab with the engine running.

Flynn had graduated to the dayroom. They wheeled him there and left him to potter. When Todd found him he was watching television. Because he could not follow the commentary he was criticising the photography, aloud and at length, so no one else was enjoying it either.

For some moments Todd just stood in the open doorway, behind Flynn's back, watching him and listening to the sound of his voice. It was difficult to say what he was waiting for. He was conscious of a sense in which this, not the firing of the shot with Flynn's name on it, marked the ending of the era, the parting of the ways.

It was four years since Todd had set off anywhere, except on the most personal business, without Flynn humping equipment and grumbling beside him. They had been closer than family, closer in some ways than lovers. They had shared their work, with its dangers and its triumphs. They had depended on one another for their livelihoods, and occasionally for their lives. Getting on the plane alone would be like leaving a part of himself behind—an irritating part, perhaps, something like a gallbladder that often seemed more trouble than it was worth, but flesh of his flesh for all that.

As if to emphasise that closeness, and thus the guilt Todd already felt over the separation, Flynn—who was not expecting him, could not see him and could not have heard anything more than the opening of the door, if that—grew aware of his presence. Todd saw the moment that he recognised the sense of familiarity stroking at his skin, like a thread of electricity in the air or some faint disturbance in the magnetosphere.

He did not come to his feet, as countless times before, in a smooth spiral glide like a mounting hawk, his long body cat-agile with the restless energy contained but barely in it, a grin of pure pleasure—or usually pleasure but not always pure—starting in the quick brilliance of his eyes and spreading across the angular planes of his face. He got up awkwardly, laboriously, leaning heavily on his good left hand, and turned slowly, moving his whole body because he could not move just his head. He had not exaggerated. He moved like an old man.

All his soul, good and bad, was still there in his eyes, an apparently unquenchable vitality. The hurts and fears of the last weeks had taken nothing away from those remarkable eyes—eyes that in a girl men would have died for; indeed, had only added depth. Before, you would have thought from his eyes that he knew it all; but now he knew more.

He came to the door, slowly, stiffly, and his eyes were steady and too intelligent. He knew—from Todd's face, from Todd's being here— what had happened. He said quietly, "You're on your way then. Back to Israel?"

Todd nodded. Flynn seemed smaller: he did not have to look up into his face.

"Ah," said Flynn. There was almost nothing else to say, for either of them. They had both known it would come, the only question was when. In a way it would be good to have it over, because it was always going to hurt.

Flynn walked Todd to the lift. Though Todd suspected it was too far for him yet, he had not the heart to send him back so they walked slowly.

Flynn said, "What's happened now?"

Todd shrugged. "More of the same. Two West Bank kids got shot in Hebron last night—young lads on their way home from the mosque or terrorist rioters, depending on who you ask. So now we'll have the street protests, and they'll turn into riots, and somebody else'll get shot so then we'll have the protests about *that*. And not only does it never change for the better, in all honesty nobody there wants it to. God help me, Mickey, if I could make one universal law for the good of mankind, it would be to make religion—like homosexuality—legal only between consenting adults in private."

They reached the lift. Flynn said, not altogether flippantly, "Look after yourself, Gil. Hebron's bandit country. I know you reckon to know your way around, but you won't have me watching your back this time."

"I know." Todd thought for a moment, chewing his lip, then decided to say it. "Mickey—"

Flynn got there first. There was a slight tinselly edge in his voice. "You're going to need a photographer. Ask at the *Jerusalem Post,* they'll put you onto someone decent. Tell him what you want—don't trust too much to his initiative, not at first. You don't want him getting above himself."

They traded a grin. Behind it Todd wondered if this was hurting Flynn as much as it was him, hoped it was not hurting him more.

"And listen," said Flynn, his voice hardening. "If you find someone who can do your job, who's free to travel and who you can get on with, hold onto him."

Flynn had been keeping the lift back by leaning his good shoulder on the open door. Now he stood back and the doors closed, and the lift carried Todd towards the street.

II

Scattered Among Heathens

And if ye will not for all this hearken unto me, but walk contrary unto me,
then I will walk contrary unto you also in fury . . . And I will scatter you
among the heathen.

Leviticus 26

THE INTERNATIONAL AIRPORT at Lod was the first reminder, if
any were needed, of how little a country was this many-promised land.
Security was as tight as ever but also as brisk, and Todd was carrying his
bag towards the taxi rank as the sun dropped like a blood orange towards Tel Aviv.

A young woman fell into step beside him. "I have a car for you, Mr.
Todd."

He looked round—and down, for she was short—in some surprise.
He had not ordered a car, and the only person who knew he was on his
way was his police contact in Jerusalem. "Who are you?"

"Leah Shimoni. This way, please." Before he guessed what she was
doing she had relieved him of his bag. Its weight did not tow her off
the vertical. She opened the back door of a sand-coloured four-by-four,
part of it camouflage and part desert dust, and tossed the bag inside.

"Excuse me," said Todd, standing his ground and daring her to do
the same with him, "but when I said 'Who are you?' I meant 'Who the
hell *are* you?' "

She got in at the driver's door, leaned over to unlock the right-hand
door for Todd. He opened it but did not get in yet. He had not got to
be a hoary old reporter by climbing into jeeps and driving off into

SCATTERED AMONG HEATHENS 65

bandit country with young women he did not know from Eve. Beirut was only four hours' drive, and the Gaza Strip a lot closer than that.

The girl looked at him through the car and frowned. She did not seem to have considered the possibility that he would refuse to go with her. She had shoulder-length brown hair cut in a rather old-fashioned bob, an unremarkable but—apart from the frown—pleasant face, and a compact, even sturdy, figure filling out a buff shirt and rolled-up shorts that could have been left over from her Army service. She was about twenty-five, going on fifty.

Finally she said, "Zev Bar Dror sent me."

Todd's life, particularly these days, was full of uncertainties but that was not one of them. He stepped back. "Oh no he didn't." Bar Dror thought too much of his day job to noise around the fact that the family holiday in Eilat each year was paid for by passing on to a British journalist information that arrived on his desk under a seal of confidentiality.

"No, he didn't," she agreed after a moment. "But I guessed he'd called you. We live in the same apartment block, and sometimes when he's trying to impress me he's indiscreet. He knows I'm interested in newspapers. So when he said in the lift this morning that he understood you were coming back to report on this business in Hebron, I checked with the airline and came out here to wait for you. Where do you want to go first?"

That sounded more like the Bar Dror that Todd knew: shooting off his mouth to young women in lifts. It still left too much unexplained. "Why did you want to see me?" But he got into her car and closed the door.

Leah Shimoni delayed answering for some seconds, until the big car had picked up momentum. When they were moving too quickly for Todd to change his mind she said, "I'm a photographer. I want Mickey Flynn's job."

It is hard to know what would have happened if she had made this announcement on the pavement, facing him. From the way the anger surged in him, swelling his chest to meet the seat belt, Todd was afraid he might have struck her. Probably he would not have done—he was not in the habit of striking women, or indeed anyone, however offensive—but he was glad of the fact that they were now travelling at forty miles an hour and any attack on the driver would have serious consequences for them both.

So he bridled his anger, saying nothing until he could feel it beginning to drop back down his throat. He looked at Leah Shimoni and caught her looking, sideways and furtively, at him. At length he said, "Do you know Mickey?" and his voice was ominously quiet.

"I know his work."

"Do you know where he is now?"

"In hospital in Holland. That's why you're here alone."

"Do you know why he's in hospital?"

"He was hurt in a riot." She frowned. "What do you want me to say —that I'm sorry? Of course I'm sorry. It was a tough break, and there aren't so many good photographers in the world that he won't be missed. But the fact is he can't work for the present, and you need someone to replace him, and I can do that." She looked sidelong at him again, resting her gaze a little longer, as if drawing confidence from the fact that he was not shouting.

She presumably knew his work too, but if she had known anything about him she would have derived less comfort from that. Like many big things, Todd was at his most dangerous when treading softly.

He said, "Mickey Flynn was shot down in cold blood by a professional rabble-rouser who didn't want to star in one of his photographs. More than a month afterwards he's still in the sort of pain you wouldn't let a dog suffer. He can just about walk. That may not last: he has a shard of bone loose in his back that could cripple him at any time. For the present?—Mickey's never going to work again, not on the streets.

"But he's not going to be replaced either—not by you, or any other bimbo with the latest fashion-accessory of a camera, or even by a real photographer. I shall need someone to take some pictures. But whoever it is won't replace Mickey Flynn, not by any stretch of the imagination, and they'll find him a hard act to follow."

A darkly rosy flush had come into Shimoni's cheeks when he called her a bimbo. Todd was not surprised. It was not the sort of language he used, except that he was upset. She kept on driving, staring straight ahead through the windscreen while anger and humiliation burned in her brown cheek. After the sideways glance that told him that, Todd did the same.

They reached the road from Tel Aviv to Jerusalem. Without asking, Shimoni turned east. Todd sighed. It would save him the bus trip, but an hour in a silent car with a fuming lady photographer seemed a high price to pay. Also, the swift and early dusk was setting in and soon there would be nothing to see either. Twenty-five miles of nothing but mutual resentment lay ahead. And shalom to you too, he thought wearily.

The Vale of Ayalon is widely held to be one of the loveliest sights in Israel. It was pitch dark by the time they reached it. Mute testimony to God's funny sense of humour, this age-old beauty spot was also the site of innumerable battles, major and minor, starting when Adam threw the apple core at Eve and continuing at monotonously regular intervals up until the Six Day War of 1967. Everything that grew here fed on the blood of millennia.

Todd was still thinking of blood and battles rather than beauty when Shimoni pulled the car over to the side of the road and stopped. He thought twenty-two years between one major conflict and the next was probably a good average for the Vale of Ayalon.

Shimoni turned the engine off and for a space there was silence. Then she said, "I'm sorry if I upset you. I didn't know about Flynn— what had happened but not, well, how serious it was. If I had known, perhaps I'd have been more tactful. I don't know, tact isn't one of my strong points, but anyway I'd have tried.

"But I'd still have been here, because I want the job and if Flynn is finished you need me more not less. I'm not a bimbo. I'll show you my equipment—none of it is in fashion colours. And I'll show you my portfolio, because there's work in there that I'm proud of and that will impress you even if you're trying hard not to be impressed. Then if you're still not interested I'll take you to your hotel and you can spend three days looking and then settle for a photographer who's less good for your job than I am. That's your prerogative.

"But don't tell me you have a monopoly on hurting. Not in this country. I've lost people I cared about, too—everyone here has, Arab and Jew and everyone else. You never saw so much bereavement crammed into three hundred kilometres by eighty. But the job goes on. It has to, otherwise the bastards who think peace is something you impose with a gun have won. You need a photographer, I'm applying for the position. May I show you my portfolio?"

Todd was not accustomed to being ticked off by slips of girls in rolled-up shorts, and he did not want the photographs to be good. But they were. Even by the meagre light in the car, supplemented as necessary by the torch from the glove compartment, he could see that they were good. More than that, he could see that they were honest.

They were not Flynn's kind of photography. Their drama for the most part was small-scale, locked up in human faces. Where Flynn's eye

saw the violence of situations, distilling it down until one frame showing one aspect of one incident stood for and somehow explained the
movement of great events on the world stage, Shimoni's zeroed in on
the pathos of individual griefs in the fine print of those events. Flynn
photographed what people were doing, Shimoni what they were feeling.

Yet she managed not to cross the shadow line dividing human interest from sentimentality, the observation of human tragedy from voyeur-
ism. Todd thought maybe the secret lay in the subjects themselves.
Partly it was the way she had picked them, partly how she had por-
trayed them, but all were recognisably three-dimensional, people with
lives beyond the immediate misfortunes which had befallen them. They
were more than the sum of their anguish. They would still be there,
still probably suffering but still surviving, long after the last copy of the
last newspaper carrying their photograph had been wrapped around the
last felafel supper and thrown away.

When he had finished looking Todd put the photographs away carefully and switched off the torch. He was not sure what he wanted to do
about this. He said, "I'm really not looking to replace Mickey Flynn,
you know."

"All right."

"Even if I was, that kind of arrangement—relationship—doesn't happen overnight. It has to evolve. You spend time looking for someone to
strike up a partnership with." Like two hours drinking with someone in
a New York bar, followed by a week drying him out, he thought wryly.

"I understand that," said Shimoni.

Todd cleared his throat. "At the same time, I am going to want some
pictures taking. I could also use some transport. Do you want to talk
business?"

Shimoni smiled, a vivid triumphant smile that was a splash of white
in the night. Even her smile was a little reminiscent of Flynn's. He
caught a last glimpse of the happiness in her eyes as she shook her head,
turned out the interior light and started the car's engine. "Not tonight.
When you've seen what I can do—not just pictures, seen me working.
The first one's on me."

They drove on to Jerusalem.

Shimoni wanted to take him to the King David. Todd invited her to
look again at his luggage. He directed her to a more modest hotel near
the Damascus Gate, handy to the Old City, the bus station and one of
the main taxi ranks. He and Flynn had stayed there often enough in the

last four years to be included in telling the Seder once when their visit coincided with the Passover; when Flynn had staggered Todd to his boot soles—though not for the first time—by knowing the meaning of the ritual questions posed by the children.

He had not had time to tell them he was coming—also not for the first time—but the Shmuel family were happy to see him and had his bag upstairs in the room he had left five weeks ago before he could ask if there was a vacancy.

They asked about Flynn and he told them. Although they knew Flynn and she did not, their reaction was identical to Shimoni's: no shock, no drama, only a brief expression of sorrow. But Asher Shmuel would remember next time he was praying at the Western Wall, and Esther, who had little patience with anyone's religion, her own least of all, and kept a sort of grudging kosher that stopped well short of a white line down the centre of the kitchen, would probably have knitted him something by the time Todd was leaving.

Shimoni went home to Ein Kerem—she lived with her brother and his wife, both of whom worked in the Hadassah Medical Centre— saying she would pick him up first thing in the morning. Todd spent the evening gossiping, with the Shmuels and their friends in the back room of the hotel, then across the road in an Old City coffee shop run by an elderly Arab of his acquaintance.

He found, as he usually found in the world's trouble spots, that there was a deal more common sense and tolerance and natural justice among the grass roots—a term more apt in Northern Ireland than in Israel— of the riven population than among their political leaders. No one in the coffee shop expected Jordan to return across the river and reclaim the West Bank. No one in the hotel saw an irreconcilable contradiction in an Israeli population of Moslem Arabs. The Arabs did not want to drive the Jews into the sea, any more than the Jews wanted to bury the Arabs in the desert. These polemic devices were recognised by both groups for what they were: political rhetoric, and old political rhetoric at that.

Oddly enough, both groups shared a common aspiration: the eleva- tion of the Arab population to full Israeli citizenship, in practice and in law. The Jews saw this as a responsibility which the Arabs would have to be coaxed and/or bullied into accepting, which might (so the tea drinkers in the hotel believed) run contrary to their view of themselves as part of an international Arab brotherhood but which was the price they had to pay for their own and everyone else's security. The Arabs, on the other hand, saw it as a right which the Jews would have to be coaxed and/or bullied into conceding, which might (so the coffee drinkers in the cafe surmised) run contrary to their view of themselves as a Chosen People a cut-and-a-half above everyone else but which was the price they had to pay for their own and everyone else's security.

Todd went to bed both exhilarated and depressed, conscious of how close an equitable settlement in Israel was and aware of how much fighting and dying would yet be done to defend illusory principles against reluctant foes.

Leah Shimoni shared her notion of first thing in the morning with the cockerels. She arrived at the hotel as Esther Schmuel made the first moves towards preparing breakfast, cutting up oranges and studiously taking no care as to which knife she cut them up with. When Shimoni explained who she had come for, Esther laughed so much she had to sit down.

It was another two hours before Todd showed his face, and then he insisted on a full forty minutes for breakfast. It was nine o'clock before they drove out of the city, heading south on the Hebron road.

When they drove they talked: not always about anything in particular, mostly getting to know each other. They talked about photography and football, their respective hobbies which were fishing and archaeology, then about politics. She questioned him about Ireland. He asked her about the Arab problem.

She succeeded in surprising him. "What Arab problem?"

"You don't think there's a problem?"

"I think there's a problem, but it's a people problem. It's the same problem faced by any multiracial society anywhere in the world. Our problem is not that we have an ethnic minority, but that essentially we have only one. That makes it more personal, makes it easier for each community to blame the other for its misfortunes. But Israel would still be a dry country without the Arabs, and sheep used to die in a bad year even before the Jews came back."

Hebron—Shimoni pronounced the *b* as a *v*—like Jerusalem is a city of limestone, floating atop its limestone mountain like an island in the archipelago that is the Judaean Hills. The old buildings below the crest and the newer ones climbing to the ridge are built of the same old rock; even the newest blocks up on the skyline are of limestone-coloured concrete.

In a monochrome city, even a little one like this, you might expect to have trouble telling one building from another. But nobody ever had to ask directions to the Mosque of Abraham, which made the concourse below it a natural venue for gatherings of all kinds.

The great square edifice loomed over the concourse like what it was: the ancient heart not only of this city but of two, possibly three peoples. The mosque was once a Crusader church, itself built on the foundations of a Byzantine basilica, but the tombs of Abraham and his family have been there since the days of Genesis. A footprint claimed as Adam's appears on a stone in the mosque. King David was proclaimed in Hebron and ruled from there for seven years.

So there has always been something going on in Hebron, and today —judging from the presence of the police loitering round the edges of the concourse—was unlikely to prove any different. So far the police, a few tourists and the usual morning worshippers were the only people in evidence. But already there was an atmosphere that could not be explained by any of that, even the oddly generous supply of police officers with not enough to do. There was a tension in the bright day as if the trouble that everyone was expecting was already here, a disembodied presence, and would happen whether or not anyone turned up to take part; as if the time and the place dictated the people and the problem, not the other way round.

Todd spotted a policeman he knew slightly and went over to say hello and sound him out. The policeman was cagy and thought he had given nothing away. But from what he did and did not say, and from the edge on his nerves which he was probably not aware of showing, Todd gained a good impression of how seriously the authorities were treating this. The military were on standby not far away.

After that Todd drifted round, apparently aimlessly, chatting to anyone who would exchange a few words of English with him. He had no gift for languages other than his own. Shimoni stayed close beside him, in marked contrast to Flynn who had been off doing his own thing as soon as he worked out how to focus and was never more than an irregular passenger on a loose orbit around his partner.

There was plenty of time yet: these things always happened late in the afternoon. Nobody knew why, when half the participants were unemployed and the other half were paid to be there whatever time they were needed. Still at midday Todd was able to take Shimoni off for a leisurely lunch in the confident expectation that, as long as they were back by three, they would miss nothing.

At three-thirty Todd suddenly realised that there were a lot more people in the vicinity of the mosque than there had been, and that a high proportion of them were young Arabs, mostly boys in their late teens. They watched the police and the police watched them. Hebron waited, holding its breath. Still nothing happened, but it was no longer a question of whether there would be trouble but of when and how it would start.

When at three-fifty someone threw the first stone, it came almost as a relief.

Todd thought, as he had thought more times than he could remember, "Well, here we go again." Then he was conscious of a difference, and supposed it was because Flynn was not here with him and some girl he hardly knew, some girl he could not yet trust to look after herself, was. Then he realised it was not that at all. For the first time in many years of finding himself in just this situation he was afraid. Not anxious. Not alert to the hazards of winging stones and baton-charging policemen. Not worried about being in the wrong place at the wrong time and seeing only closely packed backs while the day's seminal activity occurred fifty yards away and might as well have been on another planet. He was scared.

He tried to tell himself it was Shimoni, he was worried about bringing her into a riot situation when he knew so little about how she would react. But he knew that was not the problem. His fear was for himself. Events of the last few weeks—the bomb in Jerusalem, the gunman in Amsterdam—had shattered his confidence, undermined that illusion of invulnerability he had spent thirty years perfecting. It was only an illusion—he had been as vulnerable as anyone else to the physical effects of chaos supplanting order—but the confidence had seen him through; and maybe protected him too, for no one has a rougher passage through life than the man who believes himself a natural victim.

Now that confidence was gone, the seventh veil stripped from his bulky interpsichorean body, and he felt naked, like a cub reporter going solo for the first time. He had not enough eyes in his head, and those he did have were too often engaged in the impossible task of watching his own back. He thought of Flynn. He thought that if Flynn knew how he was feeling now he would laugh until he finished the job begun by a Belgian mechanic in Dam Square.

Suddenly, as if tired of waiting, the gathering of young Palestinian men and a few old Palestinian women moved towards the police, and Todd moved with them.

. . . .

Leah Shimoni got her clothes dirtied, her feet trampled and her eye blackened by someone jogging her elbow while she had the heavy camera to her face. She exposed four reels of film, a total of 144 frames, from which she developed a number of excellent photographs and two outstanding ones.

The first was published with Todd's article and became one of the enduring images of the Palestinian uprising. It showed a row of four little Palestinian girls, aged between about eight and thirteen, their backs to the camera as they watched the smart young soldiery of the Israel Defence Forces moving up to quell the unrest. One of the soldiers looked momentarily towards the girls, quiet in their long dark dresses and head scarves, and the uncertainty of the relationship between his race and theirs was caught flashing across his face. One of the four girls had her hands behind her back, and her hands were full of stones.

The second photograph was never published anywhere, but Shimoni kept it as her special treasure and only showed it to a few real friends. It showed Gilbert Todd, at the height of the riot, interposing his substantial body between an Israeli soldier and one of Hebron's battling grannies in a gallant attempt to keep them from one another's throats. His raincoat flapping in the dusty wind, Todd was wagging a critical forefinger under the nose of the soldier while he restrained the woman, dressed in long black with her hair covered by a scarf, by the simple if undignified expedient of a heavy hand flat on the top of her old head. She was a little under five feet high, and kicking his ankles to get him out of her way so she could sort out the soldier.

Shimoni had thought it was a good picture when she took it, but the sheer wealth of detail only emerged when she developed it that night in her darkroom under the stairs in the apartments where she lived. She sat looking at it for a long time, so happy with it that tears glossed her eyes.

Then she made three prints. One she gave to Todd the next day, and they chuckled and sniggered and then laughed uproariously over it like old friends. One she kept. The third she sandwiched carefully in cardboard and posted to Flynn in Amsterdam.

Todd had not thought to leave a forwarding address, so it was not until he telephoned the hospital to talk to Flynn about Shimoni a week after Hebron that he learned Flynn had gone.

His heart turned cold within him, so that he had difficulty under-standing the perfectly good English of the admissions clerk. He was not sure if she was telling him that Flynn had died, or been discharged, or what she was telling him. He demanded to speak to Dr. Van Rijn, but Van Rijn was not in the building.

He tried the clerk again. Mr. Flynn had gone, she said, checked out. Checked out, as if it were a hotel and he had paid his bill and left? Todd tried to explain to her that he could not have done that, that Flynn could hardly walk let alone do a runner. Now she had trouble with his English. But she kept insisting that Flynn was no longer a patient in the hospital.

He rang off and called the airport instead, and booked the first avail-able seat to Europe though he had to change in Rome for a flight to Holland.

Shimoni took him to the airport. They drove almost in silence. She could see how worried he was but did not understand why. She had thought it was good news when he said Flynn had left hospital; well, good for Flynn if not so good for her.

She was going to wait with him but Todd told her not to bother, by the time she had parked the car they would be calling his flight. She knew it would be longer than that but did not press him: if he preferred to wait alone, that was his right.

"You'll call me when you know what's happened?"

"Yes, all right."

"And when you come back to Israel?"

"I'll look you up."

She bit her lip. "And if you need a photographer before then."

Todd made himself smile. "I'll call you. I promise."

She believed him. At least, she believed that right now he meant it. But she had the awful leaden feeling of her future slipping through her fingertips. It had very nearly happened—what she had wanted, what she had worked for—but it was not going to happen now. Flynn, whom she had never met, never spoken to, who had sent opportunity winging unexpectedly her way, had snatched it back in the very last moment. She sighed as she drove away. The Lord was not the only one who both gave and took away.

Probably it would not have worked anyway. The thing with Flynn would always have been in the way. All she had wanted with Todd was a professional relationship, but Flynn's shadow hung over them like a dybbuk. She would never have filled Flynn's footsteps—perhaps it was better not having to try.

By the time Todd reached Amsterdam, Van Rijn had been located and told about his call and his imminent arrival. She was waiting for him in her office.

"I don't understand," he said, dropping heavily into the chair opposite her desk. His voice was bitter. "Ten days ago he could hardly move. You had me talk him into some acceptance of what had happened, because he was going to be here some time and he was never going to be fit for the life he led before. Now you tell me you've let him go, and you don't even know where he's gone?"

Van Rijn had learned medicine from dealing with patients, and patience from dealing with their relatives. She counted Todd in that: clearly there was a relationship between him and Flynn, even if it was not of blood. It might have been sexual but she doubted it. What there certainly was between them, though she was not sure either of them knew it, was love.

So she was as patient with Todd as she could manage, though he made it hard for her. "In the time you were away Mr. Flynn's mobility increased significantly. We had to cut the painkillers back daily to keep him aware of the injury. He was rather quiet for a day or two after you left, then as he felt his condition improving his mood lightened and I thought he was through the difficult part. But three days ago he came to me and said he was leaving. I asked him why but he would not say. He refused to discuss the matter with me. He asked for the prescription for his drugs, and I did not feel I could withhold it. So he took his things and left."

Todd shook his head. His face was strained, his skin drawn grey over the solid features. He was worried sick and looking for someone to be angry with. "I can't believe you just let him walk out like that. Knowing the condition he's in. All right, so he was getting better—but you're not telling me he's recovered, are you?"

Van Rijn shook her dark head sombrely. "No, I cannot tell you that. But Mr. Todd, he's a grown man with free will and the right to leave anywhere he does not choose to stay. I reminded him of the risks if he insisted on removing himself from medical supervision. That was all I could do."

"You gave him the prescription."

Her eyes on him were cold. "I do not impose my will on patients by subjecting them to pain until they submit."

She was right. Todd sighed and let go of the tension that was holding his anger together. "I'm sorry. No, probably there wasn't any more you could do. He's too big to put over your knee and spank. All the same, when I find him I'll bring him back here, whether he wants to come or not. Is that all right?"

She inclined her head. "If he comes, we will treat him. Where will you find him?"

"God knows," grunted Todd. "Not at home, because he knows I'll go there first and if he'd wanted to talk to me about this he'd have done it before. He knew where I was even if you didn't. I'll call a few people, maybe pick up a line on him. Damn him," he added with sudden venom, "pulling a stunt like this just when . . ."

Then it came together and he understood why Flynn had done what he had done, and why he had done it then. Just when Todd was picking up the pieces. Just when Todd had found someone to take his place. He sighed, a long slow whisper of breath gravid with understanding. "He saw the picture, didn't he?"

"There was a photograph, yes."

"Damn. I should have called him, told him about it before it appeared. I didn't expect he'd have seen it yet." In the background, while he spoke, his mind was doing sums. "Three days ago? He couldn't have seen it three days ago."

Van Rijn shrugged an Oriental shrug. "It arrived in that morning's post."

"The magazine wasn't out then."

"Not a magazine, a photograph—a print, yes? Of you, at Hebron. He showed me."

Oh Shimoni, Shimoni, thought Todd in the taxi on the way back to Schiphol. Why didn't you tell me what you were doing? Or maybe it would have made no difference—maybe I'd have thought it was a nice idea too. It *was* a nice idea, there was no reason for him to fling off in a huff because of it. We're not married. Anyway, he told me to find a new date. So why's he behaving this way now I have?

Despite what he told Van Rijn, he went straight to London and to Flynn's apartment overlooking the river. It was a wet spring, and the whole of the cityscape was painted in hues of sepia and grey. The neighbours watched incuriously as he climbed through the empty building towards Flynn's eyrie in the roof. With every step he wondered how, if Flynn had been here, he had managed all the stairs.

[2]

He had been there, and the stairs had given him difficulty and pain. He had been close to the end of his strength when he reached the warehouse, more tired that he could believe by the short hop from Schiphol and the taxi from Heathrow. The cabbie thought he looked about done too, and offered to help him inside with his gear. But there was not much, a grip with his clothes in it and his camera bag, and he was too tired to be bothered with the man and so paid him off. He thought he could manage alone.

He almost did not. It was a closer thing than as a fit young man bounding up and down those stone and iron steps he could possibly have imagined. Halfway up the penultimate flight his stamina was exhausted and he sat down on a step with his head in his hands, no air in his lungs and red-hot pincers fixed in his spine, and he did not see how he could make the top even if he left his bags where they were and crawled on his hands and knees. But after ten minutes' rest he tried again and made it to his own front door.

The door was barred against him. His keys opened the locks, but the chain denied him entry. There was a light on inside, and its kindly glow on the contents of his home beckoned him, and he could have wept at being able to see them and not reach them. He shouted, "Angus!" in a hoarse and rusty voice. Then something odd happened to the brick wall he was leaning on—the rough bricks went somehow soft and spongy, and at the same time the naked bulb shining in the blind passage bloomed pinkly and began to dim.

Angus thought she recognised the voice calling her name, thought she must have been mistaken, thought she had better go and see. She opened the door in time to see the eyes roll up in Mickey Flynn's white face and to grab for him as he went down.

There was a lot more of Flynn than there was of Angus so she could not catch him and carry him inside. But she went down with him, breaking his fall and keeping his head from cracking into the wall, and she stayed there, holding him, while he recovered his senses and strength enough to get himself into the flat, leaning on her as on a crutch.

Angus put him to bed. Whether it was his bed or hers at the moment was a moot point, but for now his need was the greater. She tucked the duvet up under his chin, then made them a hot drink each. She sat on the edge of the bed, drinking hers, eyeing him critically. At length she said, "Mickey, you look frigging rotten."

He had not intended to stay. He meant only to collect some clean clothes, some bits of equipment and some money, and be gone before Todd came pounding at his door—which could be a few hours, or a few days, or longer than that. But the warm drink and the bed worked their magic, and Angus—sitting quietly by his side, seeing with an artist's analytical eye the stamp of illness and exhaustion in his face and the disposition of his long limbs—watched while he fell asleep. The lids fell heavy over eyes bottomless with weariness, the fixed planes of his face softened and the long shape of him under the quilt eased as sleep stole through his veins. And all the time he slept Angus kept watch over him—not like a lover, more like a woman watching over her child.

He slept the rest of the evening away and all of the night, and began to stir with the dawn over the river and the fact that, even allowing for the extras he took to cope with travelling, his medication was now some hours overdue. Pain which had perched like a black bird on the bedpost overnight now fluttered down ponderously and settled on his shoulder, kneading its claws into flesh. The bird was like a familiar spirit to him: even when he was not aware of it, it was never far away, waiting just beyond his perception for the moment when the drugs lost their potency and allowed it in to feed on him.

Angus had watched him fall asleep and now she watched him wake. She had snatched a little sleep in between: not much, but she was used to working through the night when the spirit moved her and was untroubled by insomnia. She was watching the sky pale over the river when she heard the note of Flynn's breathing change, catch in his throat with a little whimper of half-focused distress. He might have been cold, or dreaming.

Angus twisted in her chair to look at his face, and there was a little frown between his brows and the eyelids were flickering. He lay on his good left side under the quilt, his left hand palm up beside his face on the pillow. As she watched the fingers began to twitch, then to grasp in a loose and feeble fist. Soon after that he groaned and his body moved in its long cocoon like a torpid snake.

Angus leaned forward and touched her hand to his bare shoulder. "It's all right, Mickey. You're safe here."

Before he was properly aware of her hand or voice, of where he was or what time of the day it was, he knew he needed his tablets. He groped, vaguely at first then with increasing urgency, under the covers where his pocket would have been if he had still had his jacket on. But Angus had undressed him, and his searching fingers found only his own skin.

Need roused him like a wet sponge, and he blinked awake and rolled onto his back. "Angus?"

"Here."

She found him the tablets and went for a glass of water, but by the time she returned he had chewed his way hungrily through them and already the hurt was being held in check. Angus saw the internal effect of the drug mirrored in his face, in the softening lines, in the rueful, half humorous lift of his lip, and she smiled in return.

"Are you going to tell me what the hell's going on?"

"I thought I told you last night."

She snorted impatience. "You told me nothing last night. You fainted on the doorstep then collapsed in my bed, drank my cocoa and died. I thought you were in hospital. You should be in hospital."

He rolled his head on the pillow. "No point. They've done what they can. I can manage on my own now."

"You call this managing?"

He winced, said defensively, "I was tired."

"You were dead on your feet. Honest, Mickey, you could have killed yourself." Something in the way he looked at her made her shiver clear to her spine.

He stayed there two days, resting, growing visibly stronger. As the hours passed and no one either rang or came looking for him, his anxiety about being intercepted diminished to an amused disbelief. Perhaps the first Todd would know that he had jumped bail would be when his photographs appeared. Flynn might have been aggrieved at how wrapped up in his new partner Todd had become, had he not known that Shimoni was a girl. He grinned to himself and wished the randy old goat good luck.

On the third morning, with his pills in his pocket and something like a spring in his step, Flynn walked away down the wharf, resigned to and even curiously exalted by the possibility that he would not be back again.

Nine hours after Flynn closed it behind him, Todd was hammering at the door. "You again?" said Angus.

"Is he here?"

"Who—Mickey?" she said, deliberately negligent. "No."

"But he's been here."

"Aye." She turned back into the apartment and he followed her. He had come straight from the airport and still had his case with him. He left it inside the door.

"How did he seem?"

She met his eyes then. "Frigging awful. But better when he left than when he came."

"When did he go?"

"This morning."

Half a day. "Damn." If he had called the hospital just twelve hours earlier, he would have caught up with Flynn here. "Where was he heading?"

"He didnae say."

"Did he say why?"

"Oh aye. But you willnae like it."

She had never cross-examined Flynn, never so much as asked about his intentions and his reasons. She had agreed to stand guardian of his flat, not his soul. Perhaps for the very reason that she asked no questions, brought no pressure, just stood quietly painting by the window with the light of the river on one cheek, as he regained his strength and his confidence so he began talking—reflectively, much as a man might talk to himself, or his cat. Unless he sought a response she did not offer many interruptions to what remained essentially a soliloquy; but she listened endlessly, and understood perhaps more than he would have expected or even wanted her to.

"He wasn't prepared to spend the next six months in hospital," she told Todd, "should they be the last six months of his life. Especially if they were going to be the last six months of his life. He's terrified that thing in his back's going to paralyse him. The way he sees it, if it happens when he's alone in some rooming house with the rent paid in advance, he might take a week dying but nobody's going to fill him full of tubes and Christianity and make him take fifty years over it. In the hospital it would be out of his hands: he was scared shitless they could make him live like that.

"So he was always waiting his chance to get out and disappear. He needed two things first: to be fit enough to walk out, and for you to be out of the way someplace, because he didn't trust you to stand back and let him make his own choices."

She had been right: Todd did not like it. It hurt like a fist in his belly, knocked all the breath out of him, that Flynn had been aching and yearning and maybe even praying for him to go away so that he could get on with living or dying on his own terms, without interference.

That was why Shimoni's photograph had prompted his departure. It was not pique because Todd had found a new photographer. It was because of what the Hebron photograph told him: that Todd had teamed up with a photographer who was good enough to do his job for him, and thereby to keep Todd involved and in one place while events developed instead of getting on the first plane back bemoaning the lack of local talent that made it pointless for him to stay. That one photograph had told him he had time to make his move.

Todd thought of the relief that must have come with that realisation and winced. Knowing Flynn had not trusted him with the hardest decision he would ever take was a knife under his ribs. Knowing that Flynn had been right was the twist that made the blood flow.

He coughed, found some semblance of his normal voice. "Angus, I have to find him. He doesn't know what he's doing."

The girl shook her blonde head decisively. "He knows exactly what he's doing. He always does, it's just that you don't always like it." Oh yes, Flynn must have done some talking in the two days he was here. "Look. You were on at him to accept what happened, yes? Well, he has. But he's going to deal with it his way, not yours."

"By ignoring it? He's going to end up dead in a ditch!"

"Dead in a ditch he can take. Half dead in a hospital is what he's anxious to avoid."

Todd was fighting very hard the urge to reach out and shake her: partly because he was of a generation that did not casually manhandle women, partly because he suspected she could knock the stuffing out of him. "Angus, for pity's sake. He's hurt, he's in danger, he must be scared half out of his mind. Help me find him. We can sort out then what we do next. But first I have to find him."

Angus's Celtic temper was never far below the surface and Todd's persistence was beginning to irritate her. "No, Mr. Todd, you don't have to do anything of the kind. What you have to do is face the fact that what you want for Mickey and what Mickey wants for himself are two different things, and it's what Mickey wants that counts.

"Do you think he needs you—running his life, telling him what to do? Well he doesnae. All he needs from you is to get off his case. Who the hell are you, anyway, that gives you the right to dictate to him?"

Taken aback by her sudden assault, Todd stumbled, "We're partners —friends—"

"Friends?" Her voice was scathing. "Some friend, you! You're the reason he's out there alone, going God knows where when he's barely fit to get himself to the paper-shop and back. If it wasn't for you he'd have stayed here until he was strong enough to go. But he knew you'd be after him, hunting him, haunting him, and sure enough here you are. Call yourself his friend, do you? If Mickey Flynn dies in a ditch, it'll be as much your fault as the man who shot him."

He did hit her for that: the flat of his hand across her angular cheek, hard enough to crack like a whiplash in the brick-walled room. It was unforgivable, but then it was an unforgivable thing to say, the more so because it was true. All the same, humiliation hit him like a tide, washing him up and down. He was a big, powerful man in his second half century, and he had struck a tiny young woman in her face for telling him an unpalatable truth. He had felt bad enough before: there was no way of expressing how he felt now.

He groaned and bowed his head, a heat in his cheeks, and scrutinised the deep slate-grey pile of Flynn's unexpectedly up-market carpet with rather greater intensity than it warranted. Somehow he managed to say, "Angus, I'm sorry—"

It had been a substantial swipe, enough to rock her back on her heels and imprint the shape of his fingers on her cheek, but it was not the first time she had been struck and she was less shocked by it than Todd was. She watched, quizzically, her head on one side, while he flushed alternately red and white like an aid to navigation. Then, liking him more for that than for anything he had said, she touched his arm gently. "Sit down. I'll make some cocoa."

They talked for a while longer, and understood one another better for it, but Angus still did not know where Flynn was heading. She might not have told him if she had known, but since she did not she could afford to be frank. Neither of them voiced what they both knew, that Flynn had not told her because he had guessed Todd would come here and ask. They parted on amiable terms, though Todd could still not look at her reddened cheek without a heat gathering under his collar.

Finally he went home. He played the messages on his answering machine while he had a bath. It took half an hour. The last was Leah Shimoni asking him to call her back. He did so at once, standing in his living room with a towel round his middle, steaming gently and occasionally dripping on a floral carpet whose inferiority to Flynn's, in both quality and taste, he had only this minute noticed.

He had almost given her up for out when Shimoni answered the phone, in Hebrew, gasping the words out as if she had been running. "Gil Todd," he said, "you were looking for me."

"Yes." Her voice, as she got her breath back, went quiet, even a little flat. "Have you found Mickey yet?"

"No. He went back to his place, but he'd left by the time I got there. I don't know where he's gone."

"But you're still looking."

"Oh yes." In spite of what Angus had said; in spite of her being right. "Yes."

"I called in a favour. A friend at El Al." The Israeli national airline, whose Hebrew name was capable of various high-minded translations into English but none to compare for charm, in Todd's mind anyway, with "Heavens Above!" He got a chuckle out of it every time he flew with them. "He found Mickey's name on this afternoon's flight from Heathrow."

"Mickey's in Israel?" It was the last thing he had expected. With the world to choose from, and no pressing business except apparently keeping clear of Todd, whatever would induce him to return there?—to that little country, where he knew Todd was working, forging a new partnership, where he was more likely to cross Todd's trail again than anywhere else on earth.

Then he knew. "No," he hissed in his teeth. "Oh God damn it, not that." He was not doubting her information. The moment she said it he knew it was true. More than that, he knew why Flynn had returned to Israel, and why he had taken a comprehensive camera kit with him. "Mickey! Not that."

"What is it? Gil? Do you know what he's doing here?"

"I thought I'd talked him out of it." The horror in Todd's voice reached her across a continent. "I told him if he did it he'd never work in Israel again. I told him he could get killed doing it. I suppose those threats don't carry the weight now that they did."

[3]

When Deborah Lev heard that Flynn had passed through Lod coming off the London flight, her first thought was that someone had made a mistake. Her last intelligence of him was that he was lying paralysed in a

Dutch hospital. But hope springs eternal, and it was worth a few phone calls.

One was to the cafe where she first picked him up. The waiter did not remember Flynn, but when she described him the man had no trouble recognising him. "Yes, he's here."

"How does he look?"

A certain sourness crept into the man's tone. "As if he was buying something dearer than lemonade at the last place he was in."

Flynn was still sitting alone in the corner when she arrived, his bags at his feet, his head resting on his folded arms on the table, a half empty glass in front of him. He did indeed look he had been making a day of it. But he was neither drunk nor asleep, because he saw her over the crook of his arm when she came in. He said, "I thought you might turn up."

He lifted his head so that she could see more of his face than the longish brown hair washing over his forearm, and for a moment she was shocked at the change in him. The flesh had fallen away from his face, leaving only grey skin stretched taut over the sharp bones. His eyes had sunk into deep hollows and darkened to an indeterminate sludge colour. The new stiffness in the way he moved aged him by fifteen years.

Conscience, which was not something that troubled Deborah Lev greatly, at least not these days, suddenly caught her an unexpected jab beneath the ribs. Accounts of Flynn's death might have been exaggerated, but not by all that much. Was she seriously considering sending a sick man into the hornet's nest of a PFLP training camp?

Flynn saw the unreassuring shock reflected in her eyes, and his lip quirked up in a grin that was at least half genuine. "You look like you've seen a ghost."

She sat down quickly in front of him, leaning forward. "Mickey, what are you doing here? You can't—"

He interrupted. "I don't know what I can do yet, so you sure as hell don't. What I'm here for is what we talked about before."

"No." She shook her head, the dark hair tossing briefly. "No, Mickey. Not now, not like this . . ."

He caught her eyes and she felt it like a blow. Whatever strength he had been robbed of had come from his body, not his soul. "Now," he said firmly. "Now is all I can count on. This may be the fittest I'm going to be. Next week I can't be sure of, but this week I can work and if I've only one more job in me it's going to be something big—something to make them sit up and put their coffee down all over the civilised world. A nice little secret war somewhere I could have blown the lid off would have been better still, but this'll do. Are they terrorists? Are they freedom fighters? Are they just cannon fodder to keep alive a dispute no one has any hope of solving? Here they are, judge for yourselves: every picture tells a story, which is probably just as well because the photographer hasn't a lot to say for himself these days . . ."

He seemed to hear the bitter stridency mounting in his voice and broke off abruptly. After a few moments he smiled and his voice was gentle. "I have to do this, Leila, and it has to be now. I may be fine in three months' time, but I may not. The other thing is, Gil Todd will come looking for me soon. It'll be a whole lot easier if I've dropped out of sight by then."

Lev made her mind up. She was no longer sure whose interests she was acting in, whether she was pulling Flynn's strings or he was pulling hers. The thing seemed to have developed a will and a momentum of its own, quite independent of her careful, clever plans. The only control left to her at this point was to stop it or to let it run, and concern for a man who in the very nature of the thing was a Judas goat seemed insufficient reason to stop it.

"All right, I'll fix it up. It may take a day. I know where you can go in the meantime."

She left Flynn with a man they met at the Zion Gate, who conducted him—at some speed, Flynn had trouble keeping up with him—through the dark ways, some of them little more than shoulder width, of the Old City. They crossed the Armenian quarter, then slipped neatly between the Christian and Jewish quarters into that northeastern sector where the Arabs live. One of the Arabs living there was Ismah Habach, and it was her house that Flynn was taken to by the swift, silent man who disappeared back into the city as soon as he was delivered.

There had been a third man with them, though Flynn had not seen him pass quietly between the shadows in their wake. Fahad watched until Flynn went into the house of Mrs. Habach, then he turned away quickly and hurried to the shop of Akram Kassi for a council of war. Kassi was a glazier by trade, one of the few people in Jerusalem who stood to gain from a period of sustained disorder, regardless of who was breaking whose windows and why.

Kassi left his apprentice cutting a set of windowpanes and took Fahad through into his house. "Now what are we going to do?"

Fahad shrugged. He was a small man, without the glazier's breadth of shoulder, but on the whole he had the steadier hand. "What we agreed to do: take him, be careful what we show him, hope his pictures will do us some good."

Kassi was deeply uneasy. "We had more time to get organised when she suggested it before. There weren't so many people there, only the youngsters who knew nothing and had done nothing. Now Rachid is there, working his way through half a ton of Sentex, and I think he will not take kindly to being asked to pack up and leave again."

"Rachid doesn't have to go anywhere," said Fahad. "All he has to do is stay in his workshop while we show Flynn the rest of the camp. He's not a fool, you know—Flynn. He knows there are things we cannot let him see. All we need do is keep him on a short leash."

"And if something goes wrong? If he sees something he should not have seen, what then?"

Fahad sighed. "In that case, Akram, I'd say he was a very unlucky young man."

Ismah Habach was a child of the Jihad. One of her earliest memories was of Haj Amin el Husseini, Mufti of Jerusalem, declaring Holy War against the newly independent State of Israel. That must have been the winter of 1947–48. The Jews declared the Mufti a Nazi agent, but Ismah's father considered him a very holy man.

Her father took part in the general strike of December 1947 organised by the Arab Higher Command in Palestine, though he eschewed the rioting that developed from it. He was not a violent man. He was a good man. His family had lived in Jerusalem further back than anyone could remember, had seen the British replace the Turks and now saw the Jews replace the British. He felt, as successive generations of his ancestors must have felt, that his birthright had been sold out from under his feet again. He was afraid what the consequences might be.

The Mufti told him that the Jews wanted everything that was his, including his life and the lives of his family, and that the Jews must be thrown into the sea. The Mufti was a holy man, but Ismah's father thought perhaps the world's nations which voted for a Jewish state might stand firm against the wholesale destruction of Arab culture in Palestine by their protégé.

But one day he was visiting his brother in Neve Sadij when Jewish zealots descended on the place and wrought mayhem. Ismah's father and uncle both were among the dead. The authorities' claim that the crime was the only Jewish outrage against Arab civilians during the War of Independence, despite many similar attacks on Jewish communities, impressed the international observers but not the men's families. One way or another, Ismah had been fighting the Jews since then.

She had married, and in due course lost, a Fedayeen soldier and raised for him two Fedayeen sons. One followed his father into glorious death, the younger Alam was with a PFLP group somewhere in the wilderness east of Be'er Sheva. She did not know exactly where, and because the Jews were watching for him she only saw him once a year, if that. It did not matter: they worked in the same cause, he in the desert and she in her father's house in Jerusalem.

In this small, blind-fronted house in the secret heart of the most public city in the world, Ismah Habach served in whatever ways she could. She would hide anyone on the run from anything. She would store weapons and explosives. She would tend anyone hurt in the prosecution of the forty-year-old Holy War.

She was the ideal choice to accommodate a photographer who had to be disappeared for twenty-four hours while Fahad arranged some publicity for the PFLP. She frequently took lodgers into her house, and though not many of them were Westerners, some of them did pay rent and kept nothing more than an empty suitcase under the bed.

When she had showed Flynn to his little whitewashed room she went to make some coffee. She was a surprisingly large woman for an Arab, tall and sturdily built; about fifty now, she had fierce hawk's eyes set in a strong face to which a smile did not come easily.

Flynn thanked her politely. It was like being back in school, treading warily round a new teacher until her flash point could be determined.

Ismah Habach's flash point was almost reached just ten minutes later, when she came in with his coffee and found him asleep on the bed with his boots on. Arab women are not encouraged to shout at men; still she drew in all the breath her capacious lungs would accommodate in order to scream at him; then her sparking eyes travelled up from his boots to his face.

She watched him for perhaps two minutes, the anger and the breath seeping out of her until she could no more have screamed at him than at an exhausted child collapsed on her bedspread. Then, with a nice compound of compassion and practicality, she tucked a newspaper round his feet and a blanket over the rest of him, and left him to sleep in peace.

. . . .

Sammi Akim sold newspapers on street corners, and was as much a part of the Jerusalem scenery as the Dome of the Rock. He was never seen reading the papers that he sold, in any of the three languages he sold them in. There was in fact a rumour in the city that old Sammi, with his grubby keffiyeh and his ancient tweed jacket and his leather satchel and all his papers, could neither read nor write.

Nevertheless, he had contributed countless column inches to the world's press, and though almost none of them knew his name millions of people around the globe had based their understanding of proceeding in the Middle East at least partially on his views.

Sammi was one of the most reliable "informed sources" in the business. A reporter fresh into Jerusalem wanting to establish how the local populace was reacting to any new development, or how it might view a proposed one, could either spend three days conducting a survey—bearing in mind that there was nowhere within five hundred miles where an unbiased opinion might be obtained—or he could spend small change on a couple of newspapers and ask Sammi.

Sammi had several personae: a "usually reliable source" on the subject of security, "observers close to the Knesset" when the issue was political, and "grass-roots opinion" on anything else. Alone of all the great orators, Jewish and Arab, in the long history of the conflict, Sammi could claim to have spoken for both communities with equal fervour. He had come up with some memorable quotes when representing ultra-Orthodox Jews illicitly homesteading in the occupied territories.

There were a few places Todd could have begun his search for Flynn. He could have asked the police, he could have asked Simon Meir if the Israel Defence Forces had come across him, he could have gone round some of the city's bars and cafes and made enquiries there. Instead he made a beeline for Sammi Akim's news pitch.

Todd expected the elderly newsboy to have heard that he had pulled out of Israel, and why, and so be a little surprised to see him. But Sammi greeted him casually, the rheumy eyes in his crumbling face failing to widen. It transpired that Sammi not only knew he had gone away, he knew he had come back. It was a hopeful sign, if disconcerting.

"Sammi, you know Mickey Flynn."

"It is so." The old head inclined and an unspeakable fingernail scratched his mossy nose.

"I've lost him, Sammi. The young devil's given me the slip."

"This I have heard."

Of course he had, Sammi who heard everything. "Do you know where he is?"

Sammi looked thoughtful. He rearranged his papers, so that the English-language *Jerusalem Post* kept the Hebrew and Arabic dailies a diplomatic distance apart. "Perhaps he wishes not to be found." His gaze avoided Todd's.

Damn Flynn, thought Todd, fists clenching unseen in his pockets, even the most unbiased man in the Middle East is on his side. Between them, all his friends are going to get him killed.

"He's not well, Sammi. You know what happened in Holland I suppose?" The quick furtive flare of Sammi's eyes suggested it was no more than a man deserved who was unwise enough to leave Jerusalem for uncertain foreign climes. "I have to find him. I'm worried what may happen to him if I don't."

Sammi thought some more. He looked at his papers, looked at Todd, looked up at the golden masonry of the Citadel soaring over the Jaffa Gate. Finally he broke the habit of a lifetime by asking a question. "Why did he come back?"

"He was looking for a woman." Todd caught Sammi's expression, a kind of ancient leer, and grinned too. "No, not like that. I know what you think, Sammi, but actually most of the world's cities can offer the same facilities as Jerusalem, and one or two can do better. No, it was a particular woman—someone who asked him to do a job for her. Well, for the PFLP actually."

Sammi's mouldering face went from prurient to armour-plated in a moment. Jerusalem is full of things that everybody knows and nobody talks about, at least not in the golden sunshine of a late spring afternoon within eavesdropping distance of the myriad ears and multiple allegiances of the Old City. Of course an Englishman, even one who had spent as long here as Todd, might not be familiar with the local talisman for averting the evil eye, which was to refer to them not by name, or even by cypher, but as Some People.

Actually Todd was fully conversant with this particular tradition. But he was not a superstitious man, he did not believe that speaking of the devil was enough to make him appear, and he saw no reason to bestow a kind of cosy approbation on a band of killers by referring to them as one might to a gathering of bridge players.

"I wish not to know about that," said Sammi hurriedly—a remarkable enough statement coming from the man, even if it was not true. "It is none of my business."

"Well, it's mine, Sammi," Todd said firmly, "and I shalln't drop it until I find him. Come on, who can I talk to? I'll leave you alone if you'll put me onto someone who'll help."

"Help you find him?"

"Or her. If he's gone under, she'll know where. Leila—that's all I know."

Something strange was happening in Sammi's face. It might have been horror, or amazement, or trying not to laugh. It made his face look like a fey walnut buried for three months in Jordan mud. He said, "Am I to believe this?" and put his head so far on one side his keffiyeh was defying gravity. He looked like a sparrow listening to a dirty joke.

Todd did not understand. "Why, do you know her?"

"All Jerusalem knows her. Leila is only one of her names. Another is Deborah Lev. Captain Lev to her friends."

Still Todd did not understand. "Sammi, what are you talking about?"

Sammi jerked his head in the approximate direction of Ha Kirya, the government offices out to the west of the city. "The woman. Leila?— she's no Arab, she's Shin Bet." Internal intelligence. "She works for Aaron Ben Simeon."

A frown was gathering between Todd's eyes, bewilderment gathering behind them. "She's with the IDF? Not the PFLP? What would the Army want with Mickey?"

"My friend, you miss the joke," said Sammi, quietly convulsing with mirth. "She thinks nobody knows. She works for military intelligence, and she thinks she has infiltrated certain people and nobody knows. But every Arab in Jerusalem knows who she is. Newsmen?—you and Mickey Flynn must be the last people in Palestine to be taken in by her."

Todd was still struggling with the content of this information, had not yet found time to consider the implications. "But if the PFLP know she's a spy, why don't they—?"

"Kill her?" Sammi lifted a quizzical eyebrow. "What wit would there be in that? Besides, as long as these people know who she is, they will not tell her anything they do not want her to know. Leila is no danger to anyone, and she is useful for misleading the IDF when the need arises. If she was removed they would only send someone else, who might be harder to recognise and so do some harm. No, Captain Lev is safe enough. As long as she does not strike lucky one day and see something she should not see."

For a wasted hour after he left Sammi, Todd wandered round in a daze. He was dimly aware of shops and offices emptying, of the buses and Sherut taxis filling up and running out of the city centre, but none of it touched him. For most of that hour the traffic in the wide streets thickened noisily, spun like a great mad maelstrom round the still hub of the Old City. Then at the end of that time suddenly almost everyone had gone and Todd had whole pavements to himself. It made as little impression on him as the rush hour had done.

He did not know what to do for the best. If Flynn had come here looking for Leila, as he believed, and if he had found her and gone with her, his life was in more immediate danger than the shard of bone in his back had ever posed. Her purpose in trawling for him as she had was not clear, but presumably she saw in him a means of improving her intelligence gathering. Perhaps, without knowing the reason for it, she was aware that there was a limit to how close she could get to the PFLP hierarchy and saw Flynn as a kind of robot device she could plant closer to the heart of things than she could safely go herself. Much in the way that Simon Meir used Geronimo.

If the PFLP knew she was IDF, they must know that Flynn was a threat to them. If they were still prepared to accept him into their midst, there had to be something in it for them. Publicity, of course, which was what Leila had sold them on in the first place. But they would not get the sort of coverage they wanted by allowing Flynn to return to her. Their needs and hers were contradictory: at some point conflict was inevitable. And probably that would be the first Flynn would know that he was being used as an Israeli spy.

Todd found he was sweating in the cool of the early evening. Half a dozen times he decided on a course of action, then changed his mind. He was going to the police. He was going to IDF headquarters. He would look for Leila. He would get a message to the PFLP.

Finally he called Simon Meir.

[4]

At six o'clock in the morning Fahad and another man came to the little house in the Moslem quarter and Ismah Habach showed them Flynn's room. They burst in without warning, dragged him from the bed and slammed him up against the wall. The bigger man had a handgun. He fitted the muzzle delicately over the healing scar below Flynn's shoulder, then leaned on it. Flynn's knees buckled and only the whitewashed wall kept him on his feet.

Mrs. Habach's low voice behind them cut in authoritatively. "For the love of God, that will do," she said in Arabic, and after a moment the flaring pain in Flynn's back began to subside. The deep breath he had sucked in to scream with came out in a thick, ragged pant. "His clothes are on the chair, his bag and his camera are in the cupboard." There was a creak as she put something on the bed. "He can wear these. Alam is not so tall, but wider."

It was the first indication Flynn had had since they crashed in on his sleep that they were not here to kill him. He had woken with their noise in his ears, the light blinding in his eyes, their hands on his body and a gun muzzle grinding into his back, and he had thought that he was going to die—not maybe, not sometime, but here and now. The dawn air was cool against his skin, but the whole of his body was damp with sweat.

Now here was Mrs. Habach offering him a change of clothes in a language which he did not understand but with universal gestures. If he did not know why, still he recognised a good sign when he saw one. Nobody takes that much trouble with a corpse.

The man with the gun peeled him off the wall and pushed him back at the bed. "Get dressed."

The clothes had been laundered carefully and neatly folded. They fitted where they touched. He climbed into the jeans, though his hands shaking now with reaction fumbled with the zip; but his shoulders, always stiff first thing in the morning, had gone into spasm and he could not get his arms into the shirtsleeves.

Mrs. Habach saw his difficulty, guessed the reason for it and helped him into the shirt. Her fingertips brushed the livid scar. "Who gave you that—us or the Jews?" Now she understood his weakness.

Flynn laughed shakily as he fumbled over the buttons. "What, do you think you're the only trigger-happy bastards in the world? Believe me, the choice is much wider than that. That was a Belgian fascist who didn't want to be photographed organising a riot in Holland because he wanted it to look like the work of French Communists and the South Moluccans."

She looked at him as if seeing him afresh, with something like respect. "That is a dangerous job that you do."

"Tell me about it."

Alam's shoes were too small and they would not let him keep his boots so he went barefoot, down through the house and out to a van parked at the end of the alley. There was also a car. A man was waiting in the van. Flynn was bundled into the back and the big man with the gun followed him in. Fahad, who came out of the house behind them carrying Flynn's bags, got into the car and was driven away.

"Hey," cried Flynn, indignant, "where's he going with my camera?"

The man with the gun grinned. "You wouldn't believe me if I told you." He spoke excellent colloquial English with a faint Dublin accent: he had once spent eight months setting up contacts with the IRA. His name was Kadar.

"Try me."

"OK. We're pretty sure now you're not carrying a wire. We didn't find anything in your clothes, but even if we missed one it can't do us any harm where it's going. The same applies to the camera. If we stripped it down thoroughly enough to be sure there was nothing inside except what the makers built in, it wouldn't take photographs anymore. So we'll give you a camera and film that we know are clean. They may not be what you're used to, but I expect you'll manage."

"So when do I get my stuff back?"

The grin broadened. "They'll be quite safe, you can collect them when we're finished with you. From the police. One of our people will hand them in and say she found them lying in the street. Then if there is a wire in there somewhere, the IDF will find themselves laying siege to the police station.

"Of course, if that happens," added Kadar as an afterthought, "I'll be wanting another word with you."

For Todd the long evening ached by while he sat beside the phone. A little after eleven Meir called him back. "Meet me out front in five minutes."

Meir drove a modest sports car with a sure hand and a slightly apologetic élan. Out of uniform he looked like any forty-year-old professional man, yet still Todd felt a vague unease at climbing into an open car with him, in full view of anyone who cared to watch.

By the time Todd had worked out the seat-belt arrangement, Meir was in third gear and already speeding.

"Where are we going?"

Meir's voice was almost without inflection, pitched just above the sound of the slipstream. "Where we're going, I have absolutely no business taking you. In fact we may be stopped. My personal regard for you notwithstanding, I wouldn't be taking you within five miles of the place but for the danger Mickey Flynn is in right now. Well, I don't mind putting my head on the block, it's been there before and there aren't so many volunteers for bomb disposal that they can afford to axe those they have. But I won't compromise anyone else's safety in the interests of securing Mickey's. So I need your word of honour that nothing you see or hear or learn here tonight will go any further."

Todd knew he was utterly serious. The knowledge forestalled any offence he might have felt at the request. He answered without hesitation. "You have it."

"Thank you."

"This isn't going to cost you your job, is it?"

Meir changed down to crash a traffic light. "I should be so lucky."

Aaron Ben Simeon had worked in intelligence for long enough that he had got out of the way of having his activities questioned. He certainly was not used to having them questioned by the bomb squad. He was most emphatically unused to having to explain himself to the newspapers.

He could not believe that Meir had brought a reporter to his office. "When I agreed to see you, Simon, I did not expect you to make an announcement to the press."

He did not so much shout as rumble, like a volcano working up to something big, and his short sandy hair bristled, and Todd thought he recognised a moment when he was going to have the pair of them arrested while he decided what to do about them. But Meir kept on working at him, quietly, as he might work at a device, picking away at its defences with determination and none of the extravagant gestures that turn ATOs into one-armed bandits. And in due course Ben Simeon came off the boil sufficiently to hear an explanation of his colleague's extraordinary breach of security.

Todd stepped in. "One of your agents is using my partner as a kind of stalking-horse to infiltrate the PFLP. He doesn't know that's what she's doing—he thinks she's what she claimed to be, a publicity officer for the Palestinians. He thinks he's taking photographs for a magazine. She thinks he's taking photographs for her. God knows what the PFLP think, but they know she's IDF so they must assume Flynn's a spy. His life's worth nothing if he goes with them; and Deborah Lev's can't be worth much more. You have to get in touch with her, now, and get them both off the street."

Major Ben Simeon was not too keen on being told what to do either, but he let it pass. He understood now Meir's insistence on this meeting. He frowned at Todd. "You know about Captain Lev?"

"All Jerusalem knows about Captain Lev. I got it from a news vendor on a street corner, so I think we can safely say it's in the public domain."

"Sammi Akim?" Todd made no reply. "And he actually knew her name?"

"How else would I know it?"

Ben Simeon reached for his phone. There would be other things to say and find out, but they could wait. "I'll bring her in."

"Damn her," snarled Todd, leaning over the desk, his knuckles whitening under his weight, "haul Mickey Flynn's butt in here!"

Ben Simeon looked up at him, unintimidated. He had very pale blue eyes, and when they caught him Todd stepped back in surprise at the cool strength in them. The soldier said, "I understand your anxiety. If you'll stay out of my light for just a few minutes I'll do what I can to get them both home and safe. It has to be Lev first, because until I speak to her I shalln't know where Flynn is. He may be with her, or she may have left him somewhere. We'll know soon.

"But just for the record, Todd, if I have to choose between saving a man who's gone into this for the money he can make out of a photographic exclusive and a woman who puts her life on the line every time she steps out of that door, for her people and her land—principles you may find outdated if not downright risible—and in the hope of being able to do something to stem the tide of murder and mayhem that threatens the human rights of everyone in this country, by whatever name they call it, I have to tell you that is not a choice I would find difficult to make."

Meir knew where there was a coffee machine. He took Todd away and sat him within easy reach of it, and watched the hot pungent drink put some of the colour back into his face. He said, "It'll be all right now, Gil. We'll find them."

Todd shook his head, almost too angry to talk coherently. "You have no right. Him—Ben Simeon, the bastard—all of you. This job's difficult enough without bastards like that setting us up to take the heat off them."

"We've all got difficult jobs, Gil," Meir said mildly.

"The difference is, most of us do our own dirty work. David Gichon got killed doing his. Mickey got shot doing his. What gives this Lev woman the right to trick him into doing something so dangerous she won't do it herself? That was her risk to take, no one else's. Damn it, that's what she's paid for. She had no right to use him like that."

"Sometimes the morality of how a thing is done has to take second place to the absolute necessity of getting it done." Meir tried to explain, his quiet voice cutting across Todd's rage. "Everything we do here involves the weighing of evils. Simply having the IDF on the streets costs lives: we believe it saves more, so we do the best we can and keep the casualties as low as we can, and after that we pay the price. Mickey Flynn isn't the first noncombatant to be dragged into this conflict, or the one-thousand-and-first either. I'm sorry, I liked him too and I don't want him to come to any harm.

"But the outcome of military action is decided in a large measure by the quality of the intelligence gathered before the opening salvo is fired. A lot of lives depend on the work done by people like Aaron Ben Simeon and Deborah Lev. They have to weigh that against the risks they take themselves and those they expose other people to. Involving a civilian like Flynn, they wouldn't do that lightly. They wouldn't have sent him to do anything they could do themselves. And they'd want a lot of lives to be safeguarded by it to balance the equation. I know it's hard for you to take the cosmic view right now, with Mickey in danger. But somebody has to. My job has its drawbacks, but you couldn't pay me to do Lev's."

She had been in with Ben Simeon while they were talking. Now she came into the room with the coffee machine. Todd, who had never seen her before, knew at once who she was. He was struck to the heart by how ordinary she was: not Mata Hari, not even Emma Peel, just a young woman with a difficult, dangerous, thankless job to get done.

He climbed to his feet in her presence as if she were a nun. "Mickey—?"

She had her hands shoved deep into the pockets of her white blouson, a sad defensive gesture. She was clearly shattered by the news he had brought, and its implications both for herself and for Flynn. But she was ready to start picking up the pieces.

She said, "When I started this, I thought it was something he could do, without much risk to himself, that would make a significant contribution to security here. If we can find that camp we'll take out of circulation some of the PFLP's top experts, a lot of their newest recruits, and substantial caches of arms. You couldn't quantify how many lives that would save.

"All the same," and her dark head bowed, "I didn't know then that my cover was blown. If I had I'd have stopped it. I wouldn't have handed him over to them if I'd thought they had any reason to suspect him."

That's it then, thought Todd, and somehow the shock stopped him feeling it as sharply as he might have done, the PFLP have got him, and they know the woman who sent him is IDF. Three days from now he'll turn up on a rubbish tip, with his head in a bag and unspeakable things done to his body, and the best I can hope for now is that the time bomb in his back will go off and save him the worst of the torture they undoubtedly intended to practice on him.

The woman was speaking again, her voice husky with shame and determination. "I don't know how much of this is my fault. Maybe I should have known—the clues must have been there if I'd picked them up, if I'd read them right. But if there's still time to pull him out, I'll do it. I'll see the people I left him with—maybe they'll tell me where they took him. I don't know. I wish I could promise you something but I can't—only that I'll do all I can to find him and get him out."

She spoke over her shoulder to Ben Simeon, still in English. "I'll call you in an hour. If I haven't found him by then . . ." She shrugged and walked out of the room.

The man she had delivered Flynn to at the Zion Gate thought for some moments about her request. Then he made a phone call. Then he agreed to take her to the safe house where Flynn was being kept. When she got into his car she knew there was a good chance he had instructions to kill her, and her hand was never far from the little gun hidden in the small of her back. But he took her without incident to Mrs. Habach's little house in the Old City, and waited outside while she went in.

Fahad was the last to arrive. After he left Flynn's belongings with the girl who was going to "find" them on her way to school, he shadowed the van, at some distance but still as close as he had to be in the quiet of the early morning city, until it was safely clear of Jerusalem. He turned back on the far side of Bethlehem.

When he got home, expecting to enjoy a leisurely breakfast before the day should bring its share of problems, there was a message waiting. Kassi—it was always Kassi, the glazier lacked the nerve for this kind of work—had called a meeting of councillors to consider the wisdom of taking a known IDF spy into one of their newest, most important and, because of its location within Israel instead of across some handy border, most vulnerable installations.

There were five of them there already, and they had been there long enough to talk it through informally and reach a consensus independent of anything Fahad had to say. His eyes narrowed irritably. Confound Kassi: he had never really outgrown the proposition that revolution is something you talk about. It was hard to convince him that to get anywhere you had to be prepared to act, and action invariably involved some risk.

"Did you pick him up?"

"We did. He's on his way to Bab el Jihad." They called the new camp the Gates of Holy War. Like the Jews, the Arabs tend to wax pretentious in the giving of names.

"You found nothing on him, then—no bug, nothing of that sort."

"No."

Kassi put in, "Yet we know it has to be a trap. We know where he came from."

"Indeed we do," said Fahad. "We also know that they have no idea that we know—about Flynn, about Lev. Can't you see that gives us an advantage?"

"Not if we proceed exactly as if we didn't know," retorted Kassi.

Fahad took a long breath and resolved to hang onto his patience. These men were not the enemy—not even Kassi, though sometimes he gave a good impression of it. "My brothers, I know the Jews think there is something in this for them or they would not have set it up. But there are only three ways they can gain anything: by planting a wire —a bug," he translated for Kassi's benefit, "on him, by talking to him afterwards and by studying his photographs. Well, unless they have put it somewhere it will require surgical intervention to recover it, he is not wired now if he ever was. The only thing he walked out of that house with that he also walked into it with is his own skin.

"The rest of it is in our hands. We tell him what we want the Jews to think, show him what we want them to think we have—feed them information that will set alarm bells ringing all through Ha Kirya, and have them spending time, money and ingenuity preparing to deal with one sort of threat when in fact we mean to pose them another entirely. Or we can ensure they never talk to him at all and the only pictures they see are the ones in the magazines helping us to win this war. Where is the risk in that?"

Awaz, who tended to deliberate slowly but reach the right conclusions in the end, said, "I agree, if there is no wire there is no immediate urgency—we have time to think this through. But you seem to assume that Flynn will do what we tell him. We can probably control what he sees and photographs, but if he is an IDF spy he may not be that easy to fool. Even if we put him straight onto an American plane at Amman, he'll be talking to the damned Jews before the day is out and back here helping them by the end of the week. However careful you are, he will have seen something. I cannot see that it is worth that."

"Don't underestimate what we can gain from good publicity," said Fahad. "Winning hearts and minds is what the last forty years have been about. We can't beat the IDF. They can't eradicate us. We occupy the same ground—there are no lines to be lost and taken. What we're fighting for, the only victory available to us, is support. Public opinion, in Islam and beyond, and particularly in those places where our money comes from.

"Flynn is an American with an international reputation as a press photographer. What he photographs becomes news, captures headlines. The impact of a series of pictures by him in the American press on young Palestinians training to enter the struggle for their homeland cannot be overstated. It might be worth three years' work to us. That is worth taking some risks for."

Kassi sniffed. "That is easy enough for you to say. You have no children down there for him to see and remember."

Awaz ignored him. "You think he means to publish something, then. He is not just here to gather intelligence for the Jews?"

Fahad was emphatic. "I'm sure he means to publish. I'm not altogether sure he knows he is spying."

"What?" Three or four voices posed the question, with differing degrees of disbelief.

"Perhaps I am mistaken. But I don't think he knows who Lev is. I think he believes that she is one of us, that the publicity is all she's interested in."

The hard men of the PFLP were obviously shocked. "That is a vicious way to behave. Only a Jew . . ."

"As I say," said Fahad, "I could be wrong. I shall have a better idea when I have talked to him. But either way, he will want to publish. It's what he does. Even if he is working for the Jews, mainly he is working for himself. I cannot see him making any deal that does not conclude with his photographs in some glossy magazine. That is what I want, too."

"Whatever the cost?"

"No—but if that's what it comes to, there is a way we can have the publicity without any risk at all."

That got them on his side. They could not resist the idea of a free lunch. "How? What have you planned, Jamil?"

Fahad smiled, a cool superior smile that said he was back in control. "I will explain everything, never fear. But there is time for that. First, the moment has come to decide what we should do about the woman Lev."

When Lev left Mrs. Habach's house she hurried back to the car that had brought her and asked the driver to find her a phone. He found her one and waited while she dialled. He took a gun from the glove compartment and shot her through the wound-down window, three times in the back. Then he drove away, not at any great speed, leaving her facedown in the gutter with three bright beads of blood on the back of her white nylon jacket that was supposed to look like satin.

[5]

The van travelled steadily south, with the sun climbing the sky using the irregular contours of the Mountains of Moab across the Dead Sea for a handhold. It was a calculated risk for the PFLP to move by daylight, but driving these roads by darkness was bound to provoke suspicion.

Twice the van passed through a town, the first soon after leaving Jerusalem, the second rather later in the morning. From the position of the sun Flynn knew they were heading south so these towns were probably Bethlehem and Hebron. Already they were deep into the occupied territories, and therefore surrounded by friends. It made sense for their training camp to be somewhere in these southern wastes, between the Dead Sea and the Negev.

Flynn tried to picture the topography of the region, but all there was there was mountain and desert, the occasional road, a railway line that petered out in the middle of nowhere, east of Dimona. There was a strip of Palestinian land sixty miles long by maybe twenty miles wide, with nothing in this southern half but dried river courses and barren hilltops, without even the grazing for Bedouin sheep. The place where they were taking him could be anywhere in that area. Anywhere in that area, if things went wrong, these people could kill him in the absolute confidence that only the vultures would find his bones.

Flynn shifted his position, looking through the dust-grimed window back the way they had come. The man with the gun growled, "Get away from there."

When they had burst into his room, dragged him from his sleep and slammed him up against the wall, Flynn had been afraid for his life. The memory of that was a bitterness to him now: perhaps too young to appreciate that fear was the only rational response to such a situation, he felt somehow that he should have put on a better show.

While he accepted a certain amount of pushing around as part of his job, that was different, essentially impersonal, and any revenge he felt the need of he took by getting the shots he wanted anyway. This, by contrast, was intensely personal, just him and them, and any shots they did not want him to take they would prevent him from taking. He had understood that from the start, of course. What had surprised him was how used he felt, how like a whore. In consequence he was left feeling sensitive about things that did not normally concern him, like his dignity, and his manhood.

So when the man who should have been his guide took to himself instead the mantle of captor, waving the unnecessary gun and growling orders for the sake of it, Flynn's bruised pride rebelled within him. Instead of sliding back into his seat he gritted his teeth, turned his back on the gun and, for no better reason than that he had been told not to, peered into the distance closing behind them.

Kadar had been hoping Flynn might do something like that—well, anything really that would give him the excuse to hurt Flynn. He knew that Flynn had been sent by Leila. So far as Kadar could see that made him an IDF spy, and even if Fahad meant to kill him in the end he thought it madness deliberately to take a spy into Bab el Jihad. Fahad knew how he felt and had warned him to stick to his orders; but Kadar did not like being ordered around much more than Flynn did.

He slid off his own seat, rising in a crouch behind Flynn, the weapon in his hand swinging with all the force of his powerful shoulders.

Smashing across his head the blow could have killed a man. But Kadar was not aiming at Flynn's head. He had not forgotten that interesting fresh scar in his shoulder, that Ismah Habach had prevented him from fully exploring. The blunt muzzle of the swinging gun, still accelerating, found the injury with brutal accuracy and swept on across Flynn's spine, pitching him into the locked door with pain like napalm exploding through his back.

The driver heard a cry, and the crash of meat on metal, and felt the van shake with sudden violence. He risked a nervous glance over his shoulder. "What's happening back there? Kadar? Are you all right?"

After a pause just long enough for him to consider moving up a gear and panicking, the driver got his reply. "Of course I'm all right." Kadar was breathing a little faster, that was all. He sounded pleased with himself.

The driver went back to being only a little nervous again. "What happened?"

"Nothing much. Our friend here was taking a keener interest in the scenery than was good for him, that's all. He won't do it again."

He was right about that. Flynn was facedown among the rags and old newspapers on the floor of the van, trying not to sob. It was not only the pain, though the pain was bad, beating through him in waves reinforced by the metallic vibration of the van. But worse than that was the fear that the blow had dislodged the shard of bone threatening him: that when the pain died back it would leave nothing at all—no strength, no feeling, no movement. He was afraid that he was already a cripple and just did not know it yet.

For after Kadar had hit him and yanked him back off the door and onto the floor, he had planted one large knee in the small of Flynn's back and pulled his arms behind him and tied them, then roped his legs together at the ankles. After that he had lifted Flynn's head by a handful of hair and pulled a black fabric bag over it.

So he lay, bound and hooded, on the dirty vibrating floor of an elderly van, unable to see or hear, finding it hard to draw enough air through the cloth to feed his heaving lungs, trying to establish the exact parameters of the pain still pulsing through him because if his spinal cord was gone he would feel nothing below that point. The inferno raging through his shoulders was scant comfort, the damage could be lower than that and still leave him helpless. He tried to remember if he had felt Kadar's knee in his back or had only known that it was there; if he could actually feel the rope on his ankles.

It took time, partly because of the rather random effects of the pain, partly because he was practically immobilised by Kadar's ropework. But slowly, trying hard not to imagine the reassuring signs he was desperately seeking, he decided that the aching of his arms behind his back and the chafing of his wrists were real and directly representative of the abuse of them, and that he was indeed wiggling his fingers. A few minutes later, when it struck him that his bare feet were cold, the relief was so overwhelming that he cried, silently, his tears unseen within the dreadful privacy of the hood.

The nightmare journey continued. He lost all sense of time: inside the hood there was no sun. The only reliable impression he had was of the road surface, which came to him via the chassis of the van and his right cheek against its floor, and that seemed to have been getting steadily rougher for a long time now. Eventually it stopped being a road at all and the van bounced up what might have been a wadi. Then it stopped, and a moment later the engine stopped too.

It took Flynn time to register the fact. He knew the metal floor was no longer hitting him in the face, but at first he did not miss the vibration and the soft rumble that was all he could hear of the engine through the muffling cloth. When he did recognise the silence he had to work out what it meant, that they had reached their destination. Surely to God they had not brought him this far only to drag him out and kill him?—and if they had, wouldn't they have kept the engine running? He was hurt, exhausted, disoriented and still very afraid.

Fahad, who had driven here from his meeting and caught up with the slower van at the Tel Shoqet junction, unlocked the back doors and threw them wide. Until then the deliberately dirty glass of the windows had kept the scene inside from him. Now he saw Flynn, bound and hooded, facedown among the refuse on the floor, his long body in Alam Habach's shirt and jeans trembling with cold and maybe something more, while Kadar—big tough fearless insensitive Kadar, the human equivalent of a Rottweiler—sat over him with the smug expression of someone who had done something clever.

Fahad sighed. "You big dumb camel. What did I tell you?"

Kadar shrugged. "He was trying to see where we were going."

"Have you killed him?"

Indignantly: "Of course not. I taught him a lesson, though."

Fahad had seen Kadar deliver too many lessons to be misled. "Well, get him out of there. Can he walk?"

Kadar looked surprised. "Why not?" He bent to pull the rope free of Flynn's ankles. Then he kicked his legs over the sill, tugged him upright and took the hood off.

The bright light off the white desert was more shocking than the darkness he had been condemned to. Flynn had been blind for hours; now the sudden brilliance of full day attacked his eyes and his brain like knives. He gasped and squeezed his eyes shut, and the scene swung round him in a dizzying arc.

Fahad said in English, "Come on out now," and Kadar pushed him over the sill, his hands still roped behind him. His feet found the ground but he was too weak and too dizzy to stand. He stumbled, failed to find his balance and, without his hands to save him, went down.

Fahad caught him as he fell. He was a smaller man than Flynn but there was a steely strength in his hands that caught Flynn by the shoulders and steadied his collapse, easing him to the ground with unexpected gentleness. "Easy, Mr. Flynn, easy now." He knelt beside Flynn in the dust, supporting him on one arm while his other hand picked the rope free from Flynn's wrists. "You're all right. It has been a busy day, that is all—and it's still only ten o'clock in the morning."

Insofar as he slept at all that night, Todd slept in the chair beside the coffee machine in the room not far from Maj. Ben Simeon's office. Sometimes Simon Meir was there, not talking, not trying to reassure him, just sitting quietly waiting for news, and sometimes Todd stirred from a brief and ragged nap to find him gone. No one else came to bother him.

While he was awake, and in that fuzzy grey no-man's-land between waking and sleeping, he went over—and over and over again—what he knew of the operation Flynn had been caught up in, what each of the parties to it had expected to gain from it. What he was looking for was some reason to believe that the PFLP had a use for Flynn alive.

There were the pictures. Perhaps they had gone along with Lev's proposition, even knowing who she was, because Flynn's pictures would be sufficiently valuable to them as propaganda to justify the risks. Or perhaps it was just an easy way of killing an IDF spy. If they knew who Lev was, they could not be blamed for supposing Flynn was undercover too; or for wondering what useful information he might be persuaded to part with before they blew his brains out.

Lev was not found until six o'clock. Even then Todd did not hear immediately. It was after seven that Meir came back from one of his unexplained absences, lowered himself carefully into a chair, and looked at Todd and then at the crease in the left knee of his trousers.

His voice when it came was more deeply weary than anything else. "They've shot Deborah Lev."

A lurch ran through Todd's big body as if he had been kicked under the heart. "Oh God no. Is she—?"

"Yes, she's dead."

"Mickey?"

Meir's eyes kindled for a moment. "Gil, I know Mickey's a friend of yours. Well, Deborah Lev was a friend of mine. She was thirty-two years old. She had a degree in political science, and a widowed mother, and a younger sister who's a nurse, and this morning she spent an hour bleeding to death from three bullets in her back, and not one of the hundred people living in the street where she died raised a finger to help or comfort her.

"Now I don't know, Gil, where your political affiliations lie. Maybe you think she had no business being there in the first place and deserved all she got. Maybe you think the whole of Israel isn't worth her blood or anyone else's. But more important than what you think is what she thought, which was that if Israel is to survive and know peace, the forces of lawful government have to defeat the forces of terrorism. That was why Deborah Lev was willing to risk her life daily: in no less a cause than survival.

"Gil, I don't have to tell you what this city and this land mean to us. Our people wandered in one desert or another for damn near two thousand years waiting to come back here. Even when we won that concession, it took sweat to make Israel worth having and blood to keep it. We're not unaware of the fact that the people who were living here when the UN gave it to us have legitimate grievances. We should be trying harder than we are to resolve them. But this is our home of ancient right, and we're here to stay, and even after forty years nothing is as important as defending ourselves against those who would still like to sweep us into the sea.

"That's why Deborah Lev was prepared to risk herself among those who were, not by her choice, perhaps not even by theirs, her natural enemies. She knew that, living the way she did, she would probably die in some way very similar to this, in one bloody uncaring street or another, this year or next or anyway soon. She considered the job she was doing worth it.

"So before we move on to what may have happened to Mickey Flynn in pursuit of a good photograph to illustrate his obituary, I'd like you to spare just a moment's thought, perhaps an ounce of respect, for

Captain Deborah Lev who died tonight in the unfashionable cause of protecting her family."

Todd had never heard Meir speak with such quiet passion, or for so long. It was tempting to wonder if the ATO had had something personal going with Lev, but actually that was too easy, a denial of something much more profound. Certainly he was talking about himself and Lev, but all the rest of them too, all of them who did difficult, dangerous, thankless jobs to hasten the redemption of their land.

Todd stood up and did the only thing he could think of—touched his fingers to Meir's sleeve. "Simon, I'm sorry. What with everything that's happened to Mickey, I haven't much grief left for anyone else.

"I'm not unsympathetic to what your people have been through, or the difficulties you still face. If I don't always like your solutions, I do accept that the problems are fundamental ones not of your making. And I'm not unmoved by Captain Lev's sacrifice. I'm sorry that you've lost another friend. But Simon, don't ask me to believe that what she did to Mickey was either necessary or justifiable. She tricked him into undertaking a covert operation that would always have been hideously dangerous, even if her cover hadn't been blown wide open.

"Nobody conned you into bomb disposal by saying the oil drums were full of jelly beans. Nobody tricked Lev into intelligence by representing the PFLP as a bunch of cuddly stage Arabs armed with papier-mâché scimitars. You both had all the facts before you when you chose what to do. Lev didn't give Mickey the same kind of choice. She sent him into that wolf's den believing that everything between him and them was aboveboard and that he knew the extent of the risk involved. Whatever her motives, she had no right to do that. So I'm sorry about what happened to her, but I still want to know what you're doing to rescue Mickey from this disaster the IDF dropped him in."

Simon Meir sighed. The unusual anger was already gone from him. "Sit down, Gil. There isn't much to tell. We're still looking for him— they've done a house-to-house in the street where Deborah was found —but no luck so far. That may be good news: if they'd killed him already, they'd want us to know."

Todd froze halfway into his chair, his face twisting. "Killed him already?"

It might have been a slip, or it might have been Meir's way of levelling with a man he believed needed and was entitled to the truth. "By any logical assessment, Gil, that has to be what they intend as the bottom line. Except that if it's humanly possible, we're going to find him first."

Todd went back to his hotel. He ran a shower and stood under it much longer than the needs of cleanliness dictated. Its million droplets bouncing off his skin, filling his eyes with its crystal dance and his ears with its soft Niagara roar, was a kind of sensory overload that cushioned him just a little against the brutal assault of reality. The Popular Front for the Liberation of Palestine had Mickey Flynn. They had every reason to suppose he was a spy for the Israel Defence Forces. Deborah Lev had tried to find him and had been shot dead before she could report anything she had discovered. Simon Meir thought Flynn was as good as dead if he was not found soon.

Todd thought it would take a miracle of messianic proportions for the IDF to find him now. He lifted his face into the rushing stream of the showerhead. It felt like needles, like massage, like rainfall, like tears.

Under the shower the vague outline of an idea began to coalesce in his mind.

He was about to phone Meir, so Simon would not be looking for him, when Meir phoned him. His heart lurched at the sudden sweet trilling. He did not want to pick it up. It had to be about Flynn. He did not expect it to be good news.

It was not. "The police have some things they think are Mickey's. They want you to look and see if you can identify them. I'll pick you up."

Todd said, "Is there a body?"

"No." At the other end of the line Meir winced, angry with himself for not saying that first. Though it was his opinion that there was a body somewhere, or would be soon if there was not quite yet. "There's camera equipment and some clothes. Somebody found them in an alley in the Christian Quarter first thing this morning. The police are pretty sure they're Mickey's."

"Then he is dead."

"It doesn't follow." Meir sounded less than convincing.

"You think he's wandering round naked drawing sketches of a PFLP training camp?"

"Hardly. But they could have got him some more clothes, another camera."

"Mickey wouldn't have parted with that one if he'd had any say in the matter."

Meir said, "I'll be right round."

The bag was clearly Flynn's. His name and address were on the camera. It was a formal identification the police needed, and Todd gave it them. "Where were they found?"

The police inspector read off an address that meant nothing to Todd. "It's a back alley, a shortcut. A girl spotted them on her way to school."

"Is that anywhere near where Deborah Lev—?"

Meir shook his head. "Not really, no."

"What about his clothes?"

The inspector frowned. "What about them?"

"Well, are they damaged?" Todd asked impatiently. "Torn, dirty? Are there any holes in them? Any blood?"

The man shook his head. "Nothing like that. Actually, someone folded them pretty neatly to put them in the bag."

"But they have been worn? I mean," Meir expanded, "they're not just a change of clothes he had with him?"

"I wouldn't think so, no. For one thing, there wasn't room for all of them in the bag: the boots and his jacket were in a carrier tied to the handle. Then there are the pills."

"Pills?" asked Meir; but Todd knew what they were and also what they meant, and the last wreckage of his hopes turned over and sank.

"Painkillers," explained the inspector. "Pretty strong ones, by all accounts. You wouldn't get them over the counter at a chemist's. If he needed those, he'd have wanted them with him. They were in a pocket of the jacket." He fingered the drab cloth with a certain distaste. "What is it, ex-Army surplus? You'd think a man would have more sense than wearing stuff like that here, wouldn't you?"

Meir nodded. Personally he could not see why anyone would want to wear ex-Army surplus anywhere, but he had never seen Flynn without that jacket. It might have been his security blanket.

He steered Todd towards the door with a hand on his shoulder. "Come on, Gil, I think we're finished here."

[6]

Bab el Jihad was set in a cleft of mountains that soared, palely gleaming in the bright day, towards the lilac sky. The mountains were the pale gold of a young lion, and their fastnesses were pierced by caves. The young lions of the PFLP and the people who were teaching them the art of insurgency lived in those caves, ate and slept and studied in them and only moved outside for drill and practical lessons in commando techniques.

With the nearest road six miles away, the only realistic chance of discovery was from the air, and a fighter travelling fast enough to surprise them was probably travelling too fast to see them. Lookouts on three surrounding heights kept an ear cocked for helicopters, but it was a rare occasion when the rebels had to dive for cover. It had happened only twice in the first six weeks of the camp's existence. The first time it had made them wary, but the second time they had joked about it and talked of hanging out a sign, or a Palestinian flag.

The different caves had their different purposes. There were dormitories, a refectory and adjacent cookhouse, and workshops and an armoury. And there were storerooms, one of which had been prepared to receive Flynn. Most of the caves had doors: this one also had a lock, on the outside.

Bab el Jihad was within a few miles of the lowest spot on earth, and one of the hottest. When the sun lanced down between the peaks the pale rocks baked and the air stewed and there was no wind. The caves were the most comfortable, almost the only tolerable place. Fahad sent Flynn a breakfast tray, then left him alone for a couple of hours to catch up on his broken rest.

There was a bed with a blanket folded on top in one corner but Flynn could not sleep. He was too hurt and too scared to sleep. He worked some mobility back into his arms and legs, tried to do the same for his back but only made it worse. So he lay on the thin mattress, exhausting himself in the effort to find somewhere to put himself that did not add to his mounting burden of pain.

Because now it was steadily getting worse. What Kadar had done to him, with the gun and then with the ropes, would have been easing by now, except that he was well overdue the first of his day's painkillers. He knew where they were—in the pocket of his jacket. They might as well have been on the moon.

He felt the familiar pain, seated in his spine and spreading its venom through all the connecting nerve chains, stir like a wakening dragon and flex its claws in his flesh, and stretch its scales and yawn its fetid breath in his face. He knew it was there, waited only for it to remember that he was: waited with his fists clenched, and his teeth fastened in his sleeve, and the grey woollen blanket wrapped round everything like a protective shell, for the mindless, miserable, unmanning pain to resume feeding on him. He thought of the early days in the hospital in Amsterdam, and shook with the fear that it would be like that again.

When Fahad came back, he saw the shrouded figure on the bed and assumed he was sleeping. "Come now, Mr. Flynn, rise and shine." Getting no response he reached for the blanket and said, a little more sharply, "Flynn—"

Racked already, anticipating further assault, Flynn's body convulsed, knotting at the source of his pain, and his head jerked back and a cry of rage and agony ripped from his throat: "Don't hit me!"

Startled, even momentarily offended, Fahad took a step back. "I'm not going to hit you." Then he seemed to hear the echo of Flynn's wretchedness and stepped forward again. He used his eyes, and his hands gently, and then he muttered a soft imprecation.

Outside he found Kadar. "Go tell Rachid I need him."

"What for?"

Fahad breathed heavily. "For Flynn. Because you nearly killed him, you animal. You knew he was hurt—did you have to beat him as well?"

Kadar bristled resentfully. "What does it matter? He's a Jew spy."

"It matters because he has a job of work to do for us. It matters if you want to go on getting ammunition for your favourite plaything, if we are to buy enough Sentex to keep Rachid in business. Do you think a revolution pays for itself?—like market gardening? Well it doesn't. It eats money, and if the money dries up, so does the revolution.

"Do you suppose we can fight the IDF, and the Jews' defence budget shored up by America, with only the money we raise in Palestine? Our brothers are generous, they give what they can, but they are all poor men. If we fought with swords it might suffice; if we wish to meet modern weaponry with modern weaponry, we must look further afield.

"For forty years the money to fight this war has come from the Arab nations. At first it flowed like water, then like honey; now it flows like treacle. Our warrior kin are become businessmen, and crave the approval of other businessmen more than the thanks of our wives and mothers. The world turns its face against us, and our cousins Egypt and Jordan and Syria bend like reeds with the river's tow.

"If we can no longer command their hearts, we must try to touch their souls. That is why I need Flynn, why I need him alive and why I need him to take these photographs. He will show the world how our brave children prepare to take up the struggle for Palestine. Such pictures will kindle hearts and spirits wherever Arabs dwell, and who knows?—perhaps in the high places of the West as well. We are the thorn under the skin of their support for the Jews. If one of their own tells them of our cause and our need, may we not find some of them answering?

"That is why I want you to fetch Rachid, and for Rachid to get this American on his feet long enough to get some good old-fashioned, tear-jerking, pride-wringing, pocket-emptying pictures on film. It does not matter what happens to him afterwards, but until I have seen the images I want coming out of the developer, you and everyone here handle him with care."

Kadar remained unconvinced. "It would be better to keep Rachid away from him. He is our best weapon: those pictures would have to be solid gold to be worth putting him at risk. Anyone can make a bomb, but remember what it was like before we had Rachid: half our devices exploded at the wrong time—they killed us as often as they killed Jews —and some of them never exploded at all. We have lost too many good men. You should not let a Jew spy see Rachid."

Fahad looked at him with cool contempt. "Do you really suppose he is going to leave here?"

Rachid Seleh Hantouleh was not a doctor, but he had studied human pathology during his training as a pharmacist in Egypt. He knew more about drugs than most practising physicians, and could perform simple operations if called on. This was not, of course, encouraged by the pharmacists who taught him, but then neither was his day job. An inevitable consequence of studying chemistry is learning which chemicals overreact when introduced to one another. Another is being approached by people wishing to share this knowledge.

For a long time Hantouleh avoided such contacts. He wished only to be a chemist, and had no intention of leaving Egypt to return to the land of his birth. He was not a political man.

He became involved with the PFLP almost by accident. He was paying his mother a visit when his sister begged him to help her husband who had been hurt while on active service for Palestine. It was a small thing to ask: Hantouleh believed he could oblige and still remain aloof from the struggle.

Time proved him wrong. He was asked to obtain certain materials which were not available over the hardware counter. He became interested in how they went together. His tutors, becoming suspicious, warned him to concentrate on his work. The next time he visited his mother the PFLP offered to set him up with a little bomb factory of his own, and he did not return to Egypt.

He still did not consider himself a political man. He devised bombs the way other people do jigsaws, as a philosophical exercise. It stretched his mind and disciplined his fingers. If he occasionally regretted the consequences, he told himself it was not materially different from making fast cars knowing that some of them would get people hurt or worse. His analytical chemist's brain managed to compartmentalise that aspect of what he did away to where it seldom troubled him. What in his own mind he did was make brilliant, dangerous toys for other professionals like himself—men like Simon Meir and David Gichon—to play with. He was always a little disappointed if they went off unheralded in a dark street and brought an empty building crashing down, and no one had had the opportunity to admire his craftsmanship first.

Rachid Seleh Hantouleh was the man the ATOs considered their nemesis. It was his devices, in the Jerusalem garage, which killed Gichon and came close to blowing Todd's legs off. His operation had been moved out of the city then to the safety of the training camp in the mountain wilderness by the Dead Sea.

Hantouleh handled Flynn as he handled his bombs: with skill and care, and great sensitivity of the fingertips and none of the soul. Flynn's damaged back might have been a malfunctioning tilt-switch. But when he had finished he selected a phial from the camp's extensive medical kit and slid a hypodermic into Flynn's arm with practised ease, and smiled slightly as the potent liquid worked its magic in Flynn's knotted body.

When his rapid, shallow breathing had slowed and the defensive tension of his muscles eased, Flynn breathed, "Thanks."

Outside Hantouleh explained the situation to Fahad—about Flynn's souvenir of the Amsterdam riot, and how close Kadar had come to finishing what the Belgian began. His savage slashing blow had left an angry welt across Flynn's shoulders, a little below the healing collarbone, transecting with mathematical accuracy the scar left by the bullet. Where it met the protruberance of his spine it had taken a little skin off.

"Is he all right now?" asked Fahad.

Hantouleh rocked an ambivalent hand. He was a slight, pale-skinned man in his thirties, taller than Fahad and as broad but somehow less substantial. He lacked the robust wiriness of the desert man. Hantouleh was from the Hula Valley in the north. He had mild eyes and a little moustache. "All right is an exaggeration. He's been lucky, I don't think Kadar has done him any real damage, but he's a sick man."

"Can he do the job he was brought here for?"

Hantouleh shrugged. "If he could do it yesterday, he will be able to do it tomorrow. You'll get nothing out of him today. There were some pills in his coat pocket: you'll have to get those brought down here. Will Ismah Habach still have his things?"

Fahad scowled. "No, the police will. Give him something else."

"What I've given him will hold him for now. But if I go on shooting him up with it he's going to be as high as Mount Hermon."

Fahad raised an eyebrow. "His long-term health problems are a minor consideration."

"So I supposed. That's not the point. If I give him enough to control the pain sufficiently for him to work, he'll be too spaced-out to work. He needs the drug the Dutch hospital gave him. I know what it is, I can tell you where to get some. Will you organise a thief?"

Todd spent the day in limbo. He literally did not know what to do with himself, where to put himself—in the chair in his hotel room, or on the bed, or in the bar, or walking aimlessly in the suddenly alien streets. He tried all these things by turns. None of them helped, not even the drinking. He thought about drinking enough to obliterate it, but in the morning Mickey Flynn would still be dead and he would have a hangover as well. He tried to eat something: the mere thought made him feel sick.

He thought about going home. There was nothing to stay in Israel for now. When they found the body they might want him back to identify it, but that could be days or weeks, or never. In which case, a portion of this unknown land would Flynn forever be. It was not altogether unfitting. He had spent some good times and done some good work here. Even if he had still secretly regarded it as home, it is nobody's ambition to be buried in New York.

Todd opened his case and put back into it the few things that he had taken out. Twice he lifted the phone to ask Esther to prepare his bill, and twice he put it down again. He had nothing to stay for, but he could not bring himself to leave. He lay on his bed staring at the ceiling, too numb even to hurt, and at some point he fell asleep.

Aaron Ben Simeon had taken possession of Flynn's belongings, so when the report came through he was able to check the formulation of the missing drugs against the prescription in Flynn's wallet.

It could of course be a coincidence. He got on the phone to the forensic science laboratory. They thought it unlikely that anyone would be taking the stuff for kicks—you could get a better buzz from commoner substances—though it could always be somebody experimenting. A stock-taking error was another possibility, although hospital pharmacies generally kept reliable records. No hospital could make its pharmacy a fortress against its own staff, which is why drug abuse is a recognised problem among health workers; but anyone with legitimate access was likely to know the drug was a poor substitute, in terms of what they were interested in, for other items left untouched on the shelves. An outside theft, and theft-to-order at that, seemed the least improbable scenario.

Intelligence would not normally have involved bomb disposal in such a matter. But Ben Simeon acknowledged Meir's personal interest and, after a moment's consideration, lifted the phone again.

Meir did not phone Todd. He went round to the hotel where he had left him six hours before, a tired old man drained by grief. He hammered with his fist on the door of Todd's room and kept on hammering until, slack-faced, dishevelled, looking like an elderly panda roused too soon from its beauty sleep, Todd opened it.

Meir snaked his narrow body inside before the gap seemed wide enough. Urgency fitted him like an electric glove. That brightness in his eyes could almost have been hope.

"Gil, I don't want you to read too much into this. It might mean nothing at all. But it just might mean that Mickey's still alive."

Todd had got the news so directly that even Sammi Akim had not heard it yet. His ancient face fell sombre when Todd stopped before his newsstand. "Mr. Todd. I heard about Mr. Flynn. I am deeply sorry."

"Heard what?"

Sammi looked surprised, and alarmed, and cagy. "About his things being found. His clothes, and his camera. About certain people having taken him."

"Sammi, I think he's alive."

Sammi looked suddenly, profoundly noncommittal, like a man asked about fairies by a small and eager child. "Well, I suppose perhaps—"

"The drugs he was on, that they left behind in his jacket. Somebody just stole a batch of the same thing from the hospital in Be'er Sheva. You don't steal painkillers for a dead man, Sammi."

Sammi thought about it. "No, that is so."

"I don't know if they mean to kill him. Probably, after Lev, they do.

But they don't mean to do it yet. I have a little time to find him. But I need your help."

"Mine?" Shocked, horrified, Sammi took a step backwards, bumping into his stool. "My help, Mr. Todd?"

[7]

Where Sammi sent him was not somewhere he would normally have gone. Not alone, anyway; Flynn had travelled the world visiting no-go areas the way other people visit grottos, and mostly Todd had been there beside him, grumbling, watching over his shoulder for the attacks that never came. For four years Flynn's confidence had been a better shield for them than Todd's experience.

Anyway, this was hardly a no-go area, though it was a kind of no-man's-land. Todd felt the prickle of eyes on his back and was well aware he had been spotted as an intruder. He expected to be stopped at any moment. He leaned more to the likelihood of a verbal challenge than a ballistic one, but still the flesh crept under his shirt.

What happened instead was so anticlimactic as to verge on farce. He found the address he had been given and knocked at the door. Feet scurried inside and the door was opened by a girl of about eleven wearing a print dress, a cardigan and a head scarf.

Todd said, "Is this Mr. Khalidi's house?" The girl nodded quickly, stepped back inside and said something in Arabic, and Khalidi came to the door carrying a baby.

It should have been impossible for a man in charge of a house and two children to seem sinister. The fact that Hassan Khalidi managed it suggested to Todd that he was very sinister indeed. It was not just what Todd knew about him. He had met some downright charming terrorists, in Israel and Ireland and elsewhere. Besides, Khalidi was not officially a terrorist but a representative of a political party. It made no difference. Todd knew when he was in the presence of evil.

The girl took the baby into the back of the house. Khalidi took Todd into the little front room. Todd was surprised that a man in Khalidi's position, among whose myriad enemies must be a significant number of men as ruthless as himself, should admit to his house someone he did not know from Adam. But he was doing Khalidi an injustice. Khalidi knew exactly who he was, and could have made a telling guess at why he was there.

When Todd began to introduce himself Khalidi stopped him. "I know who you are, Mr. Todd, and what you do." The man never smiled; indeed, his expression had hardly flickered since he came to the door. He was a tall, well-built man, probably in his mid-thirties, with an olive rather than brown complexion and very black hair. His eyes were set far apart and sunk very deep, which gave him the appearance of watching from cover.

His entire attitude was one of suspicious watchfulness, and he gave no indication whether what he saw made him more suspicious or less so. He was watchful, suspicious, noncommittal and, as a final disconcerting detail, he was polite—the studied, careful, skin-deep politeness of a prisoner before a parole board, a veneer, as natural and gracious as a mugger singing hymns.

Todd was conscious of a chill settling on his spine where the itch had been a few minutes before. Puzzled, he frowned. "You were expecting me?"

In the same even, expressionless voice and without the smile anyone else would have added, Khalidi said, "For the last half hour I have been expecting you."

"Do you know why I'm here?"

"Tell me." It was not a yes or a no: Todd could not guess how much of what he had to say would come as news to Khalidi.

"All right," he said. "Stop me if you've heard it." But the Arab did not.

"I suppose, to be charitable, you could call it a misunderstanding," said Todd. "My photographer, Mickey Flynn, was invited by a woman called Leila to do a spread on a PFLP training camp somewhere in Israel. The deal was, he'd be shown scenes no journalist would normally be allowed within miles of, and the PFLP would have the publicity value of the resulting scoop." He charged the word with a certain amount of sarcasm. Contrary to popular opinion it does not figure prominently in a serious newsman's vocabulary, or at all in Todd's.

"He asked what I thought, I told him not to touch it with a barge pole, so he went ahead and fixed it up." It was the abridged version, but accurate enough so far as it went. That it did not go all the way was because Todd wanted to keep this light as long as he could. He had hoped he might persuade Khalidi it was almost a joke. That was before he met him. "By the time I realised what he was doing, he'd gone—with her. Leila."

The least flicker of an expression crossed Khalidi's face but he said nothing.

Todd said, "I see the name means something to you. Well, it didn't to Mickey when he went with her and it didn't to me when I went looking for him. Until someone who was having trouble keeping his face straight let me in on the joke. That was the first I knew that Mickey had been set up by the IDF. Unless somebody's got round to telling him by now, Mickey still doesn't know. He thinks he's there to take photographs. Everybody else, on both sides, thinks he's there to spy."

"I see," said Khalidi remotely. "And why are you telling me this?"

"I want your help," Todd said simply. "I want to get word to whoever's holding him that, whatever it looks like, Mickey went into this in good faith. He didn't know he was dealing with the IDF—they went to considerable lengths to ensure that he wouldn't. None of this is his fault."

"Fault?" echoed Khalidi, with what might have been a trace of irony. "Next you'll tell me that it isn't fair."

Todd breathed heavily and a little raggedly. He simply could not afford to lose his temper with this man. "All right. Forget what's fair, let's talk about what's expedient. If Mickey Flynn is murdered in the mistaken belief that he's an IDF spy, the world's press is never going to forget it. They won't deal with the Palestinians anymore, not even through their political mouthpieces. The official sources of news in Israel will become, effectively, the only sources. In a war you can only win by propaganda, that would be the same as suicide."

There was some truth in everything Todd said; how much he could not himself judge. Would the world's press really turn irrevocably against the intifada because one of their favourite sons had been set up to be shot at by the IDF and the PFLP had obliged? They were a close-knit profession, in a world full of enemies they had to be, and Flynn had many friends among them; but was he the stuff that martyrs are made of? Would they not rather shrug, and observe that sticking his neck out that far that often he was bound to get it chopped one day; and hold a glorious uproarious wake, and then get on with their jobs as best they could, as they always had?

Todd knew he was on shaky ground. He hurried on before Khalidi had time to recognise it too. "That's why you've always kept relations with the press on a professional level: not because what we write invariably thrills you to your little chequered keffiyehs, but because you need us. You need someone to listen to you, and if we don't no one else will. If we all packed and went home tonight, no victory you are capable of achieving would be worth having."

Christ almighty, he thought then, isn't that what Mickey was saying —that night he cornered the girl in the hotel bar, and she thought he was drunk and the rest of us thought he was stringing her along? Was he serious, then?—and more importantly, was he right? *Are* we responsible for what has happened here? Am I responsible for what's happened to Mickey? Have I spent the last thirty-five years helping to excavate the hole they'll bury him in?

A tiny puzzled blink was the only indication that Khalidi had noticed Todd's rhetoric grind to a halt. There was no way he could know about the moral crisis Todd had just run up against, like a Milk Cup cyclist racing head down into a wall. But clearly he did not think Todd had stopped because he had finished. The silence between them stretched embarrassingly while Todd teetered on the edge of a shocking abyss, arms windmilling as he strove for balance and some argument that would not kick him over the brink. He had expected this to be difficult. He had had no idea how difficult.

Todd kept groping for words and eventually found some. "The PFLP knew about Deborah Lev when she offered them Mickey Flynn. I don't know why they agreed to take him. If they expected to prise Mossad secrets out of him, they're going to be disappointed. All he can do for them is what he always meant to: happy snaps for the Arab brotherhood, particularly those with deep pockets. Alive or dead, that's all he's good for. I don't want him dead before you find that out."

Khalidi raised a heavy eyebrow fractionally. "It's nothing to do with me. I still don't know what you think I can do."

"Liaise." That was Khalidi's title: liaison officer. It was another of Jerusalem's open secrets, according to Sammi Akim. "Get word through to somebody so that he walks away from this. I'll have him out of the country before the police can so much as ask after his welfare. You won't be compromised. There's even some propaganda in it for you. The IDF has always been jealous of the media's ability to move comparatively freely between the opposing elements here. Now they've used deceit to manoeuvre a news photographer with an international reputation into the front line—set him up to do their job, take their heat.

"When that comes out there'll be wigs on the green. Their only possible defence is that the thing was made necessary by the utter ruthlessness of their enemy. If it turns out that the ruthless enemy is rather less cavalier with other people's lives than the IDF, they'll never live it down."

There was no telling whether he was carrying Khalidi with him or not. His face was as darkly covert as ever, his tone as studiously polite. His eyes were like obsidian pebbles, all glossy surface and no way of seeing to their hearts. He said, "If someone has given you to understand that I can influence that sort of decision, you have been misled. I can talk to a few people for you, but I cannot say how far it will get or if it will do any good. I am a political man, not a soldier. The people you're talking about don't seek my opinions before deciding how to pursue the armed struggle."

They were phrases out of a textbook. It was like talking to a training video. Todd had no sense of getting through the surface defences and communicating with the man underneath. There was no feedback—not of sympathy, understanding and a desire to help, but equally not of anger, resentment, irritation, irony or any of the less positive responses his appeal might have provoked. It was as if they were discussing not a man's life but a Ministry of Agriculture circular on oranges. Khalidi was a man impervious to emotion: no one else's feelings got in, nor did his own, presuming he had them, get out. Todd wondered how Khalidi had come to espouse anything as passionate as a cause; or for that matter, how he had come to father children. Perhaps he got that from a manual too.

Aware that his grip on the situation was slipping dangerously, Todd shook himself and tried to concentrate on the important issue. "Mr. Khalidi, can we cut across some of the PR? Regardless of what any third person might be able to prove, you and I both know your relationship to and standing with the people who have my photographer. I want him back. He's not in great shape now: if your friends think he has any information for them, they're liable to kill him just warming up their rubber hoses. He can't help you, and he can't hurt you. You have no reason to keep him, let alone kill him."

Without the shrug that would have made the observation somehow less brutal, Khalidi said, "Wars are full of innocent victims, Mr. Todd."

"They're also full of people making mistakes." Todd felt the anger he had so far succeeded in suppressing beginning to mount. "The IDF made one when they chose Mickey Flynn to set up. The PFLP will make another if they choose to treat him as a spy, with all that implies. But Mr. Khalidi, I have to tell you that the biggest mistake of all would be for you to dismiss what happens to Flynn as just another act in the epic saga of your war. If you don't bring him safe out of this, I'll make you regret it.

"What do you want? You want me to ask nicely? OK—I'm begging you. I'd get down on my knees on the rug if it would help, except you might have to help me up afterwards. You want the kudos? That's fine too, I'll write the story so there won't be a dry eye in the circulation. I'll write it so that for three months the IDF brass won't be able to hear themselves think for the rumble of rolling heads and the resounding tinkle of shattered careers. What else? Any price I have to pay, I'll pay; but Khalidi, you do this thing for me."

He did not add "or else" but they both of them heard it. The Arab's eyebrow did its fractional elevation again. "Mr. Todd, that almost sounded like a threat."

Todd was breathing quickly. He nodded. "It did, didn't it?" He met Khalidi's inhuman black glass gaze, and for seconds that may have run into a minute neither man spoke. In the nearby kitchen the little girl was singing to the baby.

Finally, abruptly, Khalidi stood up. "I told you, I don't know how much I can do. You must leave it with me."

"But you'll try? You'll try and get him out?"

"I'll talk to some people. That is all I can promise."

"All right. Call me when you've some news. I'm staying—"

At last Khalidi cracked a cold, harsh smile. "I know where to find you, Mr. Todd."

[8]

Flynn passed an uncomfortable evening until the familiar drug in his bloodstream replaced the crude substitute as the cotton-wool round his hurts. Then he slept the deep and dreamless sleep that is most men's closest approach, short of the final one, to death.

In the morning, twenty-four hours after he arrived in the camp, Fahad woke him with coffee, fresh-baked pita bread, goat's milk cheese and apricot jam. They ate together.

"You're looking better," said Fahad.

Flynn knew how he looked: pale and stiff and slow, and so careful in his movements as to be clumsy. He had watched himself in mirrors that knew nothing of flattery. Still, all things are comparative: he felt much better than the last time he talked to Fahad.

He shrugged lopsidedly. "Before Amsterdam I could go from horizontal to vertical in even less than seven and a half minutes. On a good day."

"What happened?" Fahad had already heard most of it from other sources. He wanted to be sure he had it right because how he handled this could depend on it. When Flynn told him, reciting the facts a little like a medical textbook and a little like an alternative comedian trying out a new routine, Fahad shook his head in some wonder. "Europe is a violent place." He seemed unaware of the irony and so surprised by Flynn's little choking laugh. "Can they not put it right?"

Flynn shrugged. He was working at being offhanded about it. "This may be as right as it's going to get."

"Surgery?"

"I think my surgeon is deeply impressed by the fact that I've survived this long and wants to quit while she's ahead." He knew as he said it that he was not being fair to Van Rijn. She had not given up on him so much as he had given up on her, and that for reasons that were no reflection on her competence. He accepted her assessment that he had been getting better, and her judgement that any radical intervention at this point could do more harm than good. It was not dissatisfaction with his treatment that had made him leave the hospital.

He was haunted by the fear that he might lose control over the most fundamental aspects of his life. His returning strength had comforted him, because it supported the view that he was recovering but also because it enabled him to make provision for himself if the recovery proved not to be permanent. At a deeper level than he could talk about was the mortal dread that the shard Van Rijn suspected was indeed loose in his back would sooner or later react to an unwise movement with devastating, crippling effect.

If he had stayed under observation in hospital and it had happened there, they would have had him plugged into all their lifesaving technology before it occurred to anyone to ask whether he wanted his life saved. And if Todd was with him when it happened, the old man would draw the line at nothing including a pilgrimage to Lourdes to make him live out whatever life was left to him.

Back in Amsterdam when he first considered this, he had been utterly determined that he would die before he would settle for a life on either his back or his backside, screwed up with pain or numb with paralysis. He was less sure now, but certain of one thing: that if the worst happened, what happened next would be his decision. For that he had to stay away from doctors, and even more he had to stay away from Todd.

The other thing about it was that the hospital ethos, all questions and concern, was forcing him into a cripple's mould before it was necessary. After six months surrounded and nurtured by the trappings of invalidity he would be fit for nothing else. This way he might hasten the inevitable, but he was not going to waste whatever time he had left as a whole man. Disaster was going to have to hunt him down; he was not going to sit waiting for it, watching for the signs, attended by people watching for them too.

Except that now these people knew and they would be watching him, waiting for him to collapse in a twitching faint he would never get up from, wondering what to do with him if he did. But at least here nobody cared about him, like the hospital that was paid to and Todd who did it for free. If it happened here, he would not have to fight to die.

He grinned suddenly, savagely. "Don't worry, it might never happen. I might live to be only slightly creakier than the average ninety-three-year-old. If you can keep your friends from venting their revolutionary fervour on me."

"I am sorry about that," said Fahad. He seemed genuinely to mean it. "Kadar gets overenthusiastic at times. He thought he had good reason—well, he did have a good reason. He thought you were planted on us by the Israel Defence Forces."

"Oh come on," scoffed Flynn.

Fahad said quietly, "Mr. Flynn, you were planted on us by the Israel Defence Forces." He explained about Deborah Lev, though not what happened to her.

All the time he was talking he was watching Flynn's face. There was not a lot of colour there to start with; now there was none. His eyes widened and deepened, and seemed to search Fahad for a sign that he was joking. His attention was rivetted. Fahad was certain he was hearing this for the first time, that he had never suspected a plot. Fahad was not sure if that altered anything, but it confirmed his initial guess.

When he had finished Fahad fell silent and waited, still watching for a response. It was a little time coming. Flynn wiped the back of his hand across his mouth. His eyes rolled up to study the rough-hewn roof of the cave while a few ragged breaths struggled in and out of his chest. Then he reached out shakily and poured more coffee, spilling some of it. If, straight from the pot, it was too hot to drink he appeared not to notice as he drank it anyway.

Then he looked Fahad in the eye over the rim of the cup. The will he had been mustering while the silence crawled proved equal to the task, though no one would ever know by how fine a margin. But he did not start talking too fast, jabbering that he had known nothing about it and would not have gone along with it if he had, pleading to be believed, pleading for his life—even this damaged life which, until now, he had not known he valued. He hung onto his tongue and his dignity, and came straight to the point.

"Are you going to kill me?"

Fahad's light tenor chuckle was as shocking as a slap in the face. Flynn did not know what to make of it, what to understand by it. He waited achingly, his nerves raw, for Fahad to explain.

"Mr. Flynn," Fahad said kindly, "whatever would we want to kill you for? We knew what the Jews intended when Lev first suggested this. We would not have cooperated if we had not thought we could use it to our advantage. From where we stand, nothing has changed. You came to take photographs here, we want those photographs taken. I think when you are finished you should fly out from Amman instead of Tel Aviv, but that's the only change of plan we need make."

Aware that he could be digging his own grave, though he could not believe Fahad had not thought of it first, Flynn said, "I've seen you. I could identify you. And Kadar, and the guy with the medical kit, and Mrs. Habach."

Fahad regarded him levelly. "Are you saying that you would?"

"I'm saying I could. You know that."

Fahad grinned. "Of course I do, Mr. Flynn. But I must tell you, my face and Kadar's decorate wanted posters up and down Palestine. If the Jews ever employ a reliable optician we'll be in serious trouble. Mrs. Habach did you no harm. Should you be so ungallant as to report her, what could you say? You lodged with her one night, then left with friends."

"I'm wearing her son's clothes. Her short son's clothes."

"Some landladies offer tenants a more comprehensive service than others."

Flynn did not know whether to believe him or not. He knew better than to trust him, but Fahad could still be telling the truth. He decided that, in one way, it hardly mattered whether he was telling the truth or not. All Flynn could do was go along with it and hope for the best—trusting, but keeping his powder dry.

He looked pointedly at his bare feet. "You don't have someone on the staff whose son takes a bigger shoe size than Alam Habach?"

Todd did not dare leave his room. He had his meals sent up. He was waiting for the phone to ring so intently that when it did he startled almost clear out of his chair. But it was neither Khalidi nor Simon Meir. It was Leah Shimoni.

"I thought you said you'd call me when there was any news."

His middle-aged heart was pounding, his voice rattled with the pumping of his middle-aged lungs. When he was Flynn's age, or Shimoni's, living on the edge like this meant nothing to him. But his nerves were growing old even faster than his body.

He sighed. "There is no news, Leah. Well—no good news. Except that yesterday he was still alive."

He condensed everything that had happened into a few sentences to bring her up-to-date. He was surprised how far back he had to go, that she did not know about Lev or the PFLP. Her silence on the line was eloquent.

He said, "I'm sorry to rush you, Leah, but somebody might be trying to get me. Do you mind?—I really will call you, once I know anything."

Even so, before he could bring himself to ring off he had something to ask her. "Leah, do you ever wonder . . . ?" He stopped and started again. "Something Mickey said, that I never gave any thought to until . . ." He was finding it harder than he had thought to put the thing into words. He took a deep breath and said it. "Do you think we're at all responsible for the situations we report?—like Israel, like Ireland. How much of that is our fault, because it would go away if we weren't here?"

There was a pause. He thought he might have shocked her. And he had surprised her, in a way, but nowhere near as much as she surprised him. She said, "Gil, how old are you?"

He could not remember being asked that since his mother stopped adding to the candles on his birthday cake, and for a moment he was not sure. But he worked it out. "Fifty-three."

"Fifty-three," she echoed. "And this question never occurred to you until Mickey Flynn put it in your mind?" Her tone was incredulous and amused. Todd realised that she was laughing at him, her darkly serious face four miles away losing its struggle to remain straight. "It really was a different business when you got into it, wasn't it?"

The line crackled, or she may have been chuckling into her sleeve. Todd waited doggedly, trying not to think of the other caller who might be waiting for him.

"All right," said Shimoni. "Yes, of course we're responsible—if by responsible you mean things would happen differently if we weren't involved. Like breweries are responsible for drunken driving; like the fish are responsible for paella. If it weren't for the fact that journalists are prepared, sometimes at the risk of their own safety, to go into difficult situations and report distressing and dangerous and unpalatable facts, then indeed many acts of terrorism would be pointless because news of them would never reach those they were meant to influence.

"And in exactly the same way millions of people would starve to death, because journalists would not risk cholera and typhoid, and the gun butts of embarrassed local militia, to get the pictures that stir the conscience of the world. Unpopular minorities would scream silently under the heels of vicious regimes confident that their actions would never be called to account on the world stage.

"Even governments like yours and mine, which are essentially decent and democratic even if it sometimes takes an effort of will to believe it, would be a lot more prone to excess if they thought they would not be haunted by their errors for as long as the public memory should last. Nor should we be too ready to distinguish between causes which we believe deserve publicity and those we should wish to stifle for lack of it. That's not our judgement to make.

"So yes, I'll accept responsibility for the fact that sometimes what I do gives terrorists a boost—if I can also have the credit for some of the millions of lives saved after natural and man-made disasters, for some of the downtrodden peoples freed from tyranny, for some of the victims helped and the vicious brought to justice. We are responsible for what we do, Gil, not for what we can't prevent other people doing. Our duty is to the truth—we are not responsible for what some maniac may do with it. There is someone somewhere capable of abusing anything, even truth. That doesn't make the truth any the less worth telling."

After she had rung off, what she had said remained as a small spot of comfort in Todd's mind.

He checked with the desk but no other calls had come in for him. He waited.

Two hours later he was still waiting, and his flesh was creeping with it. Then the phone rang again, and this time it was Khalidi's voice at the other end. Khalidi did not introduce himself but, even apart from the voice, there was no one else it could have been.

"I've found your friend," he said. "In time, but only just. I think if I had stopped to pray today, he'd be dead now."

"He's all right? Thank Christ." The air seeped out of Todd slowly, like a deflating beach ball. He was standing over the phone. As the air went out, so did the strength of his body and he sat down carefully in the chair beside the window.

But Khalidi had said nothing more, and by now he should have done. Anxiety, not gone only sleeping, began to mount again. "Khalidi? Are you still there?"

"It's too soon," said the low, toneless voice, "to be thanking anyone yet. I said I'd found him, not that I'd got him out."

"You told them—about the IDF setting him up? That he wasn't involved?"

"I told them. I'm not sure how much difference it made."

Todd fought to stay calm. "All right. I'll meet with them, tell them myself."

Khalidi barked a laugh at him. "I don't think they'll meet with you!"

"But damn it, they have to—they can't—" What? Kill an innocent man? Of course they could, they did it all the time.

"You don't understand, Mr. Todd, there's a question of propriety here." He might have learned his excellent English from a solicitor's clerk. "They were put to some trouble and some risk by this. The IDF tried to hit at them through Flynn; these people knew what they were doing so it didn't come off, but if they just send Flynn back the Jews have lost nothing by trying it. What kind of a gamble is it which costs you nothing if you lose? It's an open invitation to them to try it again."

Todd did not know what was coming next, but he had a good idea he would not like it. There was a tightness in his chest that he had some difficulty speaking through. He recognised it, of course. It was fear. "What are you telling me? *Is* Mickey all right?"

"So far as I know he is." The tone was negligent, as if it had hardly occurred to Khalidi to ask. "That's not the issue here. Mr. Todd, do you speak Latin?"

"What?!!"

"A people that once ruled half the world should be better at languages," Khalidi said disapprovingly. "But perhaps you've come across
the expression 'quid pro quo'."

So that was it. Todd's heart turned over and sank, leaving a wake of
cold bubbles through his stomach. They were going to ask him to buy
Flynn's freedom. They were going to use him for their purposes as the
IDF had tried to use Flynn. Quid pro quo.

Gently, gently. No need to let Khalidi know how much this was
getting to him. His pride was his own affair: he would find ways of
repairing it once Flynn was safe. In his teeth, but he said calmly: "What
do you want me to write?"

"*I* don't want you to write anything," said Khalidi, a faint gruff note
of indignation impinging on the customary near blankness of his tone.
"You keep talking as if this was my idea. You came to me, remember,
not I to you. You asked for my help. You asked me to approach some
people and ask a favour of them; and they asked me to come back and
ask a favour in return. Quid pro quo."

Todd breathed heavily, quietly. "So what do they want me to write?"

"They don't want you to write anything either, Mr. Todd." He
added thoughtfully, "Whoever said the pen is mightier than the sword
must have been a journalist."

Todd's first reaction, when he could find a voice at all, was that he
could not do it. Clearly Khalidi was ready for that, had expected it. It
was, after all, the only normal response.

"Please, Mr. Todd," he said, "give it some more thought. It's the
best I could do—the only deal I could do for your friend's life. If you
won't go along with it, they will kill him—as an example, you see, and
to embarrass the Jews. Is that what you want? You keep telling me that
none of this was his fault, that he was set up by the IDF. So why would
you want him to pay for their crimes?"

Todd shook his head at the phone, forgetting in his savage despair
that no one could see him. "I can't do it. Do you understand? I won't
do it."

Khalidi sighed. "This means nothing to me, Mr. Todd. I'm a go-
between, that's all. As I keep telling you, I'm a political man myself.
So," he said then, briskly, "that's what you want me to tell them—that
they'll have to kill Flynn, because you won't raise a hand against the

people who set him up. Oh, that reminds me. They said, if you needed persuading, they'd send you Flynn's hand in a box. The right one—or was it the left? Anyway, after that you'd need to act quickly because their facilities are rather crude for major surgery and he'd need some tidying up. And blood, and so on."

"All right!" shouted Todd. "All right, I get the picture. Listen, I have to think about this—"

"No you don't," said Khalidi smoothly. "The last thing you have to do is think about it. If you think about it, it's premeditated. If you go out and do it as the only alternative to letting a man be hacked to death, that's acting under duress and even a Jewish court will hardly hold you responsible. The time to do this is now. Then you can have Flynn back. As soon as it's done—tonight. Will you do it?"

In a voice so small he barely recognised it as his own, Todd said, "Yes."

The satisfaction in Khalidi's voice was the most overt expression he had managed so far. "Good. This is how we do it. There's a man waiting outside your hotel in a silver car. He has the thing with him. All you need is your briefcase, it'll fit in there. Leave the phone off the hook, so I know you're not calling anyone else, and go out to the car. You'll be left at the gates, and watched to see you get inside. There's a listening device in the box too, so we'll know what's being said.

"You do understand? It has to be Meir. An empty guardroom, or the first soldier you bump into, won't do. It has to be Simon Meir. With him out of the way, we can blow up anything we want to anytime we want." He seemed momentarily to have forgotten he was a political man.

Todd whispered hoarsely, "If I do this, Flynn's home and dry?"

"Yes."

"You have no right—"

"No. But we have the need. We do what we have to. So now, do what you have to do."

Todd put the receiver down carefully on top of the chest. He looked at it stupidly, emptily, for a moment. Then he got up, slow as an old man, and reached up and took the briefcase down from the top of the wardrobe.

The explosion occurred a little after three in the afternoon. News of it went out as a stop press in the evening papers, and in full on the television's early evening news. By the main news broadcasts of the evening they had got together an obituary of the ammunition technical officer killed in the blast and were hedging carefully, since the matter was now sub judice, around the identity of the man helping police with their enquiries and the precise form that help was taking.

III

Redemption

After that he is sold he may be redeemed again.

Leviticus 25

THE CAMERA he was provided with was one of those expensive, complicated jobs that camera buffs think of as professional. In fact there is no such thing as a professional camera, only professional photographers; and by and large they tend to put their hard-earned cash into the lens rather than the number of things to twiddle on the sides.

This one had a lot of things to twiddle, and a fair number of built-in meters as well, but it was not as good a camera—because the lens was incapable of the same resolution—as Flynn's own, which he bought for perhaps a quarter of the list price of this in a closing-down sale in Beirut. Of course, he was not so naïve as to suppose that any money at all had been paid for this one.

"Will it do?" asked Fahad.

Flynn shrugged, loaded it. A Box Brownie would have done. These people were not connoisseurs, they cared nothing for the quality of reproduction, and the dramatic content of the images they sought came out of his head—well, also out of the situation but perhaps more out of his head and anyway not out of the equipment. "Let's find out."

They began with the obvious stuff, the recruiting poster shots. These were the scenes Fahad had supposed Flynn would be interested in and had set up accordingly: young revolutionaries drilling, their faces masked, their keffiyehs matching better than the rest of their uniforms, their weapons a bizarre cross section from wooden replicas at one end —the end furthest from the camera—to, prominently displayed, a very few state-of-the-art SMGs, RPGs and what Flynn thought might have been a Stinger ground-to-air missile. He could have been wrong, he had seen them in Afghanistan but not this close. Perhaps he was wrong. But if he got out of this, the IDF would be crawling all over the prints with magnifying glasses.

Apart from the putative Stinger, Flynn was not much interested in this kind of stock footage. Not that he said so: if Fahad had wanted photographs of his granny and her cat Flynn would have taken them. There are times when insisting on one's artistic independence is just plain silly. But these were not the sort of shots he, or anyone else, had made his name with. So when the trainee terrorists had posed in every way Fahad could think of, in formal ranks and in mock battles, with their armaments and in stagily ritualised unarmed combat, and Fahad had declared himself satisfied with the results, Flynn got down to some real work.

Fahad could not understand what he was after. He made no effort to create interesting tableaux. Apart from keeping half an eye on the position of the sun, he took no light readings and no measurements. Scale, whether of manpower or firepower, did not appear to attract him. He lacked, so it seemed to Fahad, an eye for the terrible beauty.

Instead he shambled round the place like a tall lean bear still troubled by his back, the camera dangling by its strap, never once holding his fingers squared before his eye in semblance of a viewfinder. But then, without warning, Fahad would find himself in the middle of a conversation with a man who was no longer beside him, who had stopped in his tracks and then shambled off deliberately in some other direction, his attention taken by some incredibly ordinary and uninspiring aspect of camp life. The kitchen, for the love of God! Whatever did the man think he was here for?

But Fahad was no fool. He knew Flynn was one of the best, perhaps the best there was, and if he did not understand what Flynn was doing it was more likely to be an error of his perception than of Flynn's. So he let him continue with his apparently aimless wandering, punctuated by occasional inexplicable activity, and expected he would understand it better when he saw the prints.

Hantouleh had laid in the materials needed to develop and print the films, and sectioned off part of the cave where he worked as a darkroom. Because Flynn, like many serious photographers even today, worked in monochrome, the facilities needed were simpler than they might otherwise have been. Perfectly good black-and-white developing has been done in blacked-out bathrooms before now.

The possibility of developing his films at Bab el Jihad had not occurred to Flynn, but when Fahad took him to the improvised darkroom he could see that there were considerable advantages—for the PFLP, not for himself. Fahad could see what had and had not been photographed instead of having to trust to Flynn's goodwill. If there was anything on a film that gave him a problem—too clear an impression of someone's face, or some clue to the camp's location—all he had to do was tear up that print. The negatives need never leave Hantouleh's cave. If, when he saw the completed portfolio, there were any gaps in the record that he would like filled, or if any of Flynn's shots failed—Fahad, like most people who keep a pocket Instamatic for family snapshots, thought that unreliable cameras and film were responsible for most failures, had no idea how few of these professional photographers actually have—he could run another film through before it was too late.

The disadvantages, from Flynn's point of view, were several and serious. He lost editorial control: anything Fahad did not like he would destroy. Since Fahad's tastes ran to ranks of marching thuglets, Flynn expected to have to fight for the decent pictures he had taken among all the partisan pap. There would be no strict need to, so probably Fahad would not risk him leaving with the negatives. But that limited the work he could do on the bench, in the trays and under the enlarger, to turn decent photographs into memorable ones. The only sanction he had was that he could refuse to put his name to anything that seriously displeased him; but he doubted he was in a strong enough position to get picky.

So after the evening meal he disappeared into the blacked-out cave with its red light bulb and began developing the films he had spent the day exposing. There were eight of them, with 36 frames on each. He could not remember taking anything like 288 shots, or even the 96 he would be left with if he had had the usual three goes at everything: one for luck, one for the idiot who blinks and one to print. But someone had pressed the shutter 288 times, and no one else had been near the camera.

Fahad gave him an hour, then went to see how he was getting on. For his pains he got shouted at through the closed door to go away, there was nothing to see yet; except Flynn did not use those words. An hour later the response was the same, except if anything cruder. Hantouleh, who had a chemist's knowledge of the developing process,

knew it would take time but not as much time as all that. When mid-
night came and went they began seriously to consider forcing the door.

At half-past the door opened of its own accord. White light flared
within, replacing the red. Flynn stood in the doorway, leaning his hand
on the frame. He looked rumpled, he looked tired. He looked as if he
had gone another three rounds with Kadar. He smelled as if he had
been bathing in the trays of chemicals. But most of all he looked
happy. Satisfied, thought Fahad, noting the bleary fume-laced eyes, the
weary grin; content, pleased with himself, even smug. But he had been
most nearly right the first time. Doing his job well made Flynn happy.

"Come on in," he said, his voice a tired drawl, "see what we've got."
He had spent five hours developing, printing, enlarging and cropping,
and the results were fanned like a spread deck of cards along the top of
the bench.

The cook-housekeepers, one noticeably stout, the other small and thin,
both of them around middle age, sleeves rolled up to their elbows in
the steamy heat of their kitchen kingdom, stood feeding vegetables to a
great bubbling pot according to some timetable and recipe existing
only in their heads, rather like the witches in the opening scene of
Macbeth.

They were embarrassed to be watched in their work, not only by
Flynn with his camera but also by Fahad. Flynn thought he might not
have been there before. Half shy, half indignant, they contrived to hide
themselves behind their head scarves and their hands and the baskets of
bread and vegetables that stocked the cookhouse cave.

For it was just a cave like the others, excavated by nature and improved upon a little by the present tenants. A crack in one wall acted as
a chimney and drew the smoke and smells of the cooking up into the
honeycombed rock, thence—presumably and eventually—to the open
air. It served, but not as well as an extractor fan. The cave was wreathed
with little blue spirals from the cooking oil, thick enough and decora-
tive enough for Flynn to incorporate them into his composition.

But the heat source, which should have been an open fire burning
chips of camel dung, was in fact a heavy-duty hot plate fuelled by
cylinder gas, whose supplier had his name stamped—in English, Arabic
and Hebrew—all over the tank. That, and the crates of Coca-Cola,
brought the scene uncompromisingly into the twentieth century.

. . . .

Lessons in urban warfare. The simplest and perhaps the most chilling image of the collection: a youth and a girl, keffiyehs drawn across their faces so that only their merry eyes remained visible, their young bodies animated with enjoyment of each other's company and their joint endeavour, giggling over a petrol bomb.

When Flynn first saw them, sitting on a rock a little aside from their group, huddled together like conspiratorial children, he could not think what they were doing. Only when he was close enough to take the photograph did he realise. They were pretending to hypnotise each other with the flame dancing from the fabric stuffed in the neck of the bottle.

Flynn had only a few words of Arabic, but he needed none at all to know what the boy was saying: "You are getting sleepy . . ." while the girl rolled her doe eyes dramatically as the lethal flame swung before them.

Then Fahad shouted at them, also in Arabic which clearly meant to quit acting the goat, that if they wanted to kill themselves that was fine but there was no need to take half the camp out with them; and the boy looked round guiltily and then snatched the flaming wick from the bottle and stamped it out on the rocky ground.

The motor mechanics. A group of men in overalls clustered round the open bonnet of an elderly car. Clearly they were enthusiasts: two of the younger ones wore baseball caps with the peaks to the back. They might have been discussing points, or timing, or when to rebore a cylinder. Actually, when the camera came close enough to focus over their shoulders and onto the engine where their hands rested or were busy, it saw that they were discussing how to wire an ignition so that when the driver turned the key a bomb under the dashboard would blow his legs off.

Rachid Seleh Hantouleh—Sinbad—making a bomb. Not his face, not even masked, but his hands, at once slender and capable, delving with infinite precision into the bowels of a device all of whose cogs and wires and terminals and connections were (or should be, if the lens was good enough) etched in the sharpest, most microscopic detail.

At some risk to all concerned Flynn switched off the dead white top light, leaving the cave where Hantouleh worked illuminated by the open door on his right. Highlights ran along the tops of the hands and the right-hand edge of all the components, meeting the shadows from the lower left in abrupt terminators.

Flynn shot the scene several times from slightly different angles. Then, unexpectedly, the light through the door was half obscured and a boy of about sixteen who did not know about the photo session within stood in the mouth of the cave bringing Hantouleh his coffee. The boy was a dark silhouette against the brilliant day behind, and so were the pot and the cup on his tray. He could not have posed better if he had been asked to. Flynn shot a last flurry of frames in which the small domesticity formed a backcloth and counterpoint to the skillful, heartless procedure continuing in the foreground. These were the best photographs of the entire shoot.

There were also proficient photographs of the weapons drill and hand-to-hand combat training which Fahad had laid on, and of other equally martial scenes that had unfolded as Flynn ambled round the camp. Fahad looked at them all, seemed pleased with them all; but the ones he kept going back to, kept extracting from the pile for another half-puzzled, half-perceptive scrutiny, were those handful of photographs which any editor and most afficionados would have recognised as bearing the distinctive Mickey Flynn stamp: intense, concentrated, perplexing, violent, alien. They were pictures that did not lend themselves to classification, images that dwelt in the mind long after they had faded from the eye.

At last Fahad looked round at Flynn with a new understanding and a new respect. "You don't pull your punches, do you?"

[2]

It was not the first night Gil Todd had spent in a police holding cell, though it may have been the most comfortable. He had forgotten there would not be any bugs. Most of the places he had been held while his credentials were checked and his independence leaned on had been carefully located on the main flight path for the area's resident insect population, and he had been bitten, stung, buzzed, walked over and explored for nesting material by more and stranger things than were dreamt of in Horatio's philosophy or anyone else's.

Here there were no ants, no caterpillars like animated feather boas, no spiders the size of a child's fist or tiny lethal scorpions. There may have been mice, a fact he deduced from the presence of a large marmalade cat which surveyed him with cool disfavour, as if it knew what he had done, whenever it sat down to wash its paws. The policeman who brought his meals gave him much the same look. In fact no one in the police station knew exactly what Todd had done, though he sometimes wondered if the cat had guessed.

There was however a general appreciation that Todd was not an ordinary prisoner being processed for ordinary, even ordinarily monstrous, crimes. For one thing, his arrest had been effected not by the police, either uniformed or CID, but by the military, and it had been made quite clear that although he occupied a police cell he remained a military prisoner.

For another, no one—military, CID, Shin Bet, not even Bet Agron the government press office—showed any interest at all in questioning him, even the minimum amount necessary to obtain a statement. It was almost as if no one cared what he had done, or if he had done anything, just so long as he stayed off the streets and behind bars.

Todd passed the hours in as much comfort as he had any right to expect, drinking tea, reading—he also had more reading material than anyone could remember a suspected person being locked up with before—and dozing on his mattress. Real sleep was out of the question, not only because of his surroundings, though he supposed that if he were here long enough it would come.

Shortly after the morning shift change Todd heard the sudden flurry of activity in the yard below, the clatter of running feet, the roar of engines, and sirens that two-toned themselves quickly out of earshot, and he guessed some new drama was unfolding in the war-weary city. In that he was right. He persuaded himself that, since he could do nothing about covering it, it was nothing to do with him, and in that he was wrong.

It was mid-morning, almost the quietest time in the average police station, that he heard the footsteps in the corridor outside his door. He knew immediately that this was something to do with him, even though there were several other occupied cells in the block and he could not see who was making those brisk, even footsteps. Still he would have been amazed if they had passed him by or stopped a door short. He supposed it was news of some kind.

He stood up, his book hanging forgotten in his hand, and waited, and part of him hoped and part of him was afraid. He was conscious of a faint thready tremble like finely engineered machinery running all the length of his body. The footsteps stopped outside his door and the lock turned.

At the desk the senior officer turned to the junior and said thoughtfully, "There's a thing you don't see too often."

Like every young policeman who had ever hoped to make superintendent, this one knew his role and had learned his lines. "What's that, Serg?"

"An accused man being visited in police cells by the man he's accused of murdering."

When the door opened and Simon Meir walked into his cell, Todd's first thought was that it was all over, that the deception had paid off and Flynn was free. His nerves leapt in anticipated celebration. Then he saw Meir's face and knew that the news was not good, and he thought then that Flynn was dead and the need for the charade therefore past. Finally he thought he had better stop guessing and find out what had happened.

"What's going on, Simon?" He was amazed at how nearly normal his voice sounded. "Have you heard something about Mickey?"

Meir shook his head. He was in his working clothes, or what remained of his working clothes when he stripped off the armour and the padding and replaced his helmet with a cap. So he had come here straight from a job without taking the time to change first.

A job? He should not have been out on a job, he should not have been here, if there had been no news yet about Flynn. That was what they had agreed: in the impossible situation in which they found themselves, that was what had been decided.

Anger surged in Todd until the tiny tremble he had been aware of was a visible shake in his hands, until his eyes burned like raked coals on Meir's face. The tremor had reached his voice by now as well. "For God's sake, Simon, what are you doing here? You're going to get him killed!"

Meir closed the door quietly behind him and leaned against it, his head bowed. Some hurt twisted the gentleness in his face, laid shadows in his mild eyes. Clearly finding it difficult, he said, "I've come to explain, Gil—and for what it's worth, to apologise."

Todd was too stung by the betrayal to listen. "To explain, Simon? To explain why you're wandering the streets as large as life when the PFLP believe I killed you? To apologise for the fact that Mickey Flynn will undoubtedly get his throat cut because you couldn't stay out of sight for just two or three days?

"Simon, I trusted you. I knew there was a chance it could go wrong, that they might somehow find out what I'd done and how I'd done it. I knew when I called you, from the hotel room next to mine while Khalidi was still on my phone, that if he found out—that we'd staged it, that everything he heard over his damn wire after I collected the bomb was playacting—he'd kill Mickey, or me, or both of us if he could manage it. It was always a gamble that we could keep him in the dark long enough.

"But at least I thought I could count on you. I never thought you'd sell us out, so quickly or so cheaply. Not after I'd put Mickey's life on the line to save yours. God damn, I should have let them have you!"

He did not mean it. Meir did not even think he did. It hardly mattered: already he felt so badly about it that Todd's bitter accusations, whether well-founded or not, could add nothing to his burden of guilt. Yet through it all he knew that he had been right, that circumstances had left him with no choice.

The target had been a building site, or rather a man working there. An Israeli Arab, he had made the money to start his own firm working as a crane driver, and as a crane driver he worked still. It was in the high cab of his great Meccano stork that the bombers found and trapped him, attaching their device where the mast rose vertically out of its stabilizers. A few people saw them doing it but supposed they were engaged in maintenance work.

When the device was armed the two men calmly stopped an apprentice bricklayer, explained what they had done and why. They said that the great crane would topple like felled timber over the site in twenty minutes' time, unless the operator tried to climb down past the device in which case the vibration would detonate it prematurely. They said that the man in the crane had brought this on himself by his antisocial behaviour in helping the Jews build Jewish settlements in the occupied territories. While the apprentice was trying to run three ways at once, they walked off the site and drove away.

"Gil, I had no option," Meir said quietly. "If I hadn't responded that man would certainly have died, and others may well have done."

"Jesus, Simon," snarled Todd, "you're not the only ATO in Israel. Could no one else have taken the call?"

"No one who was available could have tackled that device with a realistic chance of disarming it, no. It was one of Sinbad's—remember him? He killed David Gichon. David was almost as good as me"—he said this entirely without pride, merely as a statement of fact—"but he wasn't as good as Sinbad. There was no one in or near Jerusalem this morning that I could have let go to that bomb without it being murder."

"So you decided that if someone had to die it might as well be Mickey?"

For a moment Meir's statuesque patience almost crumbled. "That's not what I decided, and you know it!" He broke off and made himself breathe lightly. "Gil, I tried to keep faith with you. If it had been just the crane, or God help me the Western Wall, I'd have let it blow up. If it hadn't been one of Sinbad's I'd have let someone else take it. But there were lives at stake: at least two, the man on the crane and the man on the bomb. If I'd stuck to what we agreed, they would both have died.

"They're alive now because I did the job I'm paid to do. I'd have given a lot to get Flynn out safely, but not the lives of two men to whom I owe a duty. If Flynn dies because of this, you know how sorry I'll be but his death will have been somebody else's deed and responsibility. If I'd let that bomb go up when I could have stopped it, those deaths would have been squarely at my door.

"What it comes down to, Gil, is that I could no more sacrifice those people whose lives depended on me, even for Mickey's sake, than you could kill me, even for Mickey. I'm sorry I let you down. I still don't think I had any choice."

The worst of the fury had passed. It was not Meir's fault that Todd's plan, conceived in a few desperate moments on the telephone when he was being asked to choose between one friend's life and another's, had foundered on fate and the man's integrity, the fact that he too drew the line at buying a life with a death.

Turning away, Todd lightly touched Meir's sleeve. "Sorry, Simon. Not your fault. Not even mine. We tried—the luck was against us, that's all." He bent like an old man over the mattress and began gathering up his belongings. There seemed no point in staying any longer.

A thought occurred to him, but it was not enough to revive his hopes. "I suppose it would be naive to ask if anyone saw you closely enough to make a positive ID."

Meir shrugged economically. There was no more hope in his face than in Todd's voice. "I got in and out as quickly as I could. And you know what the gear's like, we all look the same in that. It would be hard enough for anyone there to have ID'd me. I don't think it makes any difference. They'll know it was me."

"How?"

"The device was one of Sinbad's. It didn't go off."

Todd went back to his hotel room and resumed his vigil by the phone. He was not kept waiting long.

As before, Khalidi did not give his name. As before Todd had no doubt it was him. The difference was that now the menace that had been implicit in his expressionless tone was out in the open, subtle as machine-gun fire. The man was in a vicious temper and not troubling to cover himself. It hardly mattered: Todd could not have proved to a court's satisfaction who had rung him, and Khalidi could undoubtedly pick from three separate alibis to show that it was not him.

"What kind of fools do you take us for?" demanded Khalidi by way of greeting. "Did you think we wouldn't notice a dead man defusing a bomb on a public building site?"

Todd held his tongue. He could not think of anything to say that would not make Khalidi angrier. He had spent all the time since his release trying to think of something constructive to say when Khalidi rang, as he knew he would. It would be fatuous to claim that he thought Meir was dead: the most cursory inspection of the facts indicated not only that he had to have known about the deception but that he had to have initiated it. Because of the transmitter, the only time the plan could have been laid was between Khalidi calling and Todd going out to the car, and the only way was for Todd to have called Meir in that minute and a half. It was about as inadvertent as the bombing of Nagasaki.

"Have you nothing to say?" snarled Khalidi. "Will you not tell me that the IDF set you up as they did your friend Flynn?"

"No. You wouldn't believe me."

"That's right, I wouldn't." For a moment there was only heavy breathing over the phone. "You know what you've done, don't you? You've killed Flynn as surely as cutting his throat. He's a dead man, because of you. You had the chance to save him—I gave you that chance—and you threw it away, for the sake of a Jew soldier whose life is never going to be worth more than a ten-minute fuse anyway. One day soon he's going to guess wrong and be splattered across half Palestine, and then Flynn will have died for nothing at all. I hope he haunts you."

"Listen," said Todd, just sharply enough to cut Khalidi off in mid-diatribe. "Killing Meir was your idea. I didn't volunteer. There was never any way you were going to make a murderer of me, and there still isn't. I told you the kinds of currency I can deal in: publicity, propaganda, prestige. Don't think it's a cheap option—for me it's professional suicide, but that's my choice the way other people's lives aren't. So come on, talk to me. You can't have what you wanted out of this, but you can still have something. Mickey's death is worth nothing to you."

"Oh you're wrong," hissed Khalidi. The venom positively dripped down the phone. "Flynn's death will give me personally a great satisfaction. Not because of anything he's done—because of what you've done. They'll want you to identify him, so you'll see the price he's going to pay for your treachery. After that you'll wake sweating most every night thinking about what we did to him. Well, spare a thought for me then too. Because someday, when you're not expecting it, when you think this is all in the past and you can even think of Flynn without sweating blood, what we're going to do to him, I'm going to do to you."

"Khalidi!" shouted Todd, but the dead line only hummed at him, killed at the other end. "Damn you, you son of a bitch. Damn you to hell." He replaced the phone carefully. His hand was shaking.

Almost immediately the thing rang again. This time it was Meir. "He's on his way out of the house now."

"You think he's going there?"

"That's what it sounded like to me."

"He's no fool, Simon. He won't risk leading you there. He'll look to see if he's being followed."

"I'm sure he will. And when he sees a suspicious car he'll have a shot at shaking it. And after he's shaken it he'll drive round the city for twenty minutes to make sure. After that he might change his car, but after that he'll go down there. And he'll never know that he was under surveillance every mile of the way."

"Can you do that?"

"I can't," said Meir, "but Ben Simeon's people can. A good tail is as much an art form as rendering bombs safe—or journalism, I suppose," he added doubtfully. "It takes a small orchestra of players, several different instruments, and someone to conduct. In this case Ben Simeon. They won't lose him, Gil, whatever happens, and I don't think he'll spot them. If he goes there we'll be just minutes behind."

"And if he's going somewhere else?"

"That's the gamble we took, Gil. He might not have called you at all. He might never have left his house. If he's going to visit his sister in

Ramallah we'll maybe set siege to a perfectly innocent herd of goats and a cheese dairy. In which case we'll be back in the position of having tried our damnedest and failed.

"But if you want my opinion, he's on his way to that camp. What I heard over this tap was a man so furious at being made a fool of that he couldn't wait to take his revenge. Calling you was a bad move in the first place, but he wanted you to know what he was going to do because of what you did. He wasn't going to risk you not making the connection—blaming someone else for what's going to happen to Flynn. He's only paying you back if he does it and you know.

"Look," he said then. "I'll have to be there when they find the camp in case there are any little surprises to deal with. I'm flying down to Be'er Sheva by helicopter to wait there. Why don't you come with me? It'll be better than sitting in your hotel for hours waiting to hear. It's highly irregular, of course, but so what? The book went out the window weeks ago as far as this is concerned."

"Where shall I meet you?"

"I'll pick you up."

[3]

Fahad had a problem. Common sense was pushing him one way, personal inclination another, and his least favourite ally—that deeply unpleasant piece of work from the political wing in Jerusalem—was pushing and shoving and wanting things that perhaps were not so unreasonable in themselves except that all Fahad's instincts told him that if Khalidi wanted it, it could not possibly be a good idea.

He took Kadar aside. There were many times when he disliked Kadar, but never when he was involved in discussions with Khalidi. By comparison Kadar appeared sensitive, enlightened and humane.

So he took Kadar for a stroll among the rocks and wadis after breakfast. There was a weapons drill in progress on the flat sandy area at the foot of the cliff beneath the caves. Since Flynn was sleeping late after his night's work the SMGs, RPGs, etc. had been carefully packed away in the armoury again and the drill was continuing with wooden replicas.

Rather than shouting over the bawl of orders and the blood-curdling shrieks of the recruits—which he claimed to find terrifying, but which actually sounded more like a school playground than a battlefield—

Fahad led the way into the washes. After the rare heavy rains this place was like a rock-cut Venice, urgent waters surging between the limestone cliffs, and some of it flowed a few miles to evaporate in the rich mineral soup of the Dead Sea and some of it, falling just the other side of the escarpment, flowed all the way to the Mediterranean fifty miles away. Most of the time the wadis were dry, but the important ones bore names as if they were rivers.

The wadis of Bab el Jihad, though the name appeared on no map available from the Ministry of Tourism, all drained east into the great salt lake the Jews called Yam Ha-Melah. The valley floors here were already at sea level, though the knife-edged cliffs and soaring pinnacles still lifted their heads well clear of that most fundamental mean. A barricade of rock all down its western edge hemmed in the oddly lavender-shaded lake and had done for two thousand years, and probably for seven thousand years before that. At the northern end of the escarpment a people who were neither Jews nor Arabs but probably gave birth to both were fortifying Jericho as the world's first city nine thousand years ago.

But Fahad was not primarily concerned with history, or at least only with modern history and only his own version of that. He steered his large lieutenant through the quiet gullies whose high walls and twisting course made them as private as a confessional, and said, "What am I going to do about Flynn?"

Kadar looked at him as if it were a trick question. It had never occurred to him that the subject was open to debate. "Top him," he replied succinctly. Then, because Fahad did not get much time to watch American films, he explained more carefully. "You're going to kill him. Or I will, if you prefer."

Fahad sighed. "I don't know. I mean, I'm not sure it's necessary. I'm not sure it's desirable. And then I've got Khalidi whining down the phone at me, quoting Marx and the Ayatollah Khomeini in approximately equal proportions, telling me to free him in the interests of what he calls the Greater Good—so naturally, necessary or desirable or not, I'd rather like to see him dead."

The big man frowned. "What's Khalidi's interest in him?"

"Didn't you know?—Khalidi's running for Pope. Intercessions arranged, miracles a speciality. Some friend of Flynn's asked his help, and Khalidi agreed in return for this man planting a bomb on the IDF. Apparently he has fairly unrestricted access to them; or had until yesterday, when the bomb went off killing their top ATO. Rachid's quite upset about that. Now Khalidi wants me to give Flynn back to made good his promise."

"Confound his promises," exclaimed Kadar, "what about our security? The only reason we brought him here in the first place was we never intended him to leave."

"That's true. But then again, what has he seen? Apart from you and me and Rachid, I doubt he's seen anybody he could identify. He doesn't know where this place is. There's nothing in his photographs that anyone can use against us. He really isn't much of an actual danger —except to you and me, and we're used to it."

"And Rachid. The Jews would pay for Rachid's face."

Fahad shrugged. "It wouldn't do them much good, or him much harm. All his work will be done here now. The only way they'll pick him up is by raiding this place, and if they do that it won't matter who can or can't identify him, he'll be in the same trouble as the rest of us."

"I don't like it," Kadar said stubbornly. "Khalidi or no Khalidi. Who's Khalidi to be giving you orders anyway?"

"I don't like it much myself. Nothing Khalidi says matters much to me, once I decide what is for the best he can like it or do the other thing. But if we kill Flynn there are bound to be repercussions. He's not a Jew, remember, he's an American; and he's famous; and whatever the precise circumstances, he came here to do a job for us. They're good pictures, if we put them out they'll be published whether he's dead or alive, but I think they may do us more harm than good if word gets out that after he took them we killed him."

"Does word have to get out?"

Fahad looked sceptical. "Just disappear him, you mean. Somehow I think people would guess."

"Suppose we didn't kill him but someone else did."

Fahad found it difficult to be sure in his dealings with Kadar whether the big man was cleverer and more subtle than everybody thought, or if he really did keep his brains in his boots and just struck lucky from time to time. He looked at Kadar as if seeing him for the first time. "Now that is an interesting suggestion. If the IDF killed him, there could be no reflection on us. And then all these magazines would be clamouring for the last photographs taken by Michael Diarmid Flynn before the Israelis gunned him down. There's nothing so potent as a posthumous image—did you know that, Kadar?"

Kadar's stolid, blank face suggested that he did not know what a posthumous image was, but again perhaps Fahad was misjudging him.

They walked on, Fahad talking it through—more to himself than to Kadar.

"It would be tricky," he said. "We could use a captured weapon so the bullet would be the right calibre. But once they matched it up to a gun recorded as being lost to us, nobody would believe it wasn't us who killed him. So we'd have to use a gun obtained on the day and preferably at the place that we leave him. We'd have to organise a confrontation with the IDF, with plenty of shooting in front of plenty of witnesses—a nice big riot with all the trimmings.

"We could have Flynn in the van, round a convenient corner. We'd have to shoot a soldier, borrow his gun long enough to kill Flynn with it, then put the gun back and dump Flynn's body an appropriate distance away. The obvious inference is that Flynn was photographing the riot—we'll leave the camera with him, maybe we'll find time to expose a few frames—when by a tragic coincidence he stopped a stray round from a trigger-happy soldier. By another coincidence the soldier was subsequently shot by us.

"Even if the Jews are suspicious, there's no evidence. Let the world make up its own mind. They've all seen the footage of IDF soldiers breaking Arab boys' arms, kicking old Arab men who protest: they'll assume this was more IDF excess and now they're trying to cover it up. Isn't that what you'd believe if you didn't know better?"

Kadar nodded silently.

Fahad stopped and turned to him. His eyes were sombre. "You'll have to shoot him with that gun, first time, from sufficient range to make it plausible, sufficiently accurately to kill him with one shot—because if it takes two, even our friends are going to suspect. The bullet has to stay in his body or they will know he was not shot where he was found. Is this possible, Kadar?"

Kadar nodded again. "Yes."

"You can be sure? You understand, this matters."

"Give me two men to hold him," said Kadar, "and it shall be as you say."

Fahad sighed. He raised his eyes to the lion-coloured hills. "Then Flynn is dead and no further risk to us. His pictures can be published without embarrassment. The blame for his death will fall on our enemies. Even Khalidi is off the hook—it's not his fault if the first thing Flynn does after being released is go to photograph another riot."

Kadar was watching him closely. "So why are you troubled?"

Fahad smiled at him and shrugged. "I wish it was not necessary. Or that I did not like him."

"Leave it in my hands," said Kadar, deadpan, "I don't like him at all."

By ten o'clock Flynn was awake, more or less mobile, and writing covering notes for the batches of photographs Fahad was parcelling up with cardboard for the picture editors of assorted periodicals in America and Europe.

Flynn was less than happy about this. He said he would prefer to take them with him and discuss them with the editors in person. Fahad said he was afraid of the IDF picking him up and confiscating the pictures. Even if they took him into Jordan, the possibility of interference remained. The things would be safer in the post. Once they were on their way, Flynn could follow them.

Flynn thought it hardly wise to ask, "What's to stop you killing me then?" so he did not, but the thought was uppermost in his mind. It was also uppermost in Fahad's. So together, in silence, they wrote the notes and stuck down the envelopes.

By eleven o'clock Khalidi was hearing strange rumours about the building site bomb. Trying to get a proper story, he made some calls, at the end of which he had established that (a) the device was the work of Fahad's expert and up to his usual standard; (b) an ATO arrived to work on the bomb; (c) the bomb had not exploded, and therefore (d) the ATO was almost certainly Simon Meir, hardly if at all dead after Gilbert Todd's visit of the previous afternoon.

Khalidi thought about it, anger mounting towards blind rage as he realised the deception could only have been set up at Todd's instigation and with Todd's continuing and willing assistance. He could not have been unlucky or misled. He could not have been a victim of circumstance. Within moments of agreeing to Khalidi's proposition he had begun complex manoeuvres to renege.

Final confirmation, if any were needed, came when Khalidi phoned Todd's hotel, and Todd answered.

By midday Fahad had heard from Khalidi again. Khalidi was spitting tacks and his message was not altogether clear. Fahad tried a couple of times to calm him down, without success.

"Don't let him go," Khalidi insisted, again and again. "Whatever you do, hold onto him. I'm on my way. I want him there when I arrive."

"You can't come here!" said Fahad, horrified. "For the love of God—!"

"It's all right, I'm not being followed. I had a tail but I shook him. I won't lead anyone down."

"At least let me meet you—"

"I'm on my way," said Khalidi thickly, and rang off.

At twelve-fifteen Rachid Seleh Hantouleh was sitting alone in his workshop, surrounded by the stuff of death, wrestling—with no awareness of irony—with the problem of saving life.

Matchless as he was in his chosen field, Hantouleh nevertheless had a severe limitation as a revolutionary. He had no interest in revolution. Terrorism had no appeal for him. He was a mild man, a studious man: he did not want anything enough or hate anything enough to resort to what he cared to think of as violence. For though he knew intellectually that he had been responsible for the death and maiming of many people, emotionally he looked on the creation and deployment of his devices as a game, a battle of wits and skills played with other equally enthusiastic professionals.

He had been upset to hear that his arch-opponent, the man most worthy of his challenge, was dead, the victim finally not of superior skill but of a dirty trick. Khalidi's bomb had been a joke, cobbled together probably with string and chewing gum in a back kitchen in east Jerusalem. It would not have troubled Meir for a moment if he had seen it, if it had not been smuggled into his office by a supposed friend. When he learned that Khalidi had in fact been tricked and Meir was alive and well, Hantouleh was delighted.

The point was, apart from the occasional ATO, the people Hantouleh killed were strangers, whose names he did not know, whose faces he had never seen, whose sufferings meant nothing to him and whose families mourned unguessed. To him violence meant something more personal than that, something done face-to-face or very nearly, an act of enmity. And as a nonviolent man, a man without enmity, he was appalled by what Fahad proposed doing to Flynn.

Flynn was not a stranger, nameless and faceless. He was someone Hantouleh knew, had talked to and taken meals with—had treated, for the love of God, when the consequences of earlier violence had left him half out of his mind with pain. How could Fahad ask him to care for Flynn one day, and two days later stand by while he and Kadar planned his murder? Fahad insisted it was necessary, but only Fahad bringing him here had made it so. It offended against Hantouleh's sense of fair play.

Like many mild and studious men, when roused to indignation Rachid Hantouleh was capable of almost infinite obstinacy. He could not acknowledge that the thing was unfair, and so was life, and leave it at that. The scientist in him kept him worrying at it, like a hangnail. It passed the point of mere compassion, for the man or his condition, and grew in Hantouleh's soul to a cause célèbre. It wasn't fair, it wasn't good enough, and he wasn't going to stand for it.

He saw no point in arguing further with Fahad. He knew he would be overruled. He knew, too, that his very special talents made him the safest man in the camp: safer than Kadar, safer than Fahad himself. He could hardly conceive of any deed of his so premeditatedly treacherous that Fahad would respond with more than vocal chastisement. Confident, then, in both the justice of his cause and the near invulnerability of his position, Hantouleh acted.

The storeroom allocated to Flynn was no longer locked when he was there alone, but a close watch was kept on the door. Hantouleh nodded a greeting at the watcher, tapped lightly on the door with his knuckles—he came from a background which put a premium on politeness—and went inside.

Flynn had not been fit when he walked out of the hospital, and a lot had happened to him since then. The drugs Hantouleh had acquired for him controlled the pain, but the price he paid for that was exhaustion. He simply had not the strength yet to do what he had been doing. Now that he had finished and the nervous energy which had delayed the inevitable was seeping away, he was palpably close to collapse. It showed in the grey cast to his skin, the leadenness of his body, the dullness of his eyes. With sudden anxiety Hantouleh wondered whether Flynn was capable of taking advantage of the offer he was about to make.

He was sitting on the bed, his head resting on his arms across his knees. He was too tired, too sick, too sore even to think so there was no intelligence in his eyes, only alarm, when his door opened.

"It's only me," said Hantouleh, shutting it behind him, and Flynn took up breathing again, letting his eyes fall shut on the hopelessness and the fear. "You know, then," said Hantouleh. "You know they mean to kill you."

Flynn made a little sound that was half a sigh and half a sob. His head rocked back but his eyes stayed closed. "I didn't know. I wondered."

"Politics," said Hantouleh, as if it was something he had found on his shoe. "None of them needs you dead, but all of them for their different reasons find it politic to kill you. Fahad for the propaganda, Kadar because he hates the Jews, Khalidi because he has lost face and somebody has to pay."

"Khalidi?" Flynn had not heard the name before.

"Khalidi's political. When it suits him. A friend of yours asked his help in getting you out of here. The price was a bomb—or an apology for one—sneaked into Simon Meir's office. He didn't do it, but he tricked Khalidi into thinking he had. For a while. Now Khalidi's after your blood too."

For a moment, startled, he thought Flynn was crying. But Flynn was laughing, softly, without much humour, without much hope, but with a certain wry affection. "Todd. The crazy bloody man. Maybe it's as well I'm going to die. I'll get the chance to haunt him for a change."

"Not if I can get you out of here first," said Hantouleh. He succeeded in surprising himself almost as much as he surprised Flynn, though it was what he had come here to do. "If I can distract the boy outside for five minutes, can you make a run for it? Not the way the van brought you"—he must have forgotten the precise manner of Flynn's arrival, that meant he had no idea which way the van brought him—"head for the Arad road, it's closer." He pointed.

"I will try also to distract the watchers on the cliffs. If you can pass them unseen, it could be some time before anyone checks on you. Even if you have not reached the road by then, among these hills it would take an army to find you. Except from the air, and we don't have any helicopters. If you hear a helicopter, wave it down—it will probably be the Jews looking for you anyway."

Flynn tried to visualise the route he had indicated, failed, decided it did not matter whether he could picture it or not. From here all points of the compass looked the same. The place was a desert: a rocky, mountainous desert to be sure, nothing so gently picturesque as sand dunes, but dry enough and hot enough and empty enough to qualify a dozen times over.

The possibility of escape had been at the forefront of his mind while Fahad was showing him round the camp and waiting for him to exclaim admiringly over the image of children got up for war. He had noticed how the caves ranged along the feet of two cliffs, facing one another across the sandy extinct bed of an ancient river. This was the parade ground where the recruits drilled, flinging their ill-assorted weaponry round with more dash than skill and scant regard for their own or anyone else's safety.

Most of the caves had been fitted with doors, but most of the doors were left open. The armoury and Hantouleh's workshop were the main exceptions. Otherwise the tenants of the caves put the circulation of air above the needs of privacy, which were in any event largely assured by the natural darkness within. This also meant that there was no way of knowing who was in any of them at any given time, or how many eyes might be on him, unseen in the deep shadows.

On top of the cliffs, stragetically located to see as far as possible across the hilltops and also down into the wadis, stood the guards. They changed every two hours. Even if he was not seen from the caves opposite, there would be a lot of rough country to cross before he was out of sight of the watchers. Hantouleh promised a diversion. It would take a hell of a big one to keep the watchers in the caves and the watchers on the hills occupied long enough for him to make good his escape.

"Are you serious about this?"

"Oh yes," said Hantouleh.

"Or are you getting me to make a run for it so someone can shoot me in the back with a clear conscience?"

Hantouleh's eyes were resentful. "I'm sticking my neck out for you. Fahad will guess somebody helped you; he will probably guess it was me. Well, I can take some abuse from him, but I don't need to take it from you. I'll get you out if I can because I don't see any need to kill you, certainly not to please the likes of Khalidi. You are not our enemy, and the woman who was they have already killed. It is enough."

"Leila's dead?" Flynn could not remember her other name, though Fahad had told him. He had also told him she was all right. That was when he still needed Flynn's cooperation. Of course they had killed Leila. Of course, now his photographs were in the post, they would kill him too. Maybe it did not matter if Hantouleh was leading him into a trap. If staying made his death certain he might as well take whatever risks were involved in an escape attempt, however long the odds against him.

There was however one problem. He met Hantouleh's gaze and twitched him half a smile. "If it was just me I'd try it. I wouldn't make it, but I'd try it. But there's no point you putting yourself at risk so I can begin something I know now I can't finish. If you distracted the whole of the camp personnel for half a day so I could do it at a walk, I still wouldn't make it as far as the road. I'm sorry."

Hantouleh looked him up and down with an odd mixture of concern and irritation. "I thought that. Well, if you can't you can't. Can you ride a motorbike?"

Flynn's eyes glowed. "Damn right. Can you get me a bike?"

"I don't know. Kadar has one—a big one. I don't know." Fahad might settle for shouting if he helped Flynn get away. If he helped Flynn get away on Kadar's bike, the big man would rip his arms off. "I'll see what I can work out. Don't go away."

Flynn squinted at him but it really did not seem to have been a joke.

[4]

Khalidi arrived at Bab el Jihad a little before three o'clock. He had spent thirty minutes covering the last six miles, ducking and weaving and hiding and covering his tracks. A man not inexperienced in these matters, he was confident that the tail he had lost in Jerusalem had not picked him up again and neither had anyone else. In those last six miles he nevertheless acted as if he was being followed, but nobody sprung his traps. He drove across sand once, then doubled back to drive across it again. His own tire tracks, ten minutes old now, were clearly visible but nothing else had passed that way. So he drove on to the camp, down a track that was half wadi and half quarry.

Fahad, warned of the approaching car, met him where the track converged with the ancient riverbed. "You weren't followed?"

Khalidi looked down at him with disdain. He was a much bigger man than Fahad. "What am I, a fool?"

Fahad was not intimidated by size. He knew, without having any particular desire to prove it, that he could if the need arose kill Khalidi with his bare hands, and gut him with anything sharper than a potato peeler. Khalidi's bulk and dark countenance and disdainful looks troubled him not at all.

All the same, he had to work with Khalidi, at least to some extent, so he did not answer directly. "I'll tell you when my men have checked back down the track. Do you want to tell me what you're doing here?"

"Not here," grunted Khalidi. He led the way to the armoury, a corner of which served Fahad as an office. It was the kind of rudeness

Fahad had come to expect of the liaison man, but it irked him just the same.

"You've still got Flynn?" demanded Khalidi, before Fahad was properly through his own door.

The smaller man took the time to close it before answering. "Oh yes."

"I want him dead. I want him dead now, and afterwards I don't want there to be any doubt about how he died or who killed him. I want him made an example of. Do it thoroughly."

"Thoroughly?"

"Very well," said Khalidi, meeting Fahad's inquiring gaze, "messily. Make a mess of him. Todd will have to identify him, and I want him never to forget it."

Fahad decided he had been premature in dismissing any desire to murder Khalidi. He really was, thought Fahad, a nasty piece of work—the sort of man who got terrorism a bad name. "Perhaps you'd like to do it yourself," he suggested.

Khalidi's heavy jaw came up as if he were being offered an honour. "I will do. For Palestine."

"Hassan Khalidi," said Fahad slowly, "you are an evil man, and a hypocrite, and if there was any way I could do it I'd let Mickey Flynn walk out of here, if for no better reason than to spite you. Well, I can't do that. But it's some consolation to me to know that he'll die quickly and cleanly, that Kadar will do it not you, and that his friends and everyone else will believe him the victim of a moment's carelessness by an IDF soldier.

"And if Gilbert Todd or anyone else thinks you're nothing but a windbag, all threat and no balls"—he smiled thinly—"so much the better."

If Flynn lived long enough to learn how much time, energy, expertise and sheer hard cash was being expended on his rescue, he would be deeply impressed and really rather touched. The tail on Khalidi had involved eight cars, a lorry, a motorcycle, a light aircraft and a helicopter. The helicopter in particular ran on hundred-shekel notes dissolved in alcohol.

In addition to all the drivers, pilots and observers, there were people manning the radio network linking them, people liaising with the police, people plotting maps; and Major Aaron Ben Simeon, hunched in the middle of it like a great sandy spider, vibrating his wishes out along the strands of his web and waiting for the response, playing the operation like a concerto. Those around him who were not too busy or too charitable to notice might have thought he was enjoying himself.

If the small helicopter used for spotting burned hundred-shekel notes, the big troopships waiting on the ground at Be'er Sheva consumed blank cheques. Each contained, in addition to its crew, a dozen fully armed and equipped soldiers. One of them also contained a medical team, another an ammunition technical officer and his assistant. Of course Todd was too old, too stout and looked too absurd in fatigues for anyone aboard the aircraft to believe him a bomb disposal officer in the making; but that did not matter as long as the paperwork was right. If there were fourteen bodies in the hole and fourteen personnel in the paperwork, all would be well, the sun would continue rising and setting and the grass in Jezreel would go on growing green.

Todd had travelled in military transports in many parts of the world, both on exercise and in action, from the Dakotas that were still the mainstay of tiny South American republics to the big Boeings of the USAF Strategic Air Command; and also with armed forces so small in both manpower and budget that the only transport necessary or viable was a fleet of trucks. Always he was struck by the same thing: how much hanging round there was to be done.

Even on active service, when the risks to life and limb were very real, boredom was as much an occupational hazard as bullets. It hung in the air like the smells of fuel oil and damp clothes. Among new recruits the excitement ran higher, the thread of expectation thrilling under tension, audible in the pitch of their voices as much as the querulous bravado of what they said, visible in the abrupt movements of their hands and eyes and their inability to sit still, tactile or very nearly so in the stench of adrenaline you could cut with a knife.

But experienced soldiers do not for the most part suffer from the nerves that fuel displays of this sort. It is not that they are immune from fear, more that they have learned to conserve and use the fear at those times and in those ways that it will serve and not deplete them. Fear—the concrete of imminent injury at the hands of a real foe armed with real weapons—is the edge that makes soldiers move and think faster on the battlefield than on any exercise, however realistic. If fear could be eradicated in the fighting man, more of them would die. Professional soldiers do not waste that resource on anticipation, hence the deep suffocating boredom of those waiting to fight.

Looking back, Todd thought he had spent more and more boring hours in military transports waiting for something to happen than he had in the baggage-claim areas of international airports. Even today, when the action in prospect was something personal and not just the next story, the next cheque, he was having trouble keeping his eyes open. God knew he was afraid: afraid for Flynn, for these tough silent young men drowsing with their boots thrust out in front of them, even to some extent for himself. But right now there was literally nothing he could do, and tension combined with the enforced lack of movement threatened to put him to sleep.

Beside him, looking more like a don than ever despite his military attire, Simon Meir was reading a book. A treatise on bomb disposal, wondered Todd, or something lurid to take his mind off what might be waiting for him in the desert? He craned his neck trying to see the cover. Meir noticed and smiled, angling the title, which was printed in English, his way. Todd thought then that he should have guessed. He wondered if a soldier had ever before gone into battle reading a book by Jane Austen.

Meir said quietly, "Not much longer now, Gil," and someone passed round a packet of digestive biscuits.

Hantouleh came back. He had the medical kit with him, not this time for Flynn's benefit but for that of the young man watching his door. He did not wish to provoke any speculation.

"The motorbike is with the van and Fahad's car, parked against the rockface where the wadi cuts back behind here," he said. "There's a camouflage sheet over them. The keys are in the ignition. Kadar leaves them there: he thinks no one here would dare touch it."

"No one hoping to stay here would," murmured Flynn, and Hantouleh cast him a small, tight smile.

"We'll have to do it quickly. Khalidi is here and he's after your blood, and if they put you under lock and key while they argue we'll have lost our chance. The first thing you must do is take another dose of your tablets. I know it's too soon, but for the next hour your life may depend on being able to move without wondering how much it's going to hurt."

Flynn did as he was told. Almost for the first time he was beginning to see in this a realistic prospect of escape. He did not understand why Hantouleh was helping him, and he did not care. He could cope with the likelihood that the attempt would end in failure. What he wanted was the chance to try, the opportunity to get out and fight for his life instead of waiting for death like a steer in a killing box.

He was well aware that his physical condition was a serious handicap. Surprise, and the use of Kadar's motorbike if he could get it, might just compensate. If not, there was at least the assurance that he was not going to spend the rest of his life immobile on a broken back, waiting for passing nurses to turn the pages of one book after another.

Hantouleh said, "This is what will happen. I shall have a small accident. Fahad will not believe it was an accident but he will not be able to prove differently: the most careful of us have accidents occasionally. I shall wait until there's no one near, then I shall blow the door off my cave—having just, by a lucky coincidence, stepped outside for a moment. It will be noisy, with plenty of smoke and perhaps a little flame, and everyone in the camp will come running.

"That is your chance, the only chance you'll get. I'm not going to hurt anyone else in order to save you. I'm not going to get you a weapon of any kind, and if you find you have to hit someone please remember these are friends of mine. Except Khalidi," he added as an afterthought. "If the need arises you can hit him very hard indeed. You can hit him twice."

Ben Simeon exploded, and the explosion sent shock waves through his entire staff, through most of the offices adjoining, and winging their way down the radio network towards the Negev. "What do you *mean* you've lost him?"

The observer winced and the pilot pretended to be busy working on his sick helicopter. Since he was not a mechanic, and since flying had moved on from the days when most problems could be resolved by hitting the engine a good thump with a spanner, he did not expect to succeed. But it was a good excuse for leaving his observer to deal with the major.

"We had to put down, sir. In rather a hurry." He explained precisely what it was that was overheating, and what the consequences of ignoring it would have been, but Ben Simeon had no interest whatever in helicopter engineering.

"Dear God," he exclaimed, "I'd have been better asking the Navy to shadow him in a minesweeper! All right, where are you, and what was his last course and position?" He had not finished shouting about the defective helicopter, had just deferred it until he had time to enjoy it properly.

The surest way of finding Khalidi's car again was probably to put more helicopters in the air. But common as the sight of military helicopters was in the skies over Israel, a sufficient saturation to locate a car among the wilderness roads and matchbox townships south of Hebron would inevitably be noticed. Further, if the searchers accidentally overflew the training camp they would alert the establishment there and destroy any element of surprise the IDF could have hoped for. That would be reflected in the casualty list, and the first name on it would be Mickey Flynn's.

So Ben Simeon whistled up additional ground support instead: every civilian vehicle that could be acquired, legitimately or otherwise, was poured into the area until somebody should cross Khalidi's trail.

There were two problems. One of these vehicles might inadvertently stumble on the camp itself, in which case the driver would be in real and immediate danger. And unless he could allay suspicion by some hastily thought up lie about looking for stray goats or missing the Mezad Tamar turnoff, the camp would again be on a state of alert. That meant the hard men of the PFLP fighting to the last teenage recruit, with Sinbad the explosives artiste blowing up rebel property and IDF personnel with equal abandon, and Flynn choking up his life in some back room through a six-inch slit in his throat.

The other problem was the time element. Helicopters could reach the point where Khalidi was lost within three minutes: to get road vehicles there could take literally ten times as long, by which time Khalidi might have reached his destination and disappeared from what passed in those parts for a public road system. They would know then that the camp lay within just a few miles and still lack the precise information they needed to drop out of the sky unannounced and clean up before the thing turned into a shooting war.

Despite the fact that shooting terrorists was unpopular internationally, Ben Simeon was prepared to commit his troops to such an engagement as the price of cleaning out the rat's nest that Bab el Jihad had become. But the publicity would be a lot more critical, particularly in America which Ben Simeon's political masters worried about even if Ben Simeon did not, if Flynn died than if some way of preserving him could be found.

Ben Simeon might have been horrified to learn that he shared his view of politicians with the PFLP's top bomb-maker. Or it might have been only what he would have expected, seeing a greater commonality between even enemy soldiers than between a soldier and his own side's politicians.

So it was a far from perfect solution to the dilemma. It was however, for the moment at least, the best he could do. He gave the necessary orders. "And if anybody finds Khalidi and loses him again, I will have his guts for garters and other parts of his anatomy for the pom-poms."

For a little space everyone involved seemed to be waiting.

Fahad and Khalidi were breathing heavily at one another, each waiting for the other to see sense and back down.

Flynn was waiting for the explosion that would galvanise him into whatever action he was capable of. He was perched on a crate, watching the door, rubbing the sweat from his palms with obsessive, mechanical, unconscious movements of his hands against his trouser legs.

Ben Simeon was waiting for his backup to reach the area where Khalidi had been lost and to hear that they had cut his trail again. He was passing the time working out his alternatives if that did not happen, and also who he should shout at for what and in what order.

The two men in the downed scout were waiting to be rescued. Sitting in a crippled military helicopter on top of a hill within a few miles of a major PFLP installation was not a naturally strong position and both men had personal arms within reach. The knowledge that Ben Simeon would not risk alerting the camp while moves against it were imminent left them aware that they were in for a long wait; unless a PFLP patrol, crawling on their bellies unseen among the jumbled rocks, cut it short for them.

Todd, hunched like a superannuated ActionMan in the well of the helicopter, was waiting for the crackle of the radio, the suddenly intensified atmosphere, the roar of the engines bursting into life, the clatter of rotors—anything that would signify an end to the waiting and the beginning of the end of the nightmare he had been drawn into.

Beside him, Simon Meir could hardly wait to see what Miss Bennet and Mr. Darcy were going to do next.

Rachid Hantouleh was idling at the open door of his workshop waiting for a moment when no one would be near enough to be hurt by the blast, mostly sound but a fair amount of fury, which he had set up. A ten-second delay would give him time enough to get offside himself. So he nodded at the recruits jogging past his door, and exchanged views on the weather with the larger of the two housekeepers who was passing with the remains of a meal for the goats which were the makings of another, and pointed Kadar in the direction of the armoury when he asked where Khalidi was, and wished to God they would all go away and stay away for the fifteen seconds it would take him to betray them and give a man he hardly knew a chance of surviving the day.

Why? Not really because of Flynn. Like Fahad he quite liked the man, but nowhere near enough to put himself at jeopardy. Neither had he a detailed enough interest in the Palestinian cause to worry that Flynn's murder was unworthy of it or not in its best interests; nor, obviously, was he prompted by a belief in the sanctity of human life. To himself Hantouleh argued that killing Flynn was unnecessary, unproductive and therefore unjustifiable; he managed to quite impress himself with the amount of righteous indignation he could muster on the subject.

But if he had been capable of the sort of self-examination that delves below the level of supposed motives to discover actual ones, he would have found that this sudden unexpected championing of a defenceless man had less to do with right or justice or even expediency than with shifts in the power structure as between him and Fahad.

When Hantouleh came here from Jerusalem, his joint successes in both eluding the IDF and blowing up one of their best ATOs fresh in everyone's mind, he had enjoyed a status approaching stardom. The youngsters here revered his name, studied his achievements, courted his opinions, quoted his comments and laughed at his jokes. Their tutors too, men older than himself, recognising the value of a real live hero as a teaching aid, encouraged this elevation of Rachid Hantouleh from explosives expert to minor deity. He found himself treated like a favoured elder son, a scientific authority, a master tactician and a secret weapon all rolled into one. He was flattered, and enjoyed it, and came to think of it as his right.

So when in the nature of things the honeymoon passed and Hantouleh found himself a little less celebrated, a little less special, expected to fit in more with the needs and interests of Bab el Jihad as a whole, he rather resented it. He was a clever man: he was not, particularly, a mature one. He felt that he was being taken for granted, then that he was being pushed around. He told himself that Fahad was jealous of his success, of his popularity, and felt the need to push back. He was looking for a showdown with Fahad, for acknowledgement of his continuing importance to the camp, and in the absense of anything he genuinely felt strongly about, the life or death of Mickey Flynn would have to serve.

The housekeeper had fed the goats and returned to the kitchen. Kadar had disappeared into Fahad's office, and the joggers were pounding sweatily down the far bank of the extinct river. Hantouleh went back into his workshop for a moment, then set off for a brisk walk.

[5]

It was not a big bomb, specifically designed in fact for a minimum of destruction, but it still made a flat crumping sound that could be heard and sent billowing out of the cave and up the rockface a plume of black smoke that could be seen a couple of miles away.

A couple of miles away, sitting in their crippled helicopter on the rocky hilltop where they had come down, the pilot and his observer both heard the explosion and saw the plume. They climbed down from the machine to try and work out where it was coming from. The observer brought his maps.

After a minute the pilot returned to the helicopter and got on the radio. Speaking quietly, as if someone might be eavesdropping, he said, "I can't be sure it's the PFLP place, but there's something going on in the valley below us. Somebody just put up a smoke flare."

It was the thing Ben Simeon had been waiting for, the factor that tipped the balance in favour of action, and he acted immediately. Before he had plotted the coordinates he had been given, he had the troop carriers in the air and heading east.

Todd heard the crackle of the radio he had been waiting for, and the great engines barked into life, and the vibration as the rotors picked up speed crashed through the fuselage, hammering the bodies of the men inside. All the boredom was dissipated in a moment. The young men around him exchanged expectant glances, looked towards the cockpit, rechecked their equipment that they had double-checked before.

Meir put away *Pride and Prejudice*. "Here we go," he said.

Although he had been waiting for it, the sheer volume of the explosion numbed Flynn for a second. It was of course very close, and its whole purpose was to cut across everything that anyone in the camp was thinking or doing and bring them running to see what had happened.

It worked. By the time Flynn had shaken loose his stunned senses and spasmed muscles and got to the door, the boy watching it was long gone, not even flying heels to be glimpsed. He saw people hurrying

down the riverbed past his cave and towards Hantouleh's, but none of
them looked his way. Smoke and the stench of it filled the air. He
looked up to the watch posts on the three high places: on one no one
was visible at all, on the others the guards had moved to the cliff edge
and were peering down into the camp.

Flynn looked towards the cave where Hantouleh's workshop had
been. In fact it was there still, most of it, but the immediate impression
was that nothing and no one could have survived that blast. Now the
ancient riverbed was filled with a flood of people, virtually everyone
at Bab el Jihad so Flynn imagined, converging on the scene of
Hantouleh's small diversion to find out what had happened and if they
could help. All he could see were backs, tassel-ended keffiyehs bouncing
against young men's shirts as they ran and the round shoulders of a few
older women jogging gently as they hastened, more busily than swiftly,
in the same direction.

So far as he could see no one was looking at him. He rolled his eyes
briefly heavenward, muttered the shortest prayer imaginable—"God
help me!"—and turned away from the smoke of Hantouleh's diversion
and towards Kadar's motorcycle.

He hugged the foot of the cliff, in full view of anyone who looked
his way but somehow he hoped less conspicuous here than in the middle of the parade ground, and for the same reason he walked quickly
away from the cave where he had been held but did not run. If anyone
noticed him, his escape was over before it had begun—he could not
have outrun even the stouter of the two housekeepers with his life
depending on it.

But once he reached the point where the cliff turned away from the
riverbed, where some smaller stream had once joined it and ancient
storms had chiselled a promontory out of the rock, he would be visible
to far fewer people—conceivably only the two guards remaining at their
posts. Also, he would be closer to the motorbike than anyone was to
him. It might have been the drugs, it might have been the adrenaline,
but confidence surged under his breastbone like wind.

From ground level the camouflage netting draped over the vehicles
was a pantomime, a cheap and tacky device that even a myopic camel
would never have mistaken for a sand dune. But that was to misunder-
stand its purpose, which was defence against detection from the air.
From above, it disguised the giveaway straight lines, angles and colours
that betrayed the work of men in a desert created by an older, less
systematic authority. Men in a helicopter hovering fifty feet above the

net would have thought it another rockfall on the fragmented face of nature here.

Flynn found the edge and slipped underneath, and disappeared from the view not only of hypothetical helicopter pilots but of actual watchers on the hills. For the first time in more than a minute he drew a proper breath and got it all the way down to his lungs.

The bike was there, between the van and Fahad's car, and the key was in the ignition as Hantouleh had said. Before he did anything else he lifted the two bonnets and tore out whole handfuls of wiring. Rather than risk the noise he left the bonnets up.

Then he rolled the bike off its rest, and turned the petrol on and turned the ignition. But he did not try to start it yet. He sat astride it, trying to learn the feel of it, trying to remember from his bike-riding days how the things kicked when booted into gear, how sharply they could accelerate without taking off, how tightly they could corner and remain stable. Then he tried to imagine how it would all work on sand and shale. Once he started the engine he would have no time to think about these things; getting it wrong then would kill him.

But every moment he risked that someone would check the cave and find him gone, and call the whole camp out in arms against him. He had to be out of range before that. Pausing only a last moment to breathe an ancillary prayer to the god of motorcycle maintenance (Zen, wasn't it?) he hit the electric start.

God bless Kadar and his little oily rags, the thing started first time, the deep throaty roar rising to a wail as he twisted the grip. Like David Gichon so many weeks and so much grief ago, he hissed, "Geronimo!" as he kicked it into gear.

He kept his weight forward and the front wheel did not rise as the big engine thrust the bike forward. As the camouflage net swept down on him Flynn scooped it up and over his head, and drove out into the bright afternoon.

A lot of things happened in quick succession.

Kadar recognised the wail of his favourite child and howled, "My bike!" in shock and outrage.

Fahad remembered his prisoner, saw his supposed guard ogling the smoking workshop and yelled, "Flynn!"

Both men took off at a run towards the vehicles. Fahad snatched an SMG from the man who had been on the hill but had come down at the explosion. From somewhere, possibly the wreckage of the workshop, Kadar had picked up a five-foot length of four-by-two.

Khalidi stood a moment as if rooted to the spot, and his anger as he realised what had happened was monstrous and terrible, rising through his face like a madness. Then, instead of taking off in Fahad's wake along with most everyone else, he turned on his heel and stalked to where he had left his car—on the sand, out in the open, in direct contravention of basic security.

Underestimating the amount of power between his knees, Flynn nearly ended his escape attempt on the first turn. The bike yawed wildly and Flynn lurched from one side to the other in the effort to recover his equilibrium. He twisted the grip. The engine roared at him. He kicked up a gear and raced on up the wadi, away from the camp, hugging the rock wall so closely that once his shoulder brushed against it.

He knew, of course, that by now they would have heard him. The roar of the bike bounced between the cliffs like thunder. For a moment they would not know where he was or which way he was heading in this network of gullies that ran in jumbled chaos for miles in every direction. But then they would pick up the track of the big cross-country tires in the dust, and only moments after that one or other of the watchers on the high places would glimpse the movement in the wadis that could be nothing but him and direct the pursuit onto his tail.

It might not matter. If he could keep going there was nothing in Bab el Jihad that could catch him. No one on foot could keep pace with a motorcycle, even on broken ground; no other type of vehicle could go where the bike could go. A racing camel might have given him trouble but he thought he would have noticed had there been one in the goat pen.

Two things might stop him. One was if he turned this bike over, either killing himself or so damaging himself or the machine that he could not continue, which came to the same thing. Even being careful, it was a very real possibility. He had been nineteen when he last did any serious biking, and he did not do it in a limestone quarry then. Avoiding the potholes in the streets of New York had been good sport and challenging, but no preparation for this.

The other danger was that this wadi might run out. If the stream that had carved it this deep into the rock had descended its watershed not always by gentle degrees but at some point in a vertical torrent, there would be nowhere he could go but back. He might try climbing out on foot, but he knew he had not the strength, the skill or the experience to stay ahead of the Holy Warriors on level terms, on their own terrain. If Kadar reached him first he would tear him apart.

Twice more he turned sharp corners almost like the angles of buildings, but the bike stayed under him and he was learning now what he could and could not get away with. The bike throbbed appreciatively under him. The third time he cornered almost without slowing, banking the machine into the turn just far enough that the dust was still pinned under the tires and had no chance to skid away from him, and before the smile had time to die on his face he rode into a rockslide.

It was not a sheer wall but it might as well have been. The boulders reared shoulder-high and filled the wadi as far ahead as he could see. Kadar could not have manhandled his machine over it. Flynn might as well have tried to fly out.

The deep tread on the front tire absorbed most of the impact: when Flynn picked first himself and then the bike out of the dust he found that neither was seriously damaged. The stalled engine started again at the first stab.

He took a moment longer to work on a plan of campaign before it occurred to him that his campaign had probably already foundered and the best he could do now was stay alert for any opportunity that presented itself. If he went back quickly he might reach some alternative exit, a secondary streambed which he had not noticed joining this one, before Kadar reached him. He did not know how far back they were, only that they would still be coming—probably they knew about the rockslide—and that the longer he delayed the closer they would be.

There was no emergency exit. There was only the wadi, hemmed in by high walls, blocked at one end by the rockslide and at the other by a band of armed terrorists, some of them hardly more than children but all of them aglow with the power of their cause and of the weapons in their hands. However inexpert they were, they could not all miss him.

Perhaps he did not want them to. He did not know what to expect when they got their hands on him, but it was likely that Fahad would want to know who had helped him. He owed Hantouleh better than to tell, but he was not sure how long his resolve would last if Fahad got serious about asking. Either way he was dead: there was something to be said for getting it over with.

He had stopped when he saw them. By degrees they stopped too, rage wine-dark in their faces, the prospect of action sparkling round them like an electric halo. They looked like savage children. Flynn sat astride the big bike, revving the engine till it sang, and hoped someone would take him out before he got to the point where he had to stop or ride them down. Because he really was not sure he could do that.

Suddenly, at a honking like an asthmatic goose, the wall of young faces, young bodies, split apart and the chrome and yellow bonnet of Khalidi's long car nosed through. The man in the driver's seat Flynn had never seen before. He wondered what he had done to provoke the absolute hatred in his face, in the big fists clenched whitely on the wheel. The car's engine was revving too, a bass counterpoint to the bike's tenor wail.

Flynn breathed lightly; the relief almost made him smile. A ton of steel driven by one mad Arab he could charge with a clear conscience, with his throttle wide open and with barely a thought for what could happen then. He had almost made it. He had had his chance, and done the best he could with it; a combination of fate and manpower had beaten him. He could accept that. He knew he was going to die now. In a kind of a way he was ready. The only questions remaining were how quickly and how well.

He kicked the machine into gear—any gear—and twisted the throttle with all the determination he could muster. The front wheel came up but he stayed with it, pushing it down as the machine gathered momentum. He had maybe fifty yards to build up the speed he needed. He hoped it would be enough.

Actually there was less space than that, because the car lurched forward a split second after the bike. It made no difference, the force of the collision would still be their combined velocities. If Flynn could hold his line, ignore the screaming in his head that was the chorus of every human instinct begging him not to do this.

Up to thirty people whose prime philosophy was the destruction of people with other philosophies watched in breath-abated horror as a young man with nowhere left to go hurled himself to his own destruction. Several of the women looked away. One gasped a small scream.

In the last moment, with the engine shrieking under him and the needle racing up the speedometer, Flynn's nerve failed him. The imperative for survival, ingrained as deeply as the compulsion to breathe and no easier to override, broke through his wholly rational decision to die in an overwhelming defeat of intellect by primitive animal passion. His body, with its own older set of needs and urgencies, refused to accept his mind's judgement, refused to cooperate in its own demise and momentarily snatched control. Instead of driving head-on into the advancing bonnet, already too late he snatched the handlebars away.

The near-side edge of the car's bumper hit the hub of the bike's back wheel a blow like a pile driver, and the hard metallic sound echoed off all the surrounding cliffs. The bike flew into the air, turned wheel over wheel twice and slid a little further on its side. Flynn's body made more turns in the air than the bike, hit the sand still twisting and rolled over an impossible number of times before coming to rest in a puff of dust, facedown, long limbs spread like the sails of a windmill. Alam Habach was going to need some new clothes.

As the dust settled Fahad walked forward. Like all of them in one degree or another, what he had just seen had shocked him. Deeper than the shock, he was violently angry with Khalidi, whose vicious display of ego reinforcement had ruined a good solution to a difficult problem. No one would believe in a badly aimed IDF bullet now. Deepest of all, where he could hardly see it clearly himself, was a kind of personal, human regret for the waste that the long, still, battered figure spread-eagled on the ground represented.

A startled cry dragged his attention off Flynn and back to Khalidi. After the impact he had taken the car on down the wadi and found somewhere to turn, laboriously, with much furious shuffling. Now he was coming back—presumably, thought Fahad, to see what damage he had done, though he was a little puzzled at the speed Khalidi was building up again.

Then he realised, with a thrill of the same horror that had drawn the cry he heard from the man in the crowd behind him, what it was that Khalidi intended: not to inspect the injuries he had inflicted in the unequal joust, but to inflict some more. He was not sure that Flynn was dead yet; or if he was, that the job of identifying him had yet been rendered sufficiently grim. He meant to run the car over the top of him, probably a few times, just to make sure.

"No, confound you!" bellowed Fahad, the small man thundering bull-like in his fury, and before he or any of them guessed he had strode out of the stunned crowd and put himself between Flynn's body and the racing car. He had a moment in which to wonder what the hell he thought he was doing, risking his life for a corpse; and another to recognise that Flynn was not the issue, that the issue was his authority in his own camp and the impossibility of maintaining it if jackals from Jerusalem could wander in without a by-your-leave and usurp his decisions regarding his own prisoners; and after that there was not even time for a prayer.

The car stopped. Fahad's chest, which had swelled to meet it, deflated slowly, and when he was sure he could do it without weaving he moved round from the bumper to the driver's door. Khalidi looked up at him. His dark face was suffused with hatred, he was actually panting with rage. Fahad suspected that, at that moment at least, he was clinically mad.

He worked to keep his voice calm. "I'll talk to you later." He turned away, looking for his lieutenant. "Kadar, will you see to—?"

Kadar was already bent over the broken thing on the ground, big hands unexpectedly gentle, the hardness in his face melting visibly with grief. His voice was a broken whisper. "My bike," he murmured tragically, caressing the scarred tank and twisted forks. "My bike."

Someone else was examining Flynn, rather more briskly and without the overtone of pathos. It was Rachid Seleh Hantouleh—who had not therefore, Fahad noted without surprise, perished in the wreckage of his workshop. He put his fingers inside Flynn's collar, then looked up at Fahad. There was something like a challenge in his eyes. "He's alive."

Deliberately he turned his back on Fahad then and nodded at a little cluster of young men who had stepped out of the body of the crowd, peering. "Take him back to the camp. I'll deal with him there."

The slight emphasis on the personal pronoun was not accidental, but when he turned slowly back to gauge Fahad's reaction he found, with a mixture of relief and disappointment, that Fahad was taking no notice.

Fahad was squinting into the sky and listening. "What's that?"

[6]

The helicopters came in from three sides, the clattering thunder of their engines filling the wadis with sound that echoed and reechoed off the rock walls. The first dropped its tail on the wide riverbed that served Bab el Jihad as a parade ground, and armed troops were pouring from it before it had all its wheels on the ground. The second swept down the wadi, pushing the young Palestinians—hunters only minutes before, now the quarry—back towards their base. The third continued to circle for some moments before touching down on one of the watch cliffs, for the same reason it had been chosen for a lookout—the wide field of view it commanded.

The scene below was a chaos of running men—some in keffiyehs, some in uniform, most carrying arms of one kind or another; of shouting in two languages, of the rattle and snap of gunfire which speaks always and only its own; of the bellow of the helicopter that was still airborne, weaving wasplike over the shifting action then darting in pursuit of Khalidi's yellow car as it broke through the mêlée heading for the track.

Todd watched from the rim of the cliff. He had been about to follow the soldiers down but Simon Meir pushed him, none too gently, to the ground. "Not yet."

"If he's down there—"

"If he's down there they'll find him. Without getting their silly heads shot off."

Fahad's recruits, most of whom had never been on the receiving end of an attack before, reacted to the emergency in a manner he could be proud of. Initially they scattered, offering no obvious target for the soldiers springing battle-ready from their transports. Just by running and keeping their heads down they streamed past the soldiers, or many of them did, and gained the vantage of their caves. There they regrouped and took up their positions and did their job, which was to delay the inevitable loss of the camp and kill as many Israeli soldiers as they could before dying themselves or being captured.

They were not, for the most part, anxious that their service to the Palestinian cause should be as martyrs. Most of them were under twenty-five and were keener to fight than to die. Most of them had little interest in the complexities of Middle East history and politics: their understanding of these things began and ended with slogans. Some of them were rather stupid, some of them were evil, some of them were pathologically disturbed. Most of them were desperate for some future better than the one offered by Israel. Almost all of them were scared.

But none of them were cowards. It was fashionable in government circles to describe terrorism as cowardly, and insofar as it was a weapon in the propaganda war that might deter potential terrorists from becoming active terrorists it was legitimate enough. But it was not accurate, and people who believed the propaganda were precluded from understanding the nature of the problem. Terrorism in a civil state may be many things—cruel, cynical, selfish, vicious, pernicious and evil. But it is not easy, and it is not safe, and therefore it is not cowardly.

The young people of Bab el Jihad were not cowards. Scared enough in all conscience, but believing in the myth that said that peace in their many-promised land could only come out of the barrel of a gun, they hunched down in the mouths of the caves where they had lived, and tried to remember from their abridged training what safety catches needed removing and what muzzles needed holding down, and armed with their terrible weapons and their scant expertise they went up against the professional soldiers of the IDF who, even without taking chances, needed to kill comparatively few of them in order to bring the situation under control.

And while they were defending the last ditch, and ready to die in it, their camp commandant—who had taught them everything they knew if not everything he knew—was already halfway up the rockslide at the top of the wadi, crawling on his belly among the humped boulders, inching his way unseen and unsuspected into the safety of the wilderness.

He was proud of his young fighters and sorry to have to leave them to their hopeless task, knowing that within an hour every one of them would be either dead or in custody. But above all Fahad was a realist, and he knew that if he remained at liberty he could find another twenty-five teenagers and some more caves in the secret desert and be back in business within the month. If he stayed to fight with them he would die or go to prison with them too, and be of no further use to a cause he still lived for, though it was largely habit now.

So he scrambled low among the rocks, and hoped that Hantouleh was getting out too, and that Kadar would follow as soon as he had his warriors in place and fighting. The three of them together were the nucleus of a new Bab el Jihad, even if no one else escaped.

And Khalidi? Fahad promised himself that, if no one else killed Khalidi, as soon as he had this mess sorted out he would take the time off to do it himself.

After the first hectic minutes of running and firing, the parade ground cleared as the Palestinians withdrew to the caves and the soldiers moved from one to the next, clearing them. Only the dead and injured remained on the sand.

Meir felt Todd stiffen beside him. "Simon, that's him."

"Where?" He looked where Todd pointed, to the sprawled form that was longer than the others, lying on his back where he had been dropped at the mouth of the wadi. "Yes, you're right."

"Is he alive?"

"No way of telling, from here. It'll soon be over, Gil, we'll find out then."

Flynn was out cold for no more than the first five minutes. After that he was beginning to surface, aware of the hustle and noise around him.

None of it made much sense to him yet. He was still trying to work out which end of the sky fell on him.

Fahad's new camp was going to have to manage without Kadar. Perhaps unbalanced by the loss of his motorcycle, he forgot that his role at this point was to get the kids fighting and then get himself out. With the biggest gun in the camp in his arms, with a full magazine in the breech and two more in his pockets, he strode through Bab el Jihad looking for Jews to kill.

In the event he did not kill any. He wounded two. Then three different soldiers simultaneously identified him as the leader, the hub of the defence, the one man in the camp—on either side—who could make the difference between a brief battle and the defeated teenagers herded into a corner, and a protracted firefight after which the river sand would be thick with blood and corpses. Twelve bullets hit him in the space of about two seconds, and he was dead when he hit the ground.

Projected into the midst of a battle, Rachid Hantouleh was totally out of his depth. They had discussed, when he first moved down to the camp from Jerusalem, how they should react, as individuals and in concert, to the sudden massive threat of an imminent Israeli attack. But Hantouleh was not a soldier, not even an intellectual soldier like Meir, and all he could remember through the noise and the smells of gunsmoke and fuel oil was that he was supposed to blow up his own workshop.

He had kept a device on standby for such a purpose; unfortunately it was the one which, toned down a little, he had used to blow his door off and provide Flynn's diversion. There might have been time to jury-rig a new one, but what with the running and the shouting, the guns, the crying of the injured, and this damn great helicopter parked on the parade ground out front, Hantouleh never got his nerve and his sense of purpose together for long enough to do anything about it. Shell-shocked, directionless, he allowed himself to be rounded up along with the disarmed trainees and the unarmed housekeepers in a corner of the camp away from the last few pockets of resistance.

When the camp was secured Meir moved into the caves to lead a search. He did not expect to find much that would interest him, there had not been time for anything sophisticated to be set up between the alarm going up and the IDF dropping in. But this was Sinbad's home ground now, and if he had prepared any surprises Meir did not want some enthusiastic young soldier springing them with his boot.

The other thing he was looking for, beside the hair-thin trip wires and finely balanced pressure plates that would show Sinbad had been here, was Sinbad himself. Meir had never seen him. He had never spoken to anyone who had. He had never been given a description of Sinbad, not his age nor his height nor his build. For all Meir knew about him, he might have been a pygmy, or a sumo wrestler, or a woman. Yet he thought, on the basis of no evidence whatever, that if he saw Sinbad he would know him. Something in the eyes would give him away, like catching a glimpse of his own eyes in a mirror.

The last thing he did, before setting out to search Bab el Jihad for wires the thickness of hairs and strangely familiar eyes, was tell Todd to stay put until he was sent for. Todd nodded gravely and gave him a minute's head start.

He had no difficulty reaching the riverbed, though twice he had to explain his presence to challenging soldiers. But when he got there, the injured had already been removed and only the dead remained. There was no sign of Flynn.

Todd found a soldier who spoke English. "The man who was here. The tall man, the American. Where is he now?"

"The medics stretchered him off." The soldier pointed to the nearest helicopter. "Over there."

"He was—alive?"

"Oh, he was alive all right. He seemed to be arguing."

Todd was having trouble with his face. It kept trying to grin. He nodded his thanks and turned away before he made a fool of himself, heading for the helicopter. Arguing?—it was Flynn, all right.

It was Flynn. He would not stay on the stretcher. He had stood up with every apparent intention of leaving, but his knees had buckled and the medics had steered him into a seat, given him a towel for his bloody nose and got on with other more pressing, and more grateful, casualties.

That was how Todd found him: hunched over a bloody towel, elbows and knees protruding from tears in his borrowed clothes, grit scoured into a long graze down the right side of his jaw, his eyes a little vacant and wondering as they wandered round the inside of the helicopter, but essentially intact, all his vital parts still in working order. Todd had thought never to see him again, or never alive; instead of which he was sitting here with his bloody nose and his skinned knees like a kid trying to get the hang of his first BMX.

Todd said, "Hello, Mickey."

Flynn took a moment to find him, framed in the open door. When he did he looked pleased and surprised—but not all that surprised, rather as if they had parted in a pub and then Todd had changed his mind and come back for a last nightcap. "Hi, Gil."

Todd took a long, deep breath. He considered at some length what he was going to say—how to reflect the worry, the fear, even the danger he had been put through, the trouble and expense and danger that others had faced because of Flynn—though in fairness the brunt of that had been carried by the IDF and it was their fault he was in that position in the first place. Perhaps when they came to do their totting-up the Ministry of Defence would consider the results worth the cost.

But Todd did not. He began, "You stupid, irresponsible, arrogant, egocentric, self-indulgent, mutton-headed—"

There was plenty more where that came from. Flynn interrupted the flow with a tone of mild reproof and a gaze, clearing now, that was half apologetic and half amused. "Gil, can we save this until my nose has stopped bleeding?"

For half a minute longer Todd just looked at him. The anger, a kind of displacement for relief he could not acknowledge without admitting his affection for Flynn, rose in a silent crescendo until it threatened to blow off the top of his head. Then, almost as quickly, it subsided. "Are you all right?"

"I dunno." Flynn looked round for a medic. "Am I all right?"

"You're all right," said the man working in the helicopter on a wounded Palestinian. "In fact, you're so all right I'd quite like you to go talk to your friend somewhere else and give me a bit of elbow room for dealing with real casualties."

Flynn looked at Todd and shrugged. "You heard the man—I'm all right." Actually he was not as all right as all that, he was still plainly concussed and in an ideal world would have been having his head X-rayed and his eyes peered into. At the same time, all the indications were that he had escaped serious injury, which was more than could be said for the handful of soldiers and rather more PFLP personnel receiving attention in and around the helicopter. "Tell you what, let's get some fresh air while you tell me what you've been up to."

He climbed down carefully from the machine, grinned his evil grin and draped one long arm round Todd's shoulders. "Come on, let's get out of this dump." They turned their backs on Bab el Jihad and walked slowly, at Flynn's pace, down the desert track that left the riverbed and ran eventually to the distant road. They were not going anywhere, just walking, just letting a little peace seep into their souls after the tension of the last few days.

Meir, emerging from the largest of the dormitory caves, saw them ambling off like a couple of old men gossiping in a park and smiled to himself. He approved of happy endings. He called after them, "If you get lost you'll end up walking back to Jerusalem."

Todd said, "Right you are," and Flynn raised a hand in languid salute, neither of them looking back.

Flynn said, "How did you find me?" and Todd told him.

Flynn said, "The woman—Leila, the one who set this up. She was Mossad. I think they killed her." Todd nodded.

They reached a yellow car abandoned on the track three hundred yards up from the riverbed. Flynn pointed out a dent in the near-side wing. "It belonged to a guy called Khalidi. I don't rightly know who he was, except that he turned up just in time to knock me off a motorbike."

"I know who he is," said Todd, tight-lipped. "Do you know what happened to him?"

"I don't know what happened to anyone in the last half hour, me included."

"What happened to you before that?"

Flynn sat on the bonnet of the car, steadying himself just a little on his arms, and the grin he gave Todd was a distillation of pure joy and unholy triumph. "I'll tell you what happened to me, Gil. I got beaten up. I got hit in the back with a gun. I got roped up like a Thanksgiving turkey and hauled across miles of bad road. Then I got knocked off a motorbike by a guy in a car. And you know something? I'm OK. It hasn't moved. Sure, I'm sick, sore and tired, and when this lot stiffens up I won't move for a week. But that thing in my back's where it was all along. You know what I think? I think if it didn't move for all that, it's not going to move at all."

Like Fahad, Khalidi had taken to the hills. When they heard the thunder of helicopters coming in over the cliffs he had tried to drive out. But one of the great angry machines had spotted him and flown straight at him, up the track at about head height, and he had stopped the car then and leapt from it into the shelter of the rocks.

Nor did he go alone. Khalidi was a man who attracted enemies as a pretty girl draws admirers, and not all of them were bound by Rules of Engagement. He had always known he could be a target, never entered a dark street without half anticipating assassination. The police refused

to allow him a firearm for personal protection—a decision which, char-
acteristically, he put down to racial and religious discrimination rather
than the near certainty that any weapon owned by him would end up
killing somebody whose views ran counter to his.

So he made other arrangements. He had a secret compartment
welded into his car, secure against any search that did not actually rip
the seats out, and in it he kept a shotgun, the barrels shortened to fit,
and a box of shells. He left the car in a hurry, but not so much of a
hurry that he left his gun and ammunition behind.

Not that he had any wish to fight. He was a political man after all.
His aim, indeed his duty, was to get himself away from this débâcle and
back to Jerusalem to deal with the repercussions. His first thought was
to make his way across country until he found a road where he could,
by one means or another, get help. Then he remembered that the car
could be traced to him—he did not, of course, know that it had been
followed here—and if he was not back home soon complaining loudly
about its being stolen, any later protestations of innocence would fall
on deaf ears. Also, if it was found here it really would be searched down
to its chassis, and the shotgun-shaped compartment discovered.

But for Flynn the car would still have been parked below Fahad's cave
when the helicopters arrived, and there would have been no possibility
of retrieving it. Where it was now, out of sight of the camp a quarter of
a mile down the track, three hundred yards beyond the nearest helicopter, it was not necessarily a lost cause. There was no formal guard on it.
Watching from the rocks he saw one soldier or another occasionally
glance round at it, but now that the shouting and tumult had died so
had much of the sense of urgency. It seemed to Khalidi that if he was
stealthy, and lucky, he could be on his way with it before the car was
missed. The border with Jordan was not many miles from here: he
knew that if he could cross it he could change the car for another and
defy the police to prove he had ever been at Bab el Jihad.

He was not a brave man. He would not plunge laughingly into the
valley of the shadow of death, or at all if he could help it. But if that car
stayed where it was he was going to prison for a very long time, so the
penalty for chancing nothing would be pretty high too. On his belly
again, the gun in his hand, he began inching back towards his car.

And found Mickey Flynn sitting on the bonnet, in an attitude more
usually associated with fishing gnomes, while Gilbert Todd stood in
front regarding him in the manner of a goatherd who has just dug a
favourite nanny out of a sand dune a week after giving it up for lost.

Craning forward from his cover, Khalidi heard his own name.

"When I found out what was going on, I went to Khalidi," Todd was saying. "He offered me your life in return for Simon Meir's. He wanted me to carry a bomb into Simon's office—he knew I'd been going there, reckoned I wouldn't be searched.

"I couldn't do it. We tried to make him think I had, but luck was against us. He found out. That's when he came down here after your blood. What he didn't know was, that was what we were counting on. Ben Simeon—you don't know him, Deborah Lev's chief—had him tailed here and the helicopters standing by. It was the best anyone could do in the circumstances. I couldn't kill Simon. Maybe if he'd been someone I didn't know . . ."

Flynn slid off the bonnet and straightened, a certain dignity in the battered length of him. "No. It would take more than the likes of Khalidi to make a murderer of you."

"Hardly murder—?"

"What else? Not an accident, or misadventure. I can see it was a hell of a position to be in, but actually you had no choice."

Todd snorted. "I can't imagine why I let it worry me, then."

Flynn grinned. "Me neither. I wouldn't have."

Todd looked round as the helicopter nearest them restarted its engine. It was the one to which the injured had been taken, probably it was removing them to hospital. He shouted over the noise, "I'd forgotten how much those things smell."

The helicopter firing up gave Khalidi a chance he probably would not have again. The takeoff was a diversion that would hold the attention of anyone not otherwise engaged. The crashing noise would cover the purr of a car engine starting, and any louder sounds he had to make. Even if the car was missed, a pilot flying casualties to hospital would be reluctant to turn back to search for one escaping partisan, leaving only two helicopters at the scene. Even if the commander was willing to commit them both, it would take valuable extra moments to get them into the air.

All he had to do was move the two men from in front of the car. The quickest way was also the most satisfying, and no one would hear a thing. He took careful aim, aware that the shortening of the barrels would have affected the weapon's efficiency over this kind of range, and let his finger curl sensuously around the trigger.

Even close up the blast was not much more than a hiccup, perhaps a backfire, in the helicopter's roar. But something hit Mickey Flynn from behind hard enough to thrust him bodily into Todd's surprised arms.

Flynn looked surprised too, and his eyes were glazing. He coughed and a fleck of blood appeared at the corner of his mouth. In a shocked whisper he said, "Oh Gil. Oh shit."

Then his eyes closed and his long body slumped limp against Todd's, and as Todd lowered him carefully to the ground, still with no idea what had happened, he saw that the back of Flynn's shirt and the flesh of his back were chewed up in a bloody farrago in which glinted seeds of dull lead and the white of bone.

[7]

When Meir was confident that the caves were safe to search, he left the soldiers to continue under their own officer and went to look at the workshop which had blown up, sending up the plume of smoke which had guided them here like Moses following the pillar of cloud.

But in fact the cave had not blown up. An explosion had certainly occurred inside, and the door had certainly flown off and landed, like an elderly pterodactyl lacking an airworthiness certificate, twenty feet away. But inside the damage was surprisingly limited—suspiciously limited if this was supposed to have been an accident.

The shock wave had broken a lot of glass and there was a mess on the floor, but there had been no fire and many of the chemicals on shelves round the walls and other materials stuffed into plastic dustbins had suffered no ill effects. Someone standing near the door when the thing went up might have been knocked to the ground, but should then have been able to get up and hurry away. Meir had seen the consequences of a lot of bombs, both timely and untimely in their detonation, and they did not look like this.

He looked up then, drawn by some instinct he could not name, and saw a man watching him from among the prisoners, and he had never seen the man before but it was like meeting his own eyes in a mirror.

The man looked away. Meir left the smoke-blackened cave and crossed the riverbed and, excusing himself to the sergeant of the guard, went up to the man. He said, quite quietly, without obvious triumph, "I'm Simon Meir. You're Sinbad, aren't you?"

About then the helicopter engine started up. Automatically, like everyone else, Meir glanced at it. Then he remembered Flynn who had gone for a stroll that way with his partner. If anyone both could and would identify the explosives expert they called Sinbad, it was Flynn. Failing that Meir would have to wait for forensic tests on the man's hands to confirm what he already knew.

He smiled at Hantouleh. "Don't go away." He walked down the riverbed and took the narrower track as the helicopter lurched upwards on its mercy run.

Khalidi made two serious mistakes. He did not allow sufficiently for the force of the downdraft hitting him as the helicopter took off, and his second barrel which should have done to Todd's face what his first did to Flynn's back was pushed aside by just the few degrees that made it discharge harmlessly into the dust instead.

His second mistake was to assume that he could reload the gun with cartridges from his pocket before Todd could cross thirty yards of rough ground and stop him. It must have seemed a safe enough gamble. Todd was a lot older than Khalidi, and a lot fatter, and he had just had his partner die in his arms, and the first he had known that Khalidi was there was when he looked up from the butchery at his feet after the second, abortive shot sent dust puffing into the air beside him. Khalidi had only to break the gun, take two shells from his pocket, thumb them into the breech and snap it shut. It would take less time to do than to describe, and if Todd had unfrozen enough by then to take a few steps towards him, it would just make it harder for Khalidi to miss.

Keeping his weapon in a concealed compartment in his car perhaps meant that Khalidi was less familiar with the handling of it than he might have been. All the same he was not noticeably slow. He did not drop anything, or try to put the cartridges in back to front, or catch his thumb in the breech as he snapped it shut. But Todd was coming at him sooner, and faster, than he had any reason to expect, strength and hatred driving his thick limbs, his broad face set in a mask of absolute determination. His lungs would have burst before he abandoned his race for Khalidi's throat.

He had no weapon, or anything that could be used as a weapon. His unlikely disguise as a soldier stopped far short of the rifles carried by the genuine article, or even the small-arm strapped on for the occasion by Meir who normally carried little more than a pocket-sized roll of non-ferrous tools. All Todd had were his own two hands and his fury.

Insofar as he was thinking at all, he was sure they would be enough. He hurtled up the shingle slope, hurdling the intervening rocks, and was within just a couple of strides of Khalidi, still kneeling on the ground, when Khalidi—sweating with haste and concentration—got the gun reloaded and snapped it shut.

Khalidi had time, if not much to spare, to aim the gun and fire it, and take the centre of Todd's chest out as he vaulted the last boulder at him. But finally he made a mistake. The speed with which Todd was closing the distance between them, and the murderous intensity of him, panicked Khalidi into a bad decision. Instead of taking a proper aim, he attempted to save a second by firing from the hip.

It might have paid off. If he had been calmer. If he had been standing up. If he had ever done it before, and had a clearer idea of what he had to do. But holding the gun one-handed he pulled the trigger too early, while the abbreviated barrels were still pointing skyward. The densely packed shot missed Todd by a yard, and Khalidi's sketchy grasp of the weapon was inadequate to absorb the recoil. The heavy stock rammed backwards with almost as much force as the shot flew forward, and it struck Khalidi in the thigh with a vicious blow that broke the bone.

The discharge, the sickening crack of breaking bone and Khalidi's yell of agony came in such quick succession that they merged, so far as Todd was concerned, into a wholly (if unholy) pleasing litany of violence. He reached Khalidi as the injured man fell back, his right leg above the knee twisting improbably, the gun falling from his right hand, his face screwed up in shock and pain. For a space of seconds the only sounds, apart from the receding helicopter and the bustle of the distant unseen camp, were the heaving of Todd's lungs and a low, eerie, hackle-pricking keen in the back of Khalidi's throat.

Then Todd bent over, quite slowly, and picked up the gun. He broke it open and saw the second, unfired cartridge in the breech. He closed it again. He regarded Khalidi thoughtfully. There was nothing in his face to indicate what was happening behind it. There was nothing in his eyes to suggest what he would do next. There was nothing in his eyes—a terrible nothing, an inhuman absence of emotion. Khalidi saw his eyes and whimpered.

Todd said, "Almost the last thing Mickey Flynn said to me before you killed him was it would take more than the likes of you to make a murderer of me. You want to know something? He was wrong."

Meir, coming up the track from Bab el Jihad, could not see Flynn's sprawled body for the stationary car, could not see Khalidi three-quarters prone among the rocks. He saw Todd standing still on the slope, his head bent, a sawn-off shotgun hanging slack at the end of his arm, and heard the low toneless murmur of his voice. Neither what he saw nor what he heard made any sense, but his spine pricked with an awareness of infinite menace.

"Gil? What's happened?"

Todd did not look round. Either he knew it was Meir or he did not care who it was. "It's Khalidi. He killed Mickey. Just now—shot him in the back with this thing." The heavy gun twitched in his hand.

"What?" Meir hurried towards him, past the car, and almost tripped over the blood-soaked figure in the dust in front of the bonnet. He looked down, then up again, appalled. His voice was hollow with foreboding. "Gil, what are you doing?"

"I'm going to kill him." He might have been announcing, after due deliberation, what colour he was going to paint his kitchen. "He killed Mickey, and I'm going to use this same gun to blow his head off."

"Gil, no." Meir did not doubt for an instant that Todd meant it. He groped for the words to stop him. "This is not your way. There is no justice in this."

"Justice?" Todd took his eyes off Khalidi cowering among the stones for the least moment necessary to flick Meir a glance of profound, almost disbelieving contempt. "For him? He tried to kill you. He tried to kill me. He kept trying to kill Mickey until he finally made it. Justice for him doesn't come out of a courtroom. It comes out of this second barrel of his own gun."

"It doesn't matter what happens to him," said Meir. Urgency was supplanting some of the horror in his voice. "What matters is what happens to you. Scum like that isn't worth pawning the rest of your life for."

"The rest of my life? I don't think any court in Israel is going to put that sort of price on Khalidi's head. I might get a free pardon. I might get a medal."

"I'm not thinking of the courts. I'm thinking about you, and how you're going to feel about this when your blood has cooled and your head's working properly again. You're a rational man, Gil, an ethical man. If you do this you'll make a scourge to flay yourself with every time you think of Mickey. He wouldn't want that, you know. He wouldn't do it, if Khalidi had shot you."

"Damn you, Meir!" Behind the contempt and the quiet fury it sounded as if his heart was breaking. "I don't need you to tell me what Mickey Flynn would and wouldn't do! I don't even care that you're right. I want the bastard!"

"I want him too, but not this way. Not if your soul is the price of it. Leave him to the law, Gil. The law is what the last forty years have been about, and why there was a job worth doing for you here. I've read what you wrote, I know you believe in law—if you do this now you'll make a mockery of it. What you've done, what Mickey did—it will count for nothing if you blast that garbage now. Don't waste it, Gil. It was too good to be wasted. Give me the gun."

The fingers of his left hand reached out slowly, carefully, towards Khalidi's secret weapon that was likely to prove his undoing. The fingers of his right hand were, conversely, at his belt.

Todd looked down at the heavy gun, still hanging leaden in his hand. As if by an effort of will and muscle he raised the barrels, just enough to find the man on the ground. "Like hell."

Obscenely, Khalidi began praying.

"Gil, give it to me." Meir had his own pistol in his hand. It pointed neither at Todd nor very far away.

"No."

The shot jolted all three of them. It jolted Khalidi because it hit him, just left of his sternum, and tore through the powerful, delicate chambers of his heart so that his life's blood flooded disastrously into his chest cavity; and if he was not dead when he slumped back with a soft thump on the hard ground, dark face and white eyes staring wildly at the brassy sky, he was certainly dead soon afterwards.

The same shot jolted Todd because he had not fired it, and Meir because he had.

Todd stared at the folded, deeply inert body at his feet as if he really could not believe the neat round hole that had appeared, black and only slightly bloody, in the middle of its chest. He looked too at Khalidi's gun in his own hand, as if to reassure himself that it was, as he thought, a shotgun and still with one barrel to fire.

Then he looked at Meir, who was returning his small arm quietly to its holster. There was an extraordinary calm, almost peaceful dignity about the man, and if there was sorrow in his face there was no regret.

Todd found a strange gravelly voice and said, "Why?"

Meir ghosted him a smile. "Because if I hadn't shot him, you would have. This is neater. Give me the gun." He took the shotgun and bent over Khalidi, pressing it into his dead hand. "There. That's what happened."

"W–what?"

"He shot Mickey, you fought for the gun, he got it, I shot him before he could shoot you." With the helicopter away, that last pistol shot had been heard in the camp. Soldiers were hurrying up the track towards them. Meir caught Todd's eye. "Try to remember that."

Todd blinked. Reaction was setting in: he could feel the tremor beginning in the calves of his legs. "I don't understand. The law, that the last forty years have been about—?"

Meir smiled, as if at a willing but sightly backward child. "Sometimes, Gil, it comes down to basics, and the most basic rule of all is that the good guys have to win."

Meir explained briefly to the officer commanding and, at least for the moment, that seemed to be that. Todd went along with it. He decided he would be mad not to. Khalidi had come here to kill, and had succeeded, and had been ready to kill again in order to leave. Instead he had himself been killed. The precise manner of it may not have been lawful, but it was as near justice as made any difference.

In the wake of the soldiers came the medics. A quick glance over Khalidi's body told them all they needed to know. "Nice shooting, Major. We won't waste so much as an Elastoplast on this one."

They moved round in front of the car and Todd looked away. So the sudden flurry of activity took him by surprise. He spun round, and the man kneeling by the bumper looked up as Todd looked down.

"I thought you said he was dead?"

Five minutes later they were in the air, thirty minutes later the helicopter touched down in the grounds of the Hadassah Medical Centre in West Jerusalem. Soon after that Flynn was in surgery.

Todd sat hunched in a waiting area, almost totally unaware of the passage of time. At intervals Meir pressed plastic cups of coffee into his hand, and he held each of them for a minute before putting it down to go cold along with the others.

He had been told that Flynn's condition was critical. He had been told, as if he did not know, that Flynn had lost a lot of blood, and that he had not been in the best shape to withstand such an injury to start with. But he was told (by the nurses) that the Medical Centre had some of the best trauma doctors in the world, and (by the doctors) that the standard of nursing here was second to none. The fact that Flynn had made it this far was a very real cause for hope. Patients had to try harder to die here than almost anywhere else on earth.

"That's quite true, you know," said Meir. "There isn't a hospital anywhere—not in London, not in Europe, not in the States, just maybe in Belfast—that's had as much experience in these kinds of injuries. for obvious reasons, of course."

Todd said, "Do you know what the hardest part is?"

Meir nodded. "It's going over and over the same damn facts, trying to see what you could have done differently so that things would have worked out better. And failing."

When the surgeon came from the theatre, still wearing his green pillbox and drying his hands, Todd thought at first it must be the intensity of his own hoping that was investing this rather large young man with a quite inappropriate aura of jollity. It was not conceivable that his cheeks were genuinely ruddy with good humour, his eyes sparkling with satisfaction, an actual spring in the step of his rather large and outward-turning feet.

Besides, if he had believed that those were more than figments of his anxious imagination, he would have been obliged to believe too in the badge the surgeon was sporting on the breast pocket of his white coat, which said—in English—"Doctors do it three times a day, after meals."

"I'll put you out of your misery right away," said the surgeon cheerfully. "He's going to be fine. We've taken enough lead out of his back to ballast a Flying Dutchman, and he's taken damn near enough blood to sail one in, but he's stable and he's safe, and tomorrow he'll be awake, and by the end of the week he'll be sufficiently recovered to be interested in this." He held out the flat of his hand, radiating smugness.

Todd could not identify the nondescript fragment lying there. It was too small, too rough and irregular in shape. All he could say for sure was that it was not a shotgun pellet. "What is it?"

If the surgeon had been any happier he would have been giggling. "It's a bit of bone. We found it nestling among his articular processes where, since it's not a bit of his backbone, it had absolutely no right to be, and the funny thing was it wasn't put there by today's episode. It looked as if it had been there for weeks. I presume it dates back to that first bullet wound and the broken clavicle. His back must have been giving him gyp."

Todd stared in horrid fascination at the shard. He could not believe anything so tiny could have been responsible for everything that had happened since Amsterdam. It was the sort of chip you might get stuck in your teeth from eating a chop. For the first time he understood Dr. Van Rijn's difficulty in tracking it down. "How did you find it?"

"Mostly luck," the surgeon admitted blithely. "A pellet ended up in damn near the same place, and it's a lot easier to pinpoint a bit of lead than a sliver of bone. I didn't even see it—I felt it shift under the point of the scalpel. So I hoked it out. He'll be a lot better without it."

Still Todd could not take his eyes off the thing. "You'll never know just how close that came to killing him."

The surgeon looked doubtful. "Oh, I don't think it would have killed him. It could have given him a lot of pain over a lot of years, but I don't think it would have threatened his life."

"That's not what I meant. The only reason he was in Israel, for one lot to set up and the other lot to shoot down, was that he couldn't face the kind of life he thought it was going to leave him with. He came here, and went with the PFLP, because he didn't reckon he had anything much to lose."

The surgeon thought about that, his broad cheeks creasing like a pensive cherub's. "Then I suppose you'd have to consider the possibility that the man who pumped him full of lead-shot actually saved his life."

[8]

The first time Flynn was aware of Todd sitting reading by his bed was in fact the third time he had been there. Mostly this was a reflection on Flynn's somewhat woolly state of consciousness heretofore, but it might also have had something to do with his position on the bed: facedown with a pillow under his chest, so that the vista to which he slowly woke was composed entirely of white sheeting. There was a sheet over the lower half of him too, turned back at his waist. The whole of his back was covered by a dressing. Since he could not move his head without flexing his back, and flexing his back hurt, the first few times he woke up he made a point of keeping still until he went back to sleep. It was never more than a few minutes, sometimes only seconds.

But then by degrees life began to reclaim him. He found himself listening to and making sense of the sounds of the hospital around him: footsteps on the vinyl floor, brisk for the nurses and slow for the patients; the distinctive rubbery squeak of wheelchair tires—he was not about to forget that one—and the rattle of curtain tracks; and voices, none of which he recognised.

After that he explored, not very energetically, the world of sensation: the cool of the sheet over his legs, the way the pillow had knotted under his chest, the firm pressure of the bandages against his back that increased fractionally in rhythm with his breathing; and as if at one remove, like a fire behind glass, the pain beneath the bandage that he knew was raging there but which he could feel only as a broad, unfocused distress, like mild sunburn. He thought to himself, quite lucidly, "They must have given me something for it."

Finally his rediscovery of the world reached the point where he had to take the risks inherent in opening his eyes and having a proper look round. It hurt a little, not very much. That was when he saw Todd ensconced in an armchair by his right shoulder. He thought at first Todd was reading the newspaper on his knee. Then he saw he was doing the crossword. He murmured, "Word of greeting, five letters." He thought this enormously witty and was really quite proud of himself.

Todd looked up, and the smile split his face from ear to ear. "Hello yourself."

"What happened?"

"You were shot."

"Again?" He sounded indignant.

"Khalidi this time. With a shotgun."

Flynn appeared to consider this. "Did he shoot you too, or am I still alive?"

There was nowhere for Todd's grin to expand except into his voice. "Oh, you're alive, my boy. You're going to be fine. I mean really, you're going to be OK." He explained about the pellet that had lodged itself against Flynn's spine, and the extranumery bone that had moved under the surgeon's scalpel.

Whether he could not believe it, or whether it was just morbid curiosity, Flynn wanted to see the shard. It was in a glass bottle in the locker: Todd passed it to him without comment. Flynn turned it in his fingers in front of his face. Then, fractionally, he shook his head.

"He's putting you on," he said with conviction. "That little thing? It should be about three feet long."

"Is that what it felt like?"

"No, it felt bigger, but logic dictated it couldn't be. Anyhow, us Americans are known for exaggerating."

And us Brits are known for our reserve, thought Todd, for stiff upper lips that stretch from our bald spots to our bunions. So why do I want to dance and sing like a red Indian, and hug and kiss everyone involved from the chubby surgeon to the porter in the hall who'll kick the drinks machine when it doesn't want to do coffee? I could understand it if he was my son, or a woman I cared for. But Flynn? What's he to me, or me to him come to that? Colleagues, partners, I suppose friends. Friends?—I was ready to *kill* a man when I thought he'd killed Mickey! Is that friendship? My God, is it love? Is there actually a difference?

Thinking these deep thoughts way down out of sight, for being a reserved Brit Todd would die before he would admit to an emotional range of any complexity, and particularly caring for another man with the same fondness some other Brit might feel for his dog, he said, "Well, it's out of your way now. Your back's going to look like a weather map, but scars should be all you're left with."

"No pain?"

"No reason to suppose so."

"None?"

"Hell, I don't know, Mickey. Talk to the man with the funny badge. As I understand him, the wounds will heal and after that you might get the odd twinge in cold weather but then which of us doesn't? You're OK, Mickey. The nightmare's over."

Flynn's eyes closed. After a moment Todd saw that the lashes were wet. He looked for some undamaged part of him to which he could give a comforting pat, found a small area between the bruises on his forearm. "It's all right, Mickey. Don't cry."

"I am *not* crying," said Flynn indignantly, but there was a damp spot on the sheet under his face.

Some time later Todd pushed his chair back and stood up, stretching. "I'm going to round up some dinner. I'll hardly get back this evening so I'll see you tomorrow. I must give Leah Shimoni a ring, let her know how things worked out. She's a nice kid, she'll be glad to know you're all right. I'll put out a few feelers for her. Her chance will come."

"No," said Flynn.

Todd did not understand. "What do you mean? I have to call her, I promised—last she heard you'd vanished into the Negev and I was waiting to hear from Khalidi. My God, that's two days ago. Never mind *you,* she must think *I'm* dead. What did you mean, no?"

Flynn made no attempt to look up at him. "Gil, don't be making any plans. Not for me."

"For you, for me—what odds? I know it won't be tomorrow, but we need to plan where we go from here. I think we may have worn out our welcome in Israel." It was mostly bluster: he knew Flynn had something to say that he did not want to hear. He thought if he ignored it, it might go away.

Flynn rested his forehead on the cool sheet and shut his eyes. "Gil, I'm tired and I'm sore, and I'm not up to having this conversation right now. Tomorrow, maybe. But we have things to sort out, and until they're sorted you don't make any arrangements involving me. Call Shimoni, tell her I'm fine and thanks for asking. Tell her you'll call her back in a day or two. After—"

"Mickey?"

"After your old partner decides whether you still need a new one."

Todd worried his way through a solitary dinner, called Shimoni to apologise for not calling before and promised to call back later, and went to bed still worrying.

During the night, however, he decided he was giving too much weight to the words of a man who had been living on painkillers for three months. After the latest episode, God alone knew what was circulating in Flynn's bloodstream. Just because he sounded lucid did not mean he knew what he was saying.

The next day seemed to confirm that assessment. Todd spent thirty minutes with Flynn during the afternoon and Flynn made no reference to the exchange of the previous day. They talked—lightly, of inconsequential things like hospital food and American football, avoiding the serious stuff as if by mutual consent—and Flynn was a lot clearer-headed and Todd thought perhaps he had forgotten what he had said, or else remembered and was embarrassed by it and anxious not to speak of it further.

Flynn had not forgotten, nor was he embarrassed. He was waiting for a suitable time to tell Todd what he had decided—when he could tell him face to face, eye to eye, not lying helplessly prone on a bed, having to crank his head round to make any attempt at eye contact, having Todd talk down to him literally as well as metaphorically. What he had to say was important, and difficult, and needed to be done with dignity as between free equals. It would be hard enough without having to lie facedown on a sheet like a man arguing with his masseur. He was waiting for the doctor to let him get up.

When Todd walked into the ward and saw Flynn waiting for him in a chair, approximately if not formally dressed with a T-shirt pulled over his bandages, and when Flynn rose to greet him—slowly and carefully, but hardly more so than could be explained by a good hangover—and he saw the quiet determination like a challenge in Flynn's eyes, he knew that the showdown was coming after all. He still did not know what it was about.

Flynn said, "I'm getting out of here next week. I want you to run me to the airport."

"Sure," Todd agreed readily. "Where are we going?"

In other circumstances Flynn would have found it hard not to smile at the assumption in that. Now, knowing the hurt he was about to inflict, there was no such temptation. "We're going nowhere. I'm going home."

Todd was confused. "London?"

"In the first place, I guess. I'll lie up a few weeks, get my breath back. Answer whatever questions the police forces of two countries may have about divers attempts to murder me. But then I'm really going home. To New York."

The brows pulled low over his eyes, Todd looked both puzzled and impatient. "New York? There's nothing for us to do there."

"Gil," growled Flynn, his voice thick with a kind of low passion, "will you try to understand? Or failing that, will you at least listen? I'm not going there to work, I'm going because it's my home, the town I come from. And I'm going alone."

Todd was surprised both at his decision and at the vehemence of his tone, but he was prepared to be generous, to put it down to the still fragile state of his health. "OK, Mickey. You want to go home, go home. Take a break—I'll take one too, God knows it's long enough since we had a proper holiday, phones off the hook, TV plugged out and the papers cancelled. Take three months—hell, take six if you can stick it that long. Get yourself fit again. Then give me a call and we'll—"

"Christ almighty, Gil," exploded Flynn, "what is it with you? We're not married, I don't have to file for a divorce. I'm dissolving the partnership. We're not going to be working together anymore. Fix something up with Shimoni, she'll do a good job for you—she's a better photographer than I was when we started."

"You weren't a photographer at all until I made you into one," Todd said tartly. He was beginning to understand that Flynn was serious about this, and the realisation was fuelling feelings of anger and panic.

"You gave me a job, Gil, that's all. No, to be fair, you gave me a career, and it's been profitable and mostly it's been fun and I'm grateful. But you didn't buy me, and you didn't adopt me. I'm not your child, not your heir; and I'm sure as hell not your cocker spaniel. You don't whistle me to heel."

"What are you talking about?" Todd's voice was rough, disparaging and defensive.

"You," snarled Flynn. "You buy people, and you use them. You don't want a partner, you want a property—like your car phone, like your word processor. Need a photographer?—sure, you always know where to pick up a bargain. It might need knocking into shape a bit, drying out, tuning up, but once it's working properly you'll have it forever. As long as you remember to switch it off and put it away tidily when you're not using it."

Now that it was coming it was coming fast: the resentment that he had allowed to build up because he had not had the heart to tackle it when he should have done, two or even three years ago. It had been easier to go along, let Todd play Great White Chief if he wanted to. Not until now had he realised how much sheer anger being treated like Todd's gopher had cost him. Now he was finally giving voice to it, the problem would be stopping before he destroyed the past as well as the future.

Todd spluttered, "I don't know what you mean. If it hadn't been for me—"

"Exactly!" Flynn was panting with frustration. "I've been hearing that for four years: hearing it, and seeing it in your eyes, and smelling it, and eating it. If it hadn't been for you I'd have drunk myself to death on the waterfront. If it hadn't been for you I'd never have amounted to anything. Hell, you pick a guy out of the gutter like that, make a name for him, I guess you got some equity in the rest of his life. You got the right to stop him chucking it away while it might still be some use to you!"

Their voices were sufficiently raised now to be attracting attention. Neither of them was aware of it.

"Mickey! I have never—!"

"Gil, you had no right. No right to follow me back here, no right to try and stop me. It was my choice: you had no right to try and take it away from me."

"You could be dead now!"

"Maybe. That was my risk to take, not yours to deny me. You think I don't know it was my life I was playing with? I expected to die. It was what I wanted—what I needed. If it weren't for the freak chance of a surgeon digging lead out of my back coming across the thing that was crucifying me, it might still be the only future I'd want to face."

"Suicide?—because that's what you're talking about." Todd shook his head. "It was too soon to make any decision that permanent. You weren't strong enough."

"Of course I wasn't! If I'd been stronger, there'd have been no need!" He tried to marshal his argument, to explain what he had felt, what he felt now. "You don't know what it was like—what that bastard was doing to me. I couldn't have lived like that. What I did was the quickest, easiest and cheapest way I could find of establishing whether it was going to cripple me or not; and resolving the problem if it was, and maybe leaving some good shots for the closing credits as well. You had no right to interfere in that. You were lucky, Gil, that things turned out how they did; but that still doesn't make you right."

"I was lucky? Mickey, you're twenty-eight years old! You've another fifty years' living to do. You damn nearly threw that away. You want me to apologise for saving your life? I'm not going to."

"Of course you're not. When did you ever admit to being wrong about anything?"

"Now you really do sound like my wife."

They glared at one another, nose to nose, and gradually all the temper went out of the exchange. Flynn sighed. "You don't have the least idea what I'm talking about, do you?"

That made it easy. All Todd had to do was shake his head, plead ignorance, bluff it out, and Flynn would roll long-suffering eyes at the ceiling but at least this awful emotional razor-fight would be over and they could part—he accepted now that they would part—in some residual degree of friendship. He would never forget, or forgive, what Flynn had said but he could manage a pretence until Flynn was ready to leave. All he had to do was confirm that what Flynn was saying made no sense to him. He took a slow breath.

"Actually," he said, "I know exactly what you're saying. You're saying that I take people over—that I took you over. You're saying I've played God with your life over and beyond any duty we owed each other, either as partners or as friends." He nodded. "You're right, I have. From necessity to start with—you needed somebody to sort you out those first few months—then I suppose from habit. If it bothered you, you should have said something before now.

"But I'm not sorry I didn't let you ride off into the sunset when a blind man could see you were in no condition to be making that kind of decision. The state you were in, I wouldn't have let you choose a new wallpaper, let alone choose to die.

"It wasn't luck when that shard of bone came out of your back along with the lead-shot. It was vindication. It was proof that I was right and you were wrong. You were willing to throw away the chance that you would get better because you couldn't face the possibility that you could get worse. Maybe that's what you need friends for, to take decisions you haven't the courage to take for yourself. Nothing you can say will make me regret what I did. I'm sorry if you feel I trespassed somewhere private, but I have to say I'd do the same again tomorrow."

"And if I'd spent fifty years on my back because of it?"

"You wouldn't have. You said yourself, the hammering you took, anything it was going to do it would have done then."

"But if I had?"

"In that case," snapped Todd, his patience fraying, "I might have expected to have to deal with this kind of recrimination. I might have thought it rather childish, but not altogether inexcusable from a man with no future and no hope. What I find harder to understand is the same recrimination from a man who's well on the way to recovery instead of occupying a mortuary slab, thanks in some small measure to my having indeed committed the heinous crime of which I am accused, which is caring what happens to you!" He finished with a rush and a furious glare.

And found Flynn laughing at him, softly gently laughing. Of all the facets to Flynn's complex and highly individual personality, Todd found that strange attractive gentleness hardest to reconcile. When it came, as it often did, in quick succession to the evil grin, it left him mentally floundering, like a glider pilot in thick cloud wondering which way is up. "Gil, I'm going to miss you."

As always Todd found it impossible to change tempo quick enough to keep up with Flynn. It was a moment longer before he could say quietly, "Then why go? We could do things—differently—"

Flynn shook his head but there was no longer any rancour in it. "It's time, Gil, that's all. I need some space to myself now. It's not your fault, nothing you've done." He grinned. "Not beyond being who you are, anyway. It's not even what's happened. I think it's just time—to move on, break new ground, God knows what but something. Time for a change."

Todd regarded him soberly. "You're sure. I can wait."

Flynn's grin was wicked. "You've been reading Barbara Cartland again, haven't you? No, I'm sure. Call Shimoni, work out a deal with her. And for God's sake, don't treat her like a ten-year-old with pigtails and her first Instamatic. Not everyone is as patient as me."

Todd was aware of having lost: lost the argument, lost his grip on Flynn, yet somehow not lost everything. Amazingly in view of the things that had been said, the friendship seemed to have survived— battered, bloody and bowed but still essentially intact. Rather like Flynn himself. You could not call that a defeat: maybe a draw.

"All right," said Todd, quietly ending four years and one of the legends of the international news circuit. "On two conditions."

Flynn laughed, relieved and exasperated in equal measures. "Damn it, Gil—"

"I know, I have no right. All the same, two conditions."

"Which are?"

"One, you stay off the bottle and out of The Longshoreman. I didn't go to all that trouble so you could end up in the same place in the same state, just four years older."

"I'll stay off the bottle," Flynn agreed solemnly. "The other?"

"Any time you need help, you come to me first."

Flynn smiled. "You really don't think I can manage without you, do you?"

"Your word."

"You got it."

"Good enough." Todd frowned. "Just one thing, though. If you're going to be running your own life from here on out, making your own decisions, going your own way, maybe you should start getting some practice. You think?"

"I guess." Flynn was puzzled. "What?"

Todd grinned, a grin as wicked as one of Flynn's, a distillation of pure mischief not wholly untouched by malice, that sparkled in his eyes like wine. "Take a taxi to the airport."

He turned on his heel, quite jauntily, and walked away down the ward, a sturdy slightly rumpled figure waving a laconic farewell over his shoulder without looking round. It took all the strength Flynn could muster not to call him back. He did not know if he would see Todd again.

[9]

Before Flynn left Israel, he had one last task to perform. Simon Meir collected him from the hospital. A detective inspector met them outside the Holding Centre and Rachid Seleh Hantouleh was waiting in an interview room inside.

He had been in custody for a fortnight. It felt both more and less than that: much, much more than a fortnight since he had been free, since he had had his work and his workshop, since the darkest cloud on his horizon was whether he got the respect his status demanded; but less than fourteen days because all the days ran together here, a great long waking day punctuated by meals and periods with the lights out, and periods of interrogation specifically timed to interrupt any sleep he might somehow have snared.

The prospect of interrogation had frightened him. He had heard the stories, both the versions put out by the propagandists and those quietly circulated among men who knew from personal experience, and he had always doubted—if it came to this, which he had hoped to God it would not—his ability to do what the manual recommended, take everything that was thrown at him and say nothing. He had never deceived himself that he was a brave man.

In the event, though, the hardest part of the interrogation was not what was done to him—at least so far he had suffered no actual physical abuse. It had been threatened, both tacitly and overtly, but to date the worst assault he had been subjected to was a bit of pushing and shoving. Even the disturbed nights did not bother him too much—he could not sleep when he was left to, the place was never quiet enough and neither was his mind. He lay in the darkness, listening—to the creeping silence in those odd minutes when there was nothing else—and thought about what twenty-five years each of twenty-six fortnights like this would be like.

The part he found hardest was saying nothing. He could not imagine why. As long as no one was beating answers out of you, or feeding your fingers to the power points, it seemed the simplest, the safest, the most obvious way to deal with the questions. No answers he could give would do him any good anyway. So he did not understand why, when men whose motives and morality he did not share asked him to betray himself and his friends, and asked for the most part with little or no serious intimidation, he had to fight the urge to answer until the sweat stood out on his brow.

That was the fear that rode him now when he was brought to one of these little blind barely furnished interview rooms: that one day, out of weariness or boredom or sheer force of habit, someone would ask him a question—perhaps a quite innocuous question, just something to lubricate his throat—and before he knew what he was doing he would have answered it, and the floodgates would stand open.

So when he heard footsteps at the door, and the door open, he sat still with the muscles of his jaw tight and his eyes cast down at the floor, and if it was not fear pushing his heartbeat up it might as well have been.

Someone said, "Hello, Rachid," and he recognised both the accent and the voice, and his eyes flew up in surprise and trepidation.

He had not seen Flynn shot down. But it had been common knowledge among the prisoners that Khalidi's last act in this world had been to pump lead into him from a sawn-off shotgun, and he had not supposed Flynn would have survived such an attack. He had been sorry—sorrier about Flynn than Khalidi, anyway—but his own problems had prevented him from dwelling on it. Now he stammered, "I thought you were dead."

Flynn gave him half a grin. "Reports were greatly exaggerated." From Hantouleh's blank expression he inferred that Mark Twain was not required Palestinian reading.

Before Hantouleh had recovered from the shock of seeing Flynn again he knew why he was here. It was those twenty-five years the Jews wanted him to serve, that they could only give him if they could prove he was Sinbad, the man responsible for so many bombs and so many deaths. They knew he was—Simon Meir had known the moment he saw him—but they could not prove it. He had been careful: he had left his signature on his devices but no fingerprints. Forensic tests showed he had handled explosives, but could not determine between a casual encounter and a long-term commitment. Virtually everyone arrested at Bab el Jihad had tested positive, including one of the housekeepers.

They knew he was Sinbad. They could prove he could have been. What they needed now was either a confession—he *had* to stay silent, whatever they did; even if they hurt him, it could not be worth the extra fifteen years a confession would cost him—or someone else to swear to his role. Of the twenty-three people arrested at Bab el Jihad, all of them facing prison and none of them keener on the prospect than he was, Hantouleh could not believe that no one had traded his identity for a few years remission. But no one had, not yet. His comrades, his friends, had closed round him a protective ring of silence.

Flynn was neither a comrade nor a friend. Flynn owed no allegiance to the Palestinian cause or its soldiers. Yet surely to God he might recognise a personal debt to Hantouleh? Hantouleh had rescued him, first from the depths of his pain, then—and at some risk to himself— from the imprisonment which had seemed certain to end in his death. Nothing that happened afterward, not the IDF raid nor Khalidi's murderous attack, could detract from the fact that Hantouleh had swung out over the abyss to help Flynn. Was it too much to hope that Flynn might do the same for him?

He met Flynn's eyes. He said cautiously, "You are looking better."

"Yeah. I've had some good doctors."

A tiny, sharp-taloned hope clawed at Hantouleh's heart. Was it only words, or was Flynn acknowledging that debt? Currents passed between them, full of potential and no specifics. With the soldier and the policeman there too, Hantouleh dared not ask. But surely Flynn could see the difficulty he faced, and how small a lie would rescue him from it.

He said, as lightly as he could, "Did you tell these people that I— tried to help you?"

Flynn inclined his head. "I told them. I told them you got me through when my back was killing me. And that you tried to get me out when Fahad meant to."

Hantouleh nodded slowly. "Thank you. It might save me a little time in prison." His eyes were searching Flynn's, trying to establish some sort of communication, trying to signal his need.

"I hope so," said Flynn. "It'd make me feel better about telling them the rest of it."

Hantouleh's eyes slowly saucered, his voice sank to a horrified whisper. "The rest?" Don't do this, his eyes said, please don't do this to me. I looked after you when you were hurt and in danger: don't do this to me now.

Flynn said, "About the workshop. About the bombs you made there. About the photographs I took of you making them, that are on their way back from New York. With those photographs and my testimony, you're going to be in prison until you're an old man. I'm sorry, Rachid."

The policeman cleared his throat. "Can I take it then, Mr. Flynn, that you are identifying this man as Rachid Seleh Hantouleh, known to you as the bomb-maker at Bab el Jihad, believed by you to be responsible for numerous explosive devices constructed for the PFLP over a period of time?"

Flynn said, "Yes." Something inside Hantouleh shrivelled up and wanted to scream.

"And you'll give evidence to that effect in court?"

"Yes." There was no joy in his voice. He was not doing this to pay back what he had suffered in the name of Palestinian freedom. Nor had it been forced on him: there was no indication of duress in his face or tone. In any event it was hard to imagine what form of compulsion could be exercised over an American photographer by an Israeli government whose agents had deliberately enmeshed him in events which had almost cost him his life. It seemed to follow that Flynn was here from choice.

Stricken by the bleak vista of his future stretching away in front of him, Hantouleh could only stumble, "Why?"

Flynn regarded him with something almost like pity. He explained it carefully. "Because you kill people, Rachid. Because you blow them up, and tear their arms and legs off. Because no man, woman or child living here is safe while you're on the loose, and though the people you've killed to date are your responsibility, any you kill from here on out will be mine if I don't do everything in my power to prevent you.

"You're a dangerous man, Rachid. I'm grateful for what you did for me, I'm sorry if this doesn't seem like much of a reward, but if I've anything to do with it they'll lock you up and throw away the key. The only time it'll be safe to release you is when you're a little old man with your hands bent up with arthritis."

"You dog!" choked Hantouleh. The words, thick not with anger but with terror, hardly made it out of his throat. "I should have let them kill you."

Flynn shrugged. "Maybe you should. Or maybe you should have stuck to dispensing aspirin and cough linctus. At least that way you'd have been subtracting from the sum of human misery instead of adding to it."

"That's easy for you to say," snapped Hantouleh, "your people's freedom was won so long ago you have forgotten it needed fighting for."

Flynn sighed. "Rachid, what can I tell you that you don't know already? War—any war but maybe a war of liberation most of all—is something you fight against enemy soldiers and enemy installations. Bombing civilians is terrorism."

"Vietnam?" said Hantouleh with a question mark and a sneer.

Flynn nodded. "A lot of what was done in Vietnam, on both sides, was terrorism. I didn't like it any more then than I do now."

"That too is easy to say. You were too young to have to make any choices. I wonder how well you would have defended the moral high ground if your people had looked to you for their salvation—and not in faraway Asia but from an enemy on their doorsteps, surrounding their homes, threatening their children. How smug you are now you are safe! But threatened people defend themselves as best they can, with whatever weapons they can find. You call it terrorism. I call it keeping the Jews from grinding my people's faces into the sand."

They left then, the policeman ushering them out. Hantouleh's voice, shrill with despair, followed them down the corridor. "You will not live long enough to testify against me!"

Meir drove Flynn to the airport. Neither of them was much aware of the beauty of the Vale of Ayalon, although it was daylight.

After a time Meir said quietly, "Israel cannot escape the responsibility for creating many of her own monsters. Not because we have oppressed Hantouleh and his generations so profoundly and for so long that we left them no alternative but armed rebellion. Our crime, our mistake and—if you'll pardon the analogy—the cross we shall have to bear, has been to oppress them just enough to foster the sense of grievance that all this has grown from.

"Our politicians will tell you that an Israeli Arab, or an Arab in the occupied territories, can live righteous and unafraid under the law of Israel and enjoy much that his neighbours in the Arab states cannot have, and that is true. Yet we all know, however hard we try not to say it, that Arabs are second-class citizens in Israel. We of all people should know how that feels."

Flynn cast him a shrewd sidelong glance. "You don't think that 'we of all people' line is getting a little jaded?"

Meir laughed softly, appreciatively, into the slipstream. The little sports car was approaching takeoff speed but he managed to talk audibly without raising his donnish voice. "Actually, no. Actually, the dangers of forgetting are greater than the dangers of remembering too fondly. Or why do we grow less tolerant as time goes by rather than more so?"

Flynn intoned quietly, "If I forget thee, O Jerusalem, may my right hand forget its cunning. May my tongue cleave to the roof of my mouth if I prefer not Jerusalem above my chief joy." He said it in Hebrew; it was one of those snatches he had picked up in the last four years.

Meir took his eyes off the speeding road for a dangerous few seconds in order to stare at him. The evil grin was nowhere to be seen; but that did not mean, as Meir knew, that mischief was not still Flynn's purpose. Meir sighed and switched his attention back to his driving.

After a few seconds more he said thoughtfully, "I do hope we're not going to prove better at being an oppressed minority in other people's countries than the ruling majority in our own."

They travelled another ten miles in silence, or at least without speaking. The wind sang and Flynn, who was still young enough to be intoxicated by sheer speed, hummed tunelessly along with it.

Passing Gezer, Meir shook off the veil of introspection that had descended almost visibly around him. "Er—Mickey. What Hantouleh said, about you not testifying. It was probably just spite, but he may not be the only one to think that way. You'll need to be a bit careful, at least until this is over. I mean, I wouldn't take any package tours to see the wonders of Islam if I were you."

Flynn chuckled. "I thought that. No, if I get a sudden urge to visit a pyramid, I'll make it a Mexican one."

"We could probably arrange some kind of protection for you."

"I am not having a nose job and changing my name to Schultz."

"We still haven't picked up Fahad. He could come looking for you."

"Well, he'll have to wait in line. People in my line of work make nearly as many enemies as people in yours. Fortunately it's a big world: as long as I avoid the Arab countries, the Netherlands, Ireland—and Pasadena, definitely Pasadena—I should get by."

"It would be a mistake to suppose that the extent of Arab terrorism is limited by the range of the getaway donkey," Meir said seriously. "There is a lot of money in Islam. There are some rich fanatics. They can buy people—professionals—anywhere in the world. If they decide to, they will track you down."

"Not where I'm going."

Meir wanted to warn him against that lethal complacency that kills young men who believe they are safe. "Where are you going that you think they can't follow you?"

"No idea." Again the wicked grin. "Well, London first, while I get some things sorted out; and then New York, I have a hankering to see home again. But after that, your guess is as good as mine. Easter Island, Tierra del Fuego, Machu Picchu, Angkor Wat—if you get a postcard from Bathurst Inlet, that's likely to be me too. And if I don't know where the hell I'm going, how's anyone going to find me?"

Meir understood, perhaps more than he was meant to. "Anyone?"

"Anyone," Flynn said again, firmly. He eased his long body in the cramped cockpit and his forehead creased up in a pensive frown. "You know something, though? I'm going to be thinking of him on Mother's Day."